Irregular Scout Team One

Volume 2

By

J.F. Holmes

I started writing "Even Zombie Killers Get The Blues" ten years ago on a dare. Since that time, Nick Agostine, Brit O'Neill and the rest of the Team have taken on a life of their own through eleven different books. The first book I wrote started a year or two post apocalypse, and since then I've written ten more, including the 2017 Dragon Finalist "Falling", that covered various other times, including how everything started. As a result, the timeline has gotten a bit mixed.

So I pulled all the books and sat down to make a more coherent story. In doing so I've fallen in love with the characters all over again and it's given me a chance to fill in some details. I'm hoping by redoing the series I'll present a much better story. I'll be honest, I really had no idea what I was doing writing wise when I first started and I've grown and learned a lot over the last decade.

Volume Two starts with the Team on a mission into upstate NY. It contains all three of the original books, "Even Zombie Killers Get The Blues", "Even Zombie Killers Need A Break" and "Even Zombie Killers Can Die."

If you've read any of the books before, I'm sure you'll enjoy the story all over again. If you haven't, you're in for a hell of an adventure!

~ Sergeant First Class (R) J.F. Holmes, somewhere in Upstate New York, 2023.

"LOST BOYS, SADDLE UP!"

Chapter 89

Losing a friend is hard. When that friend was one I thought of as my brother, it was even harder. The helo thundered upriver, back to Firebase Castle. I kept seeing Jonesy in my mind, swinging away at the Zombies with that big piece of metal he always carried, leading them away from us so we could board the chopper and get to safety. And then Ahmed's bullet ripping through his heart.

It seemed to happen in slow motion, in my mind anyway. In the movies, you get shot, you fall down. No blood, no gore. In real life, this sucky, post-apocalypse life anyway, you can see the blood splash out. It looked black in the light of the full moon. Again and again it replayed in my mind.

I sat leaning up against the wall of the CH-47. Brit was wrapped in a blanket and Doc was keeping an eye on her. Ahmed was up front with the pilot and SPC Mya was cleaning her weapon while she yelled nonstop in Redshirt's ear, trying to be heard over the sound of the turbine engines. She was trying to keep him awake until we landed at the base and he was admitted to the hospital.

Below me the waters of the Hudson River reflected the silver moonlight. I started to shake, my hands clenched tightly together and I threw up over the edge of the ramp. The vomit immediately blew back into the compartment from the powerful downdraft of the rotors and the crew chief shot me a dirty look. Screw him.

We had been hurt badly. Lt. Carter, attached to the mission, was dead, in a stupid, useless, suicidal charge against a crowd of Zombies. My friend and teammate for the last year, Jonesy, had saved my life again and had paid the full price for it. I could never pay him back now.

I knew what we had to do. After we had dropped off Redshirt and Brit at the base, we needed to head back and recover Jonesy's body. Zombies never eat corpses. They will only chew on you as long as you have a spark of life in you. Ahmed's shot had punched out his heart and I knew Jonesy would still be lying there.

Doc made his way over to me and handed me a helicopter crewman's headset. I put it on and plugged into the intercom system so we could talk. "Nick, we can't bring Redshirt to the hospital. As soon as they realize that he's immune to Zombie bites that kid is going to turn into the world's biggest guinea pig. They will keep him just healthy enough to produce blood for lab tests for the rest of his life."

"Tough on him. Sometimes the needs of the many outweigh the needs of the few, or the one," I said.

"Bullshit. If you believed that, you would be back in the real Army instead of scouting around out here."

I knew he had me. The kid had done good and become a member of the team and I knew what would happen once the Army Medical Research Institute of Infectious Diseases (U.S.AMRIID) got their hands on him. They would sic their pet zombies on him and keep trying to figure out why he didn't get infected and he would die soon enough from whatever other diseases developed in their rotting mouths.

"OK. He stays but Mya is going to have to look after him. You, me and Ahmed are going back for Jonesy's body tomorrow, if we can get it."

He nodded and unplugged from the intercom. We touched down on the island as the sun rose.

Chapter 90

Brit complained but she had to stay. We needed her whole and she needed serious antibiotics after her wound had opened up from her fall into the river. By the next night, she had a raging fever. After the round of antibiotics it had finally broken but she had been left exhausted and wrung out. Even her complaints had seemed like something she felt she had to do. She drifted off into a deep sleep and the PA at the medical tent had kicked us out. Redshirt was recuperating in another tent, away from the eyes of the medical personnel, guarded by Specialist Mya.

We set off downriver that afternoon, with the boat crew gunning the engine at full blast. I knew they felt bad for leaving us. If they hadn't had to return to base for repairs, Jonesy and Lt. Carter would still be alive. I didn't blame them, though; equipment broke down. It couldn't be helped.

The military ran operations on a shoestring. When the Apocalypse happened, many of the bases and depots that held spare parts for the military had been overrun. In the almost two years since then, there wasn't anyone making anything except the simple basics, like weapons and ammunition. Even our uniforms were patched and mended over and over. That and irregular maintenance (or, in most cases, no maintenance at all) had taken its toll on anything mechanical. The boats waiting for us at West Point had suffered an engine fire and an explosion, causing casualties. They had been forced to return to base, leaving us to duke it out with a horde of Zs.

The dock where we had fought as we waited for the helicopter pulled into view. Zombie bodies were scattered all over, from our rifles and the airstrikes. We pulled up and climbed out, weapons at the ready but there was no movement in sight. Ahmed kept watch with his sniper rifle as Doc and I searched for Jonesy's body. He lay where he had fallen, sprawled flat on his back, iron bar still clasped in his hands. Doc unwrapped a body bag and we tipped him over into it.

"Damn, Jonesy, you stink." My eyes were watering and I felt like throwing up. Two days in the sun and he was almost unrecognizable. At least his eyes were closed. The blood had dried black on his uniform around the hole in his heart made by Ahmed's bullet. He had always been too big to wear body armor.

"I know, right?" said Doc. "Maybe you should take a bath every now and then, Brother."

It was either that or bust out crying. It's just how you deal with it sometimes. This man had been my friend, as close to me as my own brother, or closer. We shared untold danger and saved each other's lives too many times to count and here I was about to zip up the bag and close him off from the sunlight forever. Doc motioned me aside. "I'll do it."

I turned away but I still heard the zipper as he closed it. *Goodbye, my friend, my brother.* We each grabbed a handle on the body bag and tried to lift. "Damn, he's heavy," grunted Doc. Ahmed slung his rifle and came over to give us a hand and we pulled him over to the boat. The boat crew helped us get him onboard and we headed back upriver. Not a soul or a Zombie in sight.

We buried him on the south side of Bannerman Island, just above the shoreline, so his grave got sunlight all year long. Brit stood with me and held my hand while one of the infantry sergeants, a lay preacher, spoke over the grave. He prayed for salvation of Jonesy's soul, who apparently had died doing the Lord's work. Brit squeezed my hand tight to keep me from interrupting him.

As far as I was concerned, God had turned his back on the world and I can't say I blamed Him.

******

I sat in the tent, cleaning my rifle, feeling vaguely depressed and incredibly bored. Doc lay on the cot next to me, leafing through an old Maxim magazine he had found in the ruins. On the cover was some actress who looked vaguely familiar. He reached the centerfold and flipped her open, then held her out for me to see.

"Ever seen this actress before?"

"Somewhat. One of those reality TV shows or something."

He laughed, pulled out a red marker and quickly scribbled on the picture, then held it back to me. He had reddened her eyes and put blood around her mouth.

"Holy crap!"

Doc burst out laughing. "Thought you might recognize her that way. Now if I could just find a yellow highlighter to draw in where you puked all over her. Ha ha ha!"

Redshirt sat up in his cot and Mya leaned forward. "Come on, Doc, tell us the story."

"Yeah, let's hear it!"

I shot him a dirty look but he gave me the finger. "So, some bonehead gets the idea that we should scout out Malibu. Why, I don't know. Reports of some civilian survivors holed up in one of those mansions or something. So, we parachute in and move up the grounds of this mansion, me, Nick, Jonesy, Ahmed and, um ..." he trailed off.

"Rabinowitz." I prompted him.

"Oh yesh, the Rabbi. I wonder how he's doing?"

"I heard he's getting around good on his new leg," I said.

"Cool."

"Get back to the story, old timers!" yelled Brit.

"Shut it, kids. So anyway, we are scouting this mansion, everything is cool, no signs of life till we get into the kitchen. There, standing at a table, is a woman with her back to us. Nick puts his hand on her shoulder and says, "U.S. Army, we're here to help!" and this zombie jumps up, turns around and launches herself at him! I haven't ever seen Nick move backward so fast. Just before she gets to him, he pops off a shot that catches her through the jaw and blows off the back

7

of her head. She falls on him, spraying him with her blood and brains and he throws up all down her back."

"Screw you, Doc!" I said but I smiled.

Red and Mya were laughing. "Wait, it gets better. Every time, for quite a long while, whenever we shot a Z, someone on the team would yell, U.S. ARMY, WE'RE HERE TO HELP!"

I was laughing too. It's funny how things that were so terrifying at the time turn into funny stories down the road.

The tent flap was drawn aside and a sergeant from Operations came in. "Nick, the Battalion S-3 is on the horn. They've got a new mission for your team."

"OK, be there in a few minutes. Doc, start doing Pre-Combat Checks and Inspections. Red, you up for this?"

"I'm OK, Chief."

"Alright. I'll see if Brit can get away from the medics yet on my way back." I headed out into the bright June sunlight, feeling a little better.

Chapter 91

Inside the Ops tent, the computers were driving the temperature higher. Blue Force Tracker, Intel source feeds, artillery, plasma screen for briefings and more than a dozen radios to stay in touch with the various patrols on the shore and boats transiting the river. They all combined to generate a heat that the floor fan did little to dissipate.

I walked past a table where the liaisons from the other services had set up shop. We had one each from the Navy, Air Force and Coast Guard and I made a note to get with each of them after finding out what this mission was. At the Current Ops section, I took the sat phone from the Ops Sergeant and called Task Force Empire Ops. "Empire Main, this is Lost Boys, over."

"Lost Boys, this is Empire Main, wait one, over."

After a minute, Major Flynn came on the line. After asking me how the team was doing and getting my assurances that we were OK, he expressed condolences over us losing Jonesy. Then we got down to business. "Nick, how do you guys feel about an airborne insertion?"

"Friggin hate the idea."

I could almost hear him laughing. "Well, tough crap. We need you to drop on a target."

"I could say no." No way I was going to give in so easily.

"You could and I could draft you back into the Regular Army again."

He had me by the balls. I knew that Doc and I could disappear back into the woods and Brit would go with us but dammit, I liked what we were doing. We were, in our small way, making a difference.

"OK, send me a target with an OPORDER."

"It will be in your inbox. The Navy wants back into New York and we are going to do a hold and clear as soon as they identify a target facility. You guys will be jumping in first, giving a report, then waiting for the Marines."

"Understood. I'm going to need ammo and other refit."

"Draw what you can from the infantry. We're tight up here. Empire Main, out."

I let out a deep breath. We were going to need a palette of ammunition, water, and construction materials. Replacements for some of the weapons we had lost. Maybe another trooper, perhaps that big redneck sniper from the infantry company. I headed over to the liaison table to talk to the other branches and see what support we could get from them.

*****

It's funny how you can hate a job and love it at the same time. Part of me wished we were back in Stillwater, rebuilding the house and growing some food. Another part wouldn't have missed this for anything in the world.

I had just stepped outside the Ops tent, back into the bright sunlight, when an old-school air raid siren started to wind up. Soldiers started scrambling for their fighting positions, manning machine guns and other heavy weapons set up around the island. As I passed the howitzers, I saw their crews frantically spinning the elevation wheel, lowering the barrel so it pointed out over the river. Three of them were levering the hand spike at the rear up in the air, getting ready to spin the cannon left or right. One had been set up on each side of the island, dragged there by the lone Humvee that had been brought down on the barge. Barricades made of empty ammunition boxes filled with dirt had been piled high in a circle around them, leaving just enough clearance for the barrel to direct fire on targets in the river.

I jumped down into the firing position next to our tent, joining Ahmed and Doc in the trench. We had an MK-19 40mm automatic grenade launcher. Normally useless against zombies, it would be great against anything coming across the river at us.

"What's up?" I yelled over the sound of the siren, which

was winding down.

"No idea!" answered Doc. We sat patiently, doing the old soldier thing of hurry up and wait. Not for too long, though. From around the back of the island came one of our assault boats. At the same time, I caught a glimpse of a long, low shape cruising up the river, a couple of hundred meters away, about halfway between us and the far shore.

"ATTENTION, UNIDENTIFIED CRAFT. THIS IS THE UNITED STATES ARMY. STOP AND PREPARE TO BE BOARDED." The words boomed out of a loudspeaker mounted on one of the turrets of the old castle and echoed across the water.

The boat, or ship, or whatever you want to call it, didn't stop but turned toward us. It was about sixty feet long and looked like someone had taken an old fishing boat and welded steel across the deck to make a primitive armored ship. On the front, a slit had been cut to make room for the barrel of some kind of automatic weapon. Probably a light machine gun looted from some National Guard armory. Through my binoculars, I could see a line of skulls strung across the bow.

I handed the binoculars to Doc. After a few seconds of looking, he handed them back to me and spit on the ground in front of us. "Ugh. Fucking Reaver jerkoffs." I couldn't stand them either. Zombies I killed without passion. They were what they were. People trying to survive I left alone if they let me alone and helped them out when I could. Cannibals we shot on the spot, if there was evidence of it. Mad Maxes though, were scumbags who preyed on other survivors. Looting and stealing, killing just for the sheer fun of it. Many of them were criminals who hadn't really been able to function in the real world anyway. They loved the mayhem the Zombie Apocalypse created. Some people called them "Mad Maxes". Others called them "Reavers". Didn't matter what you called them, they had no place in society if we were going to claw our way out of this mess.

"Look at that shit, they even have a frigging pirate flag

hanging off the ass end." Apparently someone in command at the base had noticed it too, because I heard a cheer go up around me and turned to look. A makeshift flagpole had been set up on the highest point of the island and up it ran the stars and stripes. At that, the ship started to turn away and the guys in the assault boat put it into high gear.

The soldier in the next hole yelled, "Hell yes, there's a new sheriff in town, scumbags!" just as the ship started firing at our assault boat with rifle and machine gun fire. Ahmed leaned forward, put his eye to his rifle scope and shot the man who was working the heavy gun on the back of the craft. The assault boat swerved away under full power. Doc racked a round into the 19 and started walking grenades toward the ship but they were just out of range. Tracers were already reaching out to it from the .50 caliber set next to us when an enormous CRACK came from the western howitzer position and the ship exploded in a muffled BOOM that echoed across the water. A high explosive round with a point-detonating fuse, fired over an open sight from the 105 mm howitzer, had impacted on the steel plate welded to the back deck and blown the ship in half. The front half started to burn while the rear sank quickly into the water. As we watched burning figures jumped from the wheelhouse into the water. Ahmed shot them as they fell, muttering a prayer for mercy as he fired.

The assault boat moved in after the front half had slipped beneath the water, leaving a patch of burning oil on the surface. I watched them through my binos as they went from body to body, pulling each one up to check for signs of life, to see if we could get a prisoner. They turned back empty.

Chapter 92

Someone, I don't remember who, once said that all warfare is logistics. That never held more truth than when fighting Zombies. One on one, maybe, you can beat a zombie, though they are strong and once they start attacking, they never, ever stop. More than one, unarmed, you're dead, or even worse, joining their ranks, if your heart doesn't give out fast enough. A baseball bat or some other kind of knocker, you can hold out for a while but having more than a few around you, you're going to get swamped, like Jonesy when he went down fighting at West Point.

The key to beating zombies is equipment and keeping your distance. Ammunition, working weapons and most important, a solid defense. I'll sit all day behind a concrete wall and poke zombies through a murder hole with a spear, provided too many bodies don't pile up and they start climbing over the wall. After that happens, of course, you're screwed.

With that in mind and not knowing where our destination was, Doc, Brit and I sat down and started working on a packing list. It was going to be an airborne insertion and I had no faith in the Navy coming to pull us out in time, so I wanted a pallet to be dropped with us. Screw that, I wanted two pallets, each a duplicate of the other. I was pretty sure we would have to settle for one, though.

What we came up with, after more than an hour of deliberating and arguing was:

- 20,000 rounds of .22 magnum ammunition for our rifles, preloaded into 50 round magazines
- 500 rounds of 7.62 for Ahmed's rifle
- 2000 rounds of straight .22 for our pistols
- 3 spare rifles and 3 spare pistols
- 1 case of thumpers
- Three AT-4 anti-tank rockets. If we needed to blow a hole in the side of a building, we were

going to need to do it fast.

I wasn't sure we were going to get that much ammo, much less the magazines but I left that up to Brit to try to wheedle it out of the fat supply sergeant up at Fort Orange.

- 5kw Generator, along with a spare parts set. Electricity was a huge combat multiplier.
- 20 gallons of gasoline. I was sure we would be able to scrounge more but I didn't want to count on it. Along with that I added 3 empty 5-gallon fuel cans and a fuel filtering unit. A lot of the gas you could scrounge from cars had gone bad with water contamination and just sitting. I also added a hand-cranked fuel pump and 20 feet of rubber hose.
- Six 100' extension cords
- 3 drills, along with screws, hammers and nails
- 2 sledge hammers and two axes
- 500 feet of ¼" steel cable, in 50' lengths. We had found this useful strung up either ankle- or chest-high. It often stopped or seriously delayed a horde of zombies.
- 2 electric saws-alls, along with a gasoline-powered demolition saw
- 5 lbs of C-4, along with blasting caps. I let Doc deal with that. I don't like explosives, never did but I wanted the ability to drop a building if I had to.
- 10 sets of halogen worklight bulbs. I could probably scrounge lights themselves, since there were hardware stores all over the city and lights were the last thing looters went after. Night vision equipment was great but I wanted the ability to light up any field of fire we had. It would save ammunition and

fighting in the light is always better for morale.

- Two 15' collapsible assault ladders. In the city, many of the older buildings had floors that were more than twelve feet apart. They could also be used to span an alley between roofs.
- Portable water purification unit., along with 30 gallons of water in 5 gallon cans.
- Three cases of MREs, along with 5 rolls of toilet paper. Never forget that.

Brit finished making a copy of the list and sent it by e-mail to the S-4 section at Fort Orange. "I'm probably going to go up there to make this happen myself," she said, "but I know a supply sergeant who owes me some, um, favors." She shot me a guilty look, the "we need to talk" thing. I nodded at her and put the thought aside.

Doc pulled out his Garmin and brought up the local hardware stores. "Well, looks like we have to go raid a Home Depot. According to the GPS, there is one in Fishkill on Route 9. I'll see if I can get some air support and fly in instead of a boat mission."

"I'm going to go over to the infantry, maybe we can get a couple more guys for this mission. I think that redneck sniper Killeen and two more riflemen would be good. They can make their own fire team. Let's plan on doing the scrounge mission tomorrow at noon. You know the drill, pre-combat checks and inspections."

We broke up and went our separate ways to start getting ready. Brit followed me on my way over to the infantry Command Post.

"Nick, we need to talk."

I hated those words. I'd rather hear a full horde screaming the zombie moan than hear a woman say that. "OK, Brit, go ahead. We went over this in Bermuda but seeing you in that water …"

"I know." She took a deep breath, then laid it out flat. "Nick, until you and I can go riding off into the sunset together, I'm not going to be with you. We can't. You're the team leader and I may love you but I expect all of us are going to die, sooner rather than later. Maybe we can call it quits someday after this zombie thing and we can rethink it but for now, you know we can't. You have way too much responsibility to think of only one person." I took off my work glove and brushed a strand of hair off her face, then ran the back of my hand across her cheek. She closed her eyes.

"Maybe someday, Brit," I said and kissed her cheek. She nodded and opened those ice blue eyes. There were tears in the corners.

"Maybe someday, Nick."

Chapter 93

"Mya, Redshirt, before we roll out, you have to go attend quarterly mandatory briefings. Sexual harassment and suicide prevention."

"I already know how to sexually harass someone," said Red.

Mya shot him a dirty look and asked me, "Why do we have to do these things if we're attached to a super special unit?"

Brit laughed. "Because you're regular Army pukes. Sucks to be you!"

"Brit, Doc is giving a class to the infantry in avoiding plague infection in Zombie Combat. You just volunteered to be his demonstrator." Now I was the one on the receiving end of the dirty look.

"Let's go, we have to finish mission prep tonight for tomorrow's hardware store run."

She stood and jumped up and down to seat her gear properly. "Good. I need more saline solution for my contacts. Can we raid Walmart tomorrow too, Oh Fearless Leader?"

"Nope, quick in and out. You're going to have to wear your birth control glasses. Maybe you should wear them now to keep the infantry guys off you."

"Now why would I want that?" she said and batted her eyes at me.

"Bite me."

"Someday."

They followed me out of the tent. Mya and Redshirt were heading over to the ops tent to get their class and Brit and I went to join up with Docs', which was already in session.

"Great, our demonstrators just showed up. This is Sergeant First Class Agostine and Civilian Scout O'Neill. Nick, Brit, we were just going over the basic background on the plague."

I made a "carry on," motion and he picked up where he

left off.

"As you were taught in basic training, we don't know the exact nature of a zombie infection. We do know that it operates on a cellular level, animating tissue where all prior electrical activity has ceased. However, it causes massive degeneration of neurons, so most brain tissue and nerves are dead, except for the most basic functions in the hypothalamus and whatever is needed for muscle function. Why that survives and a desire to eat living flesh, is unknown."

A private sitting in the first row raised his hand. Doc nodded to him.

"Is that why when we shoot them they don't feel nothing?"

"That's correct. Also, the oxygen their muscles need seems to come from some kind of metabolic reaction in the virus itself, not through respiration. Their skin, which feels slightly slimy, is covered with some kind of organic growth which aids in respiration. One reason why Zs don't like water."

After answering several more questions about the nature of the Zombie infection with a couple of "We don't know!" Doc moved on to the combat phase of the class.

We spent some time alternating between various methods of defense against a zombie attack. Most of them were based on throws from jujitsu. The best defense against a zombie that gets inside your guard is to get it off you as quickly as possible. One serious problem, though, is often the decomposition of the corpse leaves you with an arm or a leg in your hand after you've tried a shoulder throw, with the thing still trying to take a chunk out of you.

We demonstrated how an upward strike would break a zombie's jaw if you hit hard enough with the palm of your hand. I reminded them how hunching your neck up in your kevlar collar would prevent any cuts and so would the issued, detachable hood that was part of our issue uniforms now. Joes often liked to throw away equipment that was hot and bothersome but in this case, it could save their lives in a close fight.

I was demonstrating how to do a break away, with Brit acting as the Zombie, when one of the guys up front said, "I'd like to have her bite my neck!" Brit walked over to him, made a "let's go," motion, then promptly went apeshit, biting and clawing all over him. He tried hard to defend himself but she finally stepped back with his blood on her face. He had half a dozen serious scratches and one bite mark on his cheek.

"Oh my God, what the fuck is wrong with you?" yelled the burly infantryman, holding his hand to his face.

Doc stepped in between them. "Private, if you can't stop one girl you outweigh by more than a hundred pounds, what the hell are you going to do against a zombie your size, who has infection-fueled strength and could probably break you in half?"

He turned the guy around to face the rest of the group. The wound on his cheek was bleeding profusely. "Let this be a lesson to all of you, especially you kids who haven't been in a zombie fight yet: If that had been a real zombie attacking him, he would either be dead or reanimated right now and attacking you. Think about it. We're not playing games here. This isn't basic training or the playground. Nor is it Army Combatives, where you are trying to choke someone out or subdue them. This is kill or be killed, in every single encounter. Now, partner up and TRY TO DRAW BLOOD!"

I walked over to where Brit stood, wiping the blood off her face and handed her my canteen to wash up.

"I think you're getting a little slow in your old age, Brit."

"Kiss my ass, old balls," she said and grinned a bloody grin.

Chapter 94

We had air transport for our equipment-scrounging trip. To get it, I had to promise the infantry they could go along to get some Zombie fighting experience. While we were running around Home Depot with shopping carts and pallet jacks they would form a perimeter and fight a holding action against any Zs that showed up. Then, after we had loaded up on the CH-47, they would conduct a fighting withdrawal back onto the choppers. That would give them some combat experience and leave us free to do our scrounging.

That was the plan, and of course no plan survives. It was interrupted by an MH-60 from the 160th Special Operations Aviation Regiment that came flaring in for a landing as dusk settled on the river. Two guys I assumed were from Special Forces Operational Detachment (Delta) jumped out, followed by a short, good-looking woman in a flight suit. No combat gear or weapon, just a bag slung over her shoulder. Doc stood next to me as we watched them exit the bird, the two Delta Operators acting as bodyguards as they made their way to the command post.

"Should we run and hide right now? That woman is bad news," said my friend.

"No shit." Doctor Morano from the Army Medical Research Institute of Infectious Diseases. We've met before and my danger signals were firing on all motors. She walked around the command post and made a beeline for where our team had set up our hooches. I headed her off before she ran into Brit and a gunfight started right in the middle of the camp.

She waved off the body guards as we approached. "Stand down, this is the guy we're looking for." The two of them immediately shifted their attention back to scanning for threats.

"Dr. Morano. Here to get someone killed, I presume. Or kill someone."

She smiled at me. "Sergeant Agostine, so much with the

drama! You and Sergeant Hamilton. You two make a good team, running around playing white knight."

The first time I had seen her had been at Bagram Airbase, at the prison. I had signed for two prisoners who had been turned into gibbering idiots by her attempts at "biological interrogation." The other two I had turned over the day before were dead, due to "natural causes." The last time I had seen her had been on a snatch and grab of an undead. We had lost some good people on that mission, which had involved finding 'patient zero' and then watching her throw it out the back of a helo.

She smiled her sweet, evil smile at me. "I heard your team tends to run into concentrations of infected on a regular basis. I have an experimental vaccine I want you to use the next time you encounter a large group of them."

"Are you sure? That doesn't sound very evil."

"You enjoy your job, Sergeant Agostine. I enjoy mine. How are we any different?" she sneered.

I laughed. "You enjoy killing people and causing pain. I enjoy beating the enemy. I don't enjoy killing."

She gave me a blank look. Frigging sociopath. "I don't 'enjoy' it. Enough with the verbal chit chat." She handed me a bandolier of 40mm grenade rounds for the M-203. "These have been modified with an aerosol spray containing a skin contact serum. If you fire it over a crowd of infected, it should work within a few minutes. Those who are fresh corpses may be cured. Those who have decomposed past the point where life is possible, or who suffered life threatening wounds in their initial infection, should just drop."

Doc took them from her and looked them over. There were five of them. "So what's the catch? I don't trust you, Ma'am. What if I refuse to do it?"

"Doctor, not Ma'am. If you refuse, these two gentlemen will shoot you dead on the spot." The bodyguards glanced at Doc and I and I knew those guys would drill us through the head at a single word, probably a prearranged code mixed into a sentence so that we didn't have time to react.

She had us and there was nothing I could do about it. "What's to stop us from just dumping them in the river after you leave?"

"There is a transponder in each one that will tell us time of firing, location, etc. I may be evil, Nick but I'm not stupid. In fact, I'm actually a genius."

"No, you're actually a fucking sociopath. OK, we'll do your dirty work, Dr. Morano."

"Please see that you do. I'd hate to have you killed."

"I doubt that you would hate it."

"No, you're right, I'd probably record it and play it over and over."

That was one crazy ass woman. She turned and walked back to the helo that was spinning up again. One of the Delta guys looked back and gave us a thumbs up. I gave him the finger.

Specialist Mya came up behind us. "What was that all about?"

Doc handed her the bandolier. "Go get yourself a different weapon with a 203 launcher on it. We need you to replace Jonesy's firepower anyway. Then go practice with a half a dozen HE rounds into the river. Take Redshirt with you and have him show you what to do."

She looked at the rounds in the belt. "What about these?"

"Those," I answered her, "are a potential cure for the infection. We're going to fire it over a crowd of zombies and see what happens."

Her eyes got wide. I could see her professional interest as a medic had been piqued. "Coool!"

We were cleaning weapons an hour later when we heard a blood-curdling scream of agony carry across the island. Doc, Brit and I jumped up and ran as fast we could in the direction of where Mya and Redshirt had been lobbing 203 rounds into the river.

She lay on the ground, with Redshirt standing there ten feet away from her. We were the first to get there. Doc made to push past Red but he tackled the big man and tried to hold him back.

"DOC, NO!" he yelled in his ear, "It's poisoned! Nerve agent!"

Doc's face went pale and he stood. The rest of us halted where we were. Mya lay on the ground, twitching in agony. She had vomited and her back arched in spasms, her scream fading as her jaw opened and closed. Beside her a 203 round lay on the ground, one of the ones from the bandolier Morano had given us. We stood and watched until Brit pulled her pistol from her leg holster and shot Mya through the heart, twice. She arched one last time and fell still.

"She said she wanted to check out the shells with the medicine in them, see how they worked. She took one out and I guess she handled it wrong or something. Next thing I knew, she staggered and yelled at me to run, said it was nerve gas and then said something like V, then she fell to the ground and started vomiting and she screamed once." V meant VX, a nerve agent. As a medic, Mya knew what was happening to her.

He turned around and threw up in the bushes. I handed him a canteen. The infantry guys showed up and Brit motioned them back. Doc filled them in and they away way. This part of the island would remain off limits, along with her corpse. We wouldn't even be able to bury her. At least not for a while.

"She saved your life, Red. You would have been dead if you tried to help her."

Doc came up. "VX nerve agent. Bad shit, Nick. Persistent oil-based. If we had fired that and it had misfired, or blown back at us, we could have all been wiped out. What the fuck were they thinking?"

"They were thinking they needed to do a field experiment and they didn't care who happened to get burnt in the process."

I looked back at Mya lying dead in the moonlight. I would file a report back to JSOC and I'm sure we would see

Doctor Morano again. I had an urge to wrap my hands around her throat but we would have to be very, very careful around her.

Chapter 95

"GO! GO! GO!" The back ramp was down before we hit the ground. A swirl of dust and ash obscured the LZ, lifted by the rotor wash of the other CH-47. The other Chinook had touched its back wheels down thirty seconds before us, dropping off two squads of infantry, then lifting back off. One more squad and a heavy weapons team filled the canvas seats in our chopper, along with the rest of the Lost Boys. As soon as the ramp touched, the guys filed out in two lines, breaking left and right to add to the perimeter. Then the heavy weapons team carried out their M-249 SAWs and the head-high tripods they were mounted on, along with crates of extra ammo. The infantrymen quickly started pushing debris into some kind of perimeter, unraveling concertina wire in a big loop around the front doors of the Home Depot and pounding stakes to hold it into the parking lot.

The heavy weapons team had four M-249s that they set up to cover likely areas of approach. Each light machine gun was mounted on a tripod which held the weapon roughly five and half feet off the ground, just about the average height of a zombie head. Yeah, aimed shots were better than automatic fire but sweeping a packed mass of a zombie hoard with a couple hundred rounds a minute at head height, if you've got the ammo, can work wonders. The infantry worked hard to push any moveable cars to create channels for zombies to be herded into and machine gunned. Already single shots were popping off from the Designated Marksmen teams, taking out a few Zs that were stumbling around on the road.

The doors of Home Depot were shattered and I breathed a sigh of relief. Sometimes a closed storefront would hide a pack of zombies that had become trapped in the store. This one had been hit by looters but I was pretty sure that we would be able to find everything we needed. I led the way in the stack, followed by Brit, Doc and Redshirt. We all carried shotguns for quick snapshots down the aisle. Ahmed stayed outside with the two infantry guys we had picked up,

Corporal Killeen and Specialist Desen, doing some very long-range sniping.

We moved through the front of the store, coming up dry. That was the easiest part. The hard part would be going down through the aisles, with limited visibility, making noise stumbling over debris and trying to keep our footing. Stepping into the first aisle, we snapped on head-mounted and weapon-mounted flashlights. Even in bright daylight, the store was dark and gloomy. We could have used NVGs but if you looked back at the bright sunlight at the front of the store they tended to blank out.

Down the center aisle, we split into two teams; Doc and Redshirt together in one and Brit and I in the other and headed in separate directions. We would meet back in the front of the store after confirming ID.

Brit led the way, shotgun at the ready. The flashlights created a jumpy, dancing pattern of shadows and my heart was pounding.

"Are you up to this?" I whispered as I noticed her favoring her leg that had been wounded a few weeks before.

"Suck it, fat boy," she whispered, without looking back at me. I grinned in the darkness. She was okay.

We had made it through the tools section, moving aisle by aisle. Brit poked a small periscope with a PVS-14 NVG attached to it around each corner, looking for the faint heat signatures a zombie gave off. Shining a light down the aisle could miss something hiding in shadows. Looking around one corner, she held up one hand, palm down, then two fingers, then a walking motion towards herself. Okay, two zombies, ambulatory, moving toward us. I brought my shotgun up to my shoulder and put my knee on her back to let her know I was ready.

As soon as I felt her move, I swung past her right and turned left down the aisle. My flashlight swept up the floor to center on the head of the right-hand zombie and I fired twice. I heard Brit's gun boom next to me at the same time. Her first shot spun the left-hand zombie, the second shot taking off the back of its head. Mine was also down but still trying to crawl forward with half its face blown off. I walked up and hit it in the head with the hammer I carried.

"CLEAR, two zulu down."

"Roger, two zulu down," came Doc's response over the radio.

We met back up at the front of the store, each team peeling off to get the assigned items, Brit pushing a shopping cart and me a pallet. Outside, the firing was picking up, going from occasional shots to almost continuous single shots. We ran down the aisles, throwing things we needed into the cart and onto the pallet while keeping an eye out for any Zs we might have missed.

"Do we have everything?" I asked, slightly out of breath from pushing the heavy cart as fast as possible.

"I need new mechanic's gloves."

I held up a pair in her size. "I grabbed you a pair. Let's get the hell out of here."

"Pink? I'm not wearing pink gloves."

"They were the only thing in your size, sweetcheeks. You can dye them when we get back to camp. Besides, pink looks good on you." She gave me a dirty look and we walked out into the bright sunlight, followed a minute later by Doc and Redshirt.

Outside it had evolved into a full-fledged firefight. Zs were piling up on the perimeter, climbing over bodies to get at the fresh meat shooting at them. The machine guns were hammering out a steady symphony of bursts, waiting for a cluster of Zs to show themselves over the pile. Brass lay all over the parking lot. I grabbed the infantry platoon leader where he was directing fire and shifting people and yelled in his ear.

"SIR, WE ARE GOOD TO GO!"

"ROGER THAT!" and he shouted for his platoon sergeant, making a whirling motion with his hand over his head. Then he popped smoke right in front of the pallets and shopping carts. While we waited for the birds, the team secured all the loose items in each pallet or cart with a tarp, duct taping them down heavily. Once on board, the crew chief would strap them down.

Now came the hard part: Withdrawing under pressure. As the helo set down, we joined the perimeter, firing along with the infantry at the massive horde pouring out of the city of Newburgh. Next to me a young trooper panicked, trying to reload his magazine as a Z came straight at him. He dropped the weapon and turned to run but tripped on the broken pavement. I shot the Z coming at him but another was right behind him. It grabbed his ankle and started to viciously bite on his leg, dragging him out of the perimeter. His scream was cut short as Redshirt put a burst into his chest. A stream of tracers from the machine guns tore through at head level of the crowd of zombies but a bullet caught another trooper in the back of the head as he stood up to swing his knocker at them. He fell forward on his face and lay still.

We shortened the line as each squad peeled back into the choppers. As the heavy weapons crew collapsed their tripods and ran into the last chopper, we followed them in. I counted off the whole team, getting a thumbs-up from each, then boarded myself. The last squad practically fell onto the ramp, getting a hand up from the guys already onboard.

As we lifted, zombies rushed the helos and the crew chief opened up with his minigun. A hundred rounds a second and only a few fell to head shots. More fell from limbs being torn off.

We flew out over the river. Across from me, a young kid stood up and staggered over to me.

"I HOPE IT WAS WORTH IT, YOU MOTHERFUCKER!" he yelled at me. I guess one of the guys who had died was a friend.

"I DON'T KNOW IF IT WAS OR NOT!" That took the wind out of him and he sat back down, tears running down his face.

Truth was, I didn't know.

Chapter 96

The mood in the infantry was ugly when we got back. They helped us unload our supplies but little was said. The company commander called me, the platoon sergeant and the platoon leader aside and asked what had happened. When we got to the part about the two soldiers who had been lost, he said nothing but his eyes narrowed and his jaw clenched.

"I'm sorry about that, Sir. I know you guys were supporting us." It sounded contrite but I wasn't sure what else to say. This was a new company, most of them privates straight out of basic training at Joint Base Lewis-McChord outside Seattle.

He nodded. "It's OK, sergeant. You and I have both been around this fight long enough to know that people are going to die. They're dead because of their own mistakes and lack of training." At that, he looked hard at the platoon leader, who flushed red.

"Can't always stop a man from panicking, captain. It happens. Most of these kids have never dealt with a zombie horde. Hell, some of them might not have even seen one outside the rifle range at Basic Training. Isn't that why you sent them with us on this scrounging raid in the first place? Two men died but it might save a lot of lives later."

He was silent for a minute, then he nodded his head toward me. "I'm going to make sure none of them has a problem with supporting your team in the future."

"Thanks, appreciate it."

He walked away and climbed on top of some ammo crates that were sitting by the LZ. He waited until his guys had all stopped what they were doing and he had their attention. "Listen up. We lost two soldiers today. Good guys. Kemp and Coburn. They were friends of yours. They were also my soldiers. I know you're upset by what happened but they are dead. Get that into your heads. This isn't Call of Duty and you don't respawn. Soldiers die and in this shitty war, some of you will die on almost every mission we go on.

I hope not. I really, really do." He paused for a second and took off his glasses, rubbing them on his T-shirt and then putting them back on.

"Just remember this about your buddies. They aren't zombies, stumbling around in the dark with their souls trapped in a rotting body. Sergeant Agostine's soldier did the right thing by shooting Coburn. If not, he would have been a danger to all of you if he had turned Z while inside the lines. He saved your lives. Don't hold it against him or the rest of his team. Your job is to go where you are told and kill what you see. You did that today and I'm proud of you." He paused for a minute to let that sink in, then he pointed back to me.

"Their job is to go alone, unsupported into infected territory and get information so that more of you don't die when we do assault into hostile territory, and when a scout team goes dark, it means they're dead. All of them. The information they bring back is worth more than its weight in gold. If they need our help, they will get it. What they do out there alone will save your lives."

He jumped down and walked back toward the Command Post. I saluted him as he walked past. There are officers and then there are Leaders.

The rest of the day was spent packing everything onto some pallets. We had grabbed two of most things, because I had seen a chute failure often enough on cargo drops in Afghanistan and if we lost one, I wanted back up. We would jump with as much ammo as we could carry and stack the pallets with more too.

At 1900 I headed over to the CP for a mission planning session. All the service reps were there and a Lt. Commander was leading the briefing. He jumped right in. "As you know, the Navy holds Portsmouth Naval Shipyard in Maine and Guantanamo Bay in Cuba as the only bases on this side of the Atlantic. Bermuda is still holding steady but it's six hundred miles off the coast and doesn't have the port facilities we need. We have a carrier strike group based out of Portsmouth but we need a deep-water port that can hold the whole fleet if necessary." He used a laser pointer to illustrate each of the places he was talking about on a large map of the east coast.

"Naval Intelligence wants reconnaissance of each of the large ports on the east Coast. Yesterday we lost contact with a scout team in Philadelphia, presumed overrun. We also have teams set to go into Jacksonville, Florida and Baltimore, Maryland tonight and tomorrow, respectively.

I interrupted him. "Sir, do you know what team that was? Who was in charge?"

"Let me check my notes. Um, JSOC IST 3. Doesn't give any names."

"Ok, thanks." The Zombie Killers were Joint Special Operations Command Irregular Scout Team 1. I knew who led Team 3; in fact I knew all the guys on it. Correction, I had known all the guys on it. Damn.

He continued on. "We need your team to go check out the New York Container Terminal on Staten Island. The usual drill." He tacked up a black and white photograph of the terminal, a wide-open area with cargo cranes and warehouses.

"I've been there before," I said. "Back in '07, prior to going to Iraq, to familiarize ourselves with container operations. Nice wide-open space. For a minute I thought you were going to drop us into Manhattan."

"We thought about it, right up until Team 3 disappeared."

"Nice. Why not insert from boats? Seems like it would be a lot easier."

The infantry company Supply Sergeant chimed in. "Gas shortage and a boat shortage. We're having a real hard time getting gasoline for the patrol boats and spare parts, too. Aviation fuel we have a shit ton of, courtesy of the Navy."

I chewed that around for a bit. "OK but how do we get out?"

"Well, if the facility looks usable based on your report, you will be relieved by a reinforced Marine Rifle Company from the *U.S.S New York* flying in on Ospreys. From there, the Navy will expand its presence in the city and you will be retasked."

"What if the place is unusable?" I asked.

"Then the same Ospreys will pick you up and take you back here to FOB Castle."

"How long can we expect to be on the ground before pickup?"

He turned to the Marine sitting in the front row who leaned back and said, "Just give us a call and we'll come get you."

"Right and the check is in the mail. You better."

Chapter 97

I hated flying. I didn't mind helos but a plane? No damned way. Just ordinary flying turned me white with fear. Tonight we were bucking violent winds, the tail end of a storm front that had blown through.

As the C-130 lurched in another downdraft Brit threw up her hands in the air and screamed at the top of her lungs, "YEEEEHHHHHAAAAAA! We're on a goddamn roller coaster from Hell, Nick!"

I bent forward and stared at the floor in front of me, trying to ignore her and whispering a prayer for safety as we lurched through the sky. Across from me, Ahmed slept. Doc was reading a medical textbook by the light of a headlamp. Redshirt looked out the window as we flew down the Hudson River Valley from Albany.

I took a minute to study the three new people on our team. Corporal Killeen and Specialist Desen were two regular Army infantry soldiers whom I had picked out to accompany us, out of the half dozen volunteers we had gotten. Killeen was the big redneck sniper who had been shooting with Ahmed on the boat when the airborne trooper was killed. Desen was his spotter. The two went everywhere together and with the wide-open spaces of the cargo terminal, I wanted some longer range hitting power. He carried an M14 EBR-R, a modified M-14 rifle that fired the heavier 7.62 round and had better range and hitting power than our M4A2s (the M4s firing .22 magnum rounds). I had watched him shoot on the barge and he was good. The only thing I wanted to know was where he was able to find dip. I knew guys who would kill for it and here he was, spitting in between the seats when the C-130 crew wasn't watching. His partner, Desen, was one of those small, wiry guys who looked like he never ate anything and could run your ass into the ground. He chain smoked on base but I knew a guy like that could make himself so unseen a whole zombie horde could walk right past him.

Directly next to them sat our newest civilian Zombie Killer. He had shown up on the island at dusk the day before, paddling a canoe from the far shore of the river. Sasha Zivcovic, or "Ziv," so he called himself, said he was looking to kill Zs. He claimed he had been surviving up in the Hudson highlands and had heard the gunfire and come down to investigate. Looked like a tough character and had readily agreed to come with us to the city when I explained what we were about.

"We're going to be jumping into the City. What experience do you have with airborne operations?" I already knew he was tough if he had been surviving this close to the hordes in the city but I didn't want someone without any jump experience getting hurt on a static line drop. In answer, he rolled up his sleeve to reveal a tattoo of a parachute with the number 63 on it. Over it were several Cyrillic letters and over that, an old scar I recognized as a crudely sewn-up bullet puncture.

"Serbian Army. 63rd Parachute Battalion. Bosnians, Croats, Zombies, all the same," he said in a thick eastern European accent.

"OK then, I guess you're qualified. Ever jump with a T-11 chute?"

"Six hundred and fifty-two times. Eleven times into combat in war."

Jeez, where the hell did we find these guys? I guess it figured though, war veterans survived where others didn't. We knew the world could go to shit any time and half expected it. I introduced him to the team and shook their hands in a reserved, standoff manner. When he got to Brit, he stared at her for a minute, left her hand hanging, then turned to me.

"You have woman on your team?" he growled.

"Yes we do. She is third in command, after myself and Doc." Out of the corner of my eye I could see Brit starting to get angry. Not a good way to start off, brother.

"She is soldier? Maybe lesbian. They make good

fighters. Very angry." He eyed her up and down and she glared back at him.

"I'll cut your effing balls off! Lesbian, my ass. Nick, dump him. We don't need him," she said, obviously pissed.

"Ha, she has spirit. I like that in woman." He grinned at her, showing bad European dental work.

Problem was, we did need him. I tried to smooth things over before one of them knifed the other. "Yes, Brit is a damn good soldier and I have every confidence in her. She has saved me more times than I can count. Is it going to be a problem?"

He spoke after a moment. "No, no problem. This is America, I forget sometimes, you are not old country." After that he had said little, just pitched in and helped organize the pallets for loading on the C-130.

Now he sat across from me, eyes closed, ignoring the bumping ride of the plane. I hoped he would be an asset to the team. We could use a good fighter to replace Jonesy but the attitude toward Brit might be a problem. That and he might be full of shit about his combat experience but I didn't think so.

The ride smoothed out as we approached the city, passing through the clouds into clear air. The crew chief came back to lower the ramp prior to the pallet drop and gave me a "three minutes," sign. We stood up, a tough thing to do with chute and equipment and staged ourselves at the jump door on the side of the plane, doing the usual pre-jump checks. I was jumpmaster, so I went out last, making sure everyone had a good exit. If anyone held up at the door, I wanted to be able to kick them in the ass. Being last out, I could also watch how the others landed. We were jumping onto a park about five hundred meters east of the container facility; jumping onto hard concrete was a good way to get a broken leg. The team used static lines instead of jumping off the back ramp because Brit and Ahmed had only gone through a rushed, one-week airborne qualification jumping from helicopters up at Fort Orange. Good enough to get them out the door and onto the ground without breaking their necks but that was about it.

The pallets went out first, off the back ramp. They would drop directly onto the port grounds, showing an IR beacon so we didn't have to haul them from the Drop Zone. A slow turn back out over lower New York Harbor and the pilot lined up on our DZ.

Over the rush of air from the slipstream and the droning engines, the Crew Chief yelled to me "THIRTY SECONDS!" I felt that icy knot build up in my stomach, it happened no matter how many times I had done this before and then the light turned green.

Chapter 98

One thing I loved about the Zombie Apocalypse, and I won't deny it, was how dark it got at night. With very few places using electricity, you could see the stars burning brightly in the night sky. They distracted me for a moment as I looked up to check my canopy. Then I looked down and counted chutes. We were dropping from eight hundred feet above ground level and that ground came up awfully fast.

One, two, three ... I reached six. Dammit! Below me in the moonlight I saw a body plummeting towards earth, spread eagle, his chute a tangled mess. His reserve chute came out but he still hit hard, with a sickening crunch I could hear from several hundred feet away.

As soon as I was on the ground and had gathered up my chute, I jogged over to where the soldier still lay prone. Doc was already bent over him, giving him a quick once over. Around me, the team gathered in a circle, pulling 360-degree security.

"It's Desen. Compound fracture of the right leg." grunted Doc as he worked to cut off Desen's pant leg. He untied his boot, then put on a rough splint. "We're going to have to carry him."

He lay there groaning as Doc shot him up with some morphine. "Don't worry about it, trooper. You just sit tight and we'll get you out of here once we're done with the scout."

Ziv came over and looked down at Desen, then turned to me. "If he compromises us, we kill him, yes?"

In the darkness, I doubt he could see my expression but I'm sure he could tell from the tone of my voice how pissed I was. "He's my troop. I decide what happens to whom. Got it? Now get back to your position."

"Sure, boss. Whatever you say." He shuffled back to his side the circle. What the hell? Yeah, sometimes we had to do things that you wouldn't consider in the old world. But you don't freaking talk about it right in front of the guy.

"OK. Ahmed and Killeen, you two carry him, the rest split up his gear. Let's go." Way to start off a mission.

We set off towards the Northwest. In our NVG's we could see the infrared strobe from the two pallets that had dropped down before us, directly onto the container yard. Brit led on point, stopping every few hundred meters to listen for any Zombie howls. The place was eerily silent and I hoped it would stay that way. The day before, a U.S. Navy destroyer, the *U.S.S Reuben James*, had bombarded the other side of Staten Island for more than an hour with its 76mm main gun. Hopefully the noise had drawn off most of the Z's present. They were scheduled to provide Naval gunfire support if we needed it but small caliber Naval guns didn't have much effect on zombies. Rumor had it that the *U.S.S New Jersey*, one of the old Iowa class battleships, was being refitted to fire 16 inch BB rounds. In the spring we had scouted and raided the Watervliet Arsenal, with engineers stripping out all the machine tools and sending them back west. Meanwhile, we made do.

Brit made it to the gate at the container yard without encountering a single Z and we quickly cut a hole in the fence. Each of us slid through, dragging Desen on a collapsible stretcher.

"Brit, Ahmed, Red, you scout out the closest building. Clear it and then report back to me. Killeen, Ziv and I will go to the next closest. Doc, stay here with Desen, be ready to move to whichever building we decide forts up best."

Brit and her team took off running towards a building that looked like it was the operations center for the place. We passed them just as Ahmed fired into the door lock with a loud cough and they piled into the first room.

Our target was a large garage. I didn't expect much trouble there but I wanted to keep an eye on Ziv and Killeen. The first door we tried was open and we cautiously stepped into the deeper darkness. Through my NGVs, I immediately saw the softly glowing heat shapes of two zombies stumbling towards us, attracted by the noise. I sighted down my rifle to shoot and my optics were suddenly obscured by the bright heat source of a warm, live body. I felt, more than heard, one of my team members run past me.

I dropped my rifle barrel down to the floor and watched as Ziv rushed them and swung left, then right, knocking them both across their skulls with a three-pound hammer. He spit on them and muttered something, then came stalking back to us.

Ignoring Ziv, Killeen and I continued to sweep the rest of the building, coming up empty.

"Outside, let's go." I kept my voice tight but I was furious.

In my ear, Brit's voice crackled over the radio. *"Building clear. Three Zulus down. Looks like a good place to fort up, over."*

"Roger, be there in two mikes, over."

"Roger, out."

We stepped outside and I stopped Zivcovic.

"Ziv, hang on a second."

He stood silently. Killeen kept walking, not wanting to be part of the conversation he knew was coming.

"Let's get something straight. We aren't glory hounds. We're not here to kill every zombie on earth. We're here to scout. That means doing the job quickly and at the least risk to ourselves. I know you have been living on your own, surviving for years now but we are a team. Do you understand?"

"Are you coward, Nick?"

Was this guy shitting me? Coward? I took a deep breath. "No, Ziv, I'm not a coward. No one on this team is but we have one job to do and I want every one of us to come back alive. That means you work as part of a team, or I leave your ass here on Staten Island. Do you understand me?"

He snorted, then sighed. "Yes, I understand. You Americans, such technology whores, so weak. But I will do as you say."

"Good. You're a good fighter. We can use you but go

off on your own again and I'll put a bullet in you. True story."

"It's been done before and I am still here."

"Me too, Ziv. Listen, we need you and the time for lone wolf is over. This conversation is done." I turned my back and left him standing there.

I keyed the mike to raise Brit. "Brit, take Red, get over to the pallets, get the supplies, see if you can get some transport running."

"Roger that."

"Ahmed, you and Killeen have overwatch. Ziv and I will be there in a minute to start forting up. Tell Doc to keep an eye on Desen."

I headed over towards the office building, not looking back to see if Ziv was following. In the east, the sky was starting to lighten.

Chapter 99

Sunrise brought a wind, like it always did. The air was full of pollen and Brit started sneezing as she pulled up in a pickup truck, the back filled with supplies from the two pallets. We had included spare car batteries, a foot pump, Fix-A-Flat, fresh gasoline, everything needed to get two or three vehicles running. Brit had found a fairly new Ford F-300 pickup with a winch on front. She knew what to look for.

We quickly unloaded and began forting up the building. It was two stories and we started by boarding up the windows with plywood and two by fours. The generator, running quietly with a special muffler, had sandbags around it to further dampen the sound. Doc ran an air-powered nail gun, tacking up the plywood. The sound of hammers would carry too far in the summer air. Ahmed ran a steel escape cable from the roof out to the nearest building while Red and Ziv worked on demolishing the stairway up to the second floor.

On the roof, Killen sat in overwatch with Brit on the spotting scope, watching for Zs that might come stumbling into the yard. Occasionally a muted pop came from the end of Killeen's rifle and I could hear Brit calling out sightings. She leaned over and called down to me "Hey Nick, this guy really can handle a rifle. I think I might like him to show me how he handles his gun." I gave her a salute and she started sucking on her finger.

We took a break at 12:00 and sat down to figure out our next step. Our mission was to see what shape the container yard was in. From the first look, it was a wreck. Next to some of the cranes I could see the bow of a half-sunken freighter rising over the edge of the docking area. That we already knew about from satellite recon and it was the Navy's problem. Our interest was in the cranes themselves and the loading bays for the trucks. We had been tasked with getting a complete rundown on how workable they were and I expected it to take about two full days. If we had the time. I expected the undead would start showing up tonight, so we had to hustle.

"OK, we have two things to accomplish. Desen is stable and he can shoot. He stays here. Killeen, he's your teammate, you keep an eye on him. Ahmed stays here, so the two of you can provide rotating overwatch. Red is staying also." He was currently up on the roof, keeping an eye out. "Start into shifts, Red and Ahmed, Killeen and Desen."

Doc spoke up. "I'm not sure Desen is up for it. I think he might have a broken rib but I can't be sure without an x-ray."

"I'm alright. I can fight." said Desen, then started coughing. "Ow. Fuck, that hurts. Someone gimme a smoke." Brit handed him a cigarette and he drew it down to the filter, then lay back and passed out.

"Like I said, Desen is out of it."

"OK, then. Can you three handle providing overwatch on the gate area and cover us as we scout?"

Ahmed nodded. "We can do that."

I turned to Brit and Ziv. "You two will be coming with me. First things first, the cranes. I'm not sure how we can tell if they're working without any power but we can inspect the cables and machinery. Ziv, do you have any engineering experience?" I wanted to bring him into the team. His loner attitude bothered me and the more useful I could make him, the better.

"In parachute regiment, we learn how to build things so we can blow them up. Mostly bridges, some buildings. Machinery, no."

"OK, well, if you see anything out of place, anything, let one of us know." I turned to Brit. "Camera, pictures of EVERYTHING."

"You betcha, Chiefarooney."

Ziv barked out a laugh, short and harsh. Brit shot me a "sorry," look.

"OK, check your ammo, make sure you have water, any extras you want to bring. SP is in fifteen mikes. Poop or piss or smoke, whatever you gotta do. Remember, we won't be more than five hundred meters from the fort. Stay away from the edge of the docks, I'm not jumping in after anyone. Again."

*****

Doc took a break from cleaning his pistol and said, "1200 BBC news!"

Ahmed spoke up. "Can we get it on the SINCGARS down here?"

"No, we would have to use the Harris radio if they were broadcasting on those freqs but they aren't. Brother, this comes courtesy of the U.S. Navy, broadcasting on the AM radio. Just started last week, up and down the east coast. Lady and gentlemen, AM 890, WU.S.N!"

He walked over to the pickup truck, started it and turned on the radio. We gathered around just as he tuned it in.

"...the BBC News. The Allied Expeditionary Force launched its first area-clearing drive. British, Free French and Spanish Exile army units started moving forward from Gibraltar into Southern Spain. Latest reports have them driving ten miles and establishing a defensive line. General Sir Richard Trask, Allied Forces Commander, said casualties had been light and were on timeline to be in Madrid by September.

A Russian nuclear submarine surfaced outside U.S. territorial limits in Hawaii on Tuesday, requesting asylum. This is the third Russian Navy unit to sail to the United States after the fall of Vladivostok two months ago. The Russian government in exile has issued a general order for national military units to turn themselves into the nearest Allied military base.

In Asia, United States surveillance satellites detected three nuclear detonations in the Himalayan Mountain region of southwestern China. All communication with official Chinese government sources have ceased since these detonations."

I watched Ziv's face as we listened to the broadcast. His normal expressionless mask was turning into a deep scowl.

"... merican Airborne troops have launched directly from securing the Mexican oil fields to an Airborne assault to secure the locks of the Panama Canal Zone. The 82nd Airborne Division, supplemented by elements of the 3rd Canadian Light infantry Division landing by ship, are fighting their way through Panama City. Casualties are reported to be heavy.

Other American forces are reported to be making progress in an effort to approach New York City, reaching the Military Academy at West Point. A rail line has been reopened between Albany and Buffalo."

Brit jumped up and waved her arm in the air. "Hey, that's us!!!! Woot woot, Lost Boys in the house!"

We all grinned at her antics, then Doc shushed us. "Shut it, you foolish woman!" he snapped as Brit continued doing a war dance around the truck.

"...United Nations Agricultural Bureau has forecast another year of food shortages, despite intensive planting in the Pacific Northwest of North America and the United Kingdom. UN estimates have placed the total world population at five hundred million, worldwide. This has been the World News from the BBC."

Ziv had walked away before the news ended and sat at the doorway. I walked over and sat down next to him.

"Guess you haven't had much news over the last few years, huh?"

He sat smoking a cigarette, then taking a swig from a flask. Ordinarily I would have said something about the alcohol but not right now.

"It is all gone, no?"

"Europe? Yeah, pretty much. England is OK, they took in a lot of refugees in. There were some pretty bad riots a year or so in but they have it under control now. Some of the Scandinavian islands, parts of Denmark. Africa is, well, Africa."

"Serbia?" he asked.

"No one has heard anything out of Central Europe in more than a year. Did you have a lot of family there?"

He nodded. "We Serbs have big families." Standing up, he ground the cigarette out and capped the flask, then started checking his weapons.

"Well, at least all those bastard Croats and devil Bosnian pagans are burning in hell now. I always thought I would go back and we would finish the job but God has beaten me to it."

I had nothing to say to that. As far as I could recollect, the Serbs had as much blood on their hands as any of them, if not more. Whatever. That feud was done, after a thousand years. Death and the Zombie Plague treated everyone as equals.

Chapter 100

In the end, the container yard was a bust. Not a Z to be seen and our main objective, the cranes that lifted the containers from the ships to the trucks, sat mute. From everything we could tell, they seemed in good condition but I couldn't answer the Navy's main question of whether they worked or not. I had brought up that specific point when we were getting our mission brief but I was told to just do my best. Of course, when I reported this, they blew their stack.

"Swabbie six niner, this is Lostboys six, over."

"Lostboys, use proper callsigns, over."

I ran my finger down the Signal Operating Instructions that I had taped to my forearm.

"Ah, Rapier seven two, this is Lostboys six, over."

"This is Rapier six, you are sending unsecure, please authenticate, over."

Great, the frigging admiral in charge of the Navy Task Force was sitting off New York Harbor and he wanted me to send different word codes to make sure I was really me. Who the hell else would be calling him? Plus, he was a jerk anyway, which I knew from personal experience.

"Rapier six, I authenticate your daughter has a birthmark on her right breast, just below her nipple, over."

Brit shot me a dirty look. I grinned at her. "Hey, you weren't the only one to have a good time in Bermuda last year."

The radio stayed silent for a minute, then the fleet executive officer came on. *"Roger, Lost Boys, this is Rapier five, I also can confirm. Send your traffic, over."* Ha ha, that would be Captain Reynolds. Fighter pilot, good guy and man, could he drink. I gave them a quick lowdown on the terminal. The loading docks were all secure, buildings looked good but we were unable to determine if the cranes worked without power, as we had said in our initial briefing.

"Lost Boys, this is Rapier Six. What do you mean you can't determine if they work, over?" He sounded pissed.

"I mean without a massive generator to tie into the power infrastructure, there is no way to determine. They look functional, over."

Captain Reynolds came back online. *"Lost Boys, what is your tactical situation, over?"*

"Rapier, we are secure at this time. When can we expect exfil, over?"

"Twenty- four to thirty-six hours, unless your situation deteriorates. QRF is tied up in Philadelphia, over."

Great. Would have been nice if they could have come and get us right away.

"This is Lost Boys, twenty- four to thirty-six, out." I gathered the team around. Killeen was up on the roof, pulling overwatch.

"Well, here's the deal. The Marines can't get here for a day, day and half. If we sit tight, nice and quiet, there shouldn't be much of a problem. Nearest residential area is more than half a mile away and I think our sniper teams have already cleared out the local Zulus."

"A lot less than usual." observed Ahmed. "Something doesn't seem right. This was a heavily populated area. The number of wanderers alone should be in the hundreds."

Doc chimed in. "I remember the evacuation out of the City didn't cover Staten Island, since the Goethals Bridge had become jam-packed with crashed vehicles on day one of the plague. Place was a madhouse. Boats running out, gunfights, riots. Army just basically wrote it off after day three."

"Well, regardless, it seems quiet here. We've hunted the whole compound out, killed maybe another six Zulus outside the gate. Doc, how is Desen doing?"

"Seems OK so far but he needs proper medical attention. I've splinted the leg and given him antibiotics and painkillers but the longer he doesn't get it set properly, the bigger the chance of infection and improper healing."

"Keep an eye on him. Position improvement, overwatch from the roof. As soon as it's dark, sleep rotation. I've got a weird feeling but hopefully by this time tomorrow we'll be turning this place over to the jarheads."

Killeens' voice crackled over the radio. "Sarge, we got movement, human heat sources, vehicle noises and engine heat. Two vehicles, no, three. Stopped about three hundred meters back. Looks like scouts moving up either side of the street. I count two scouts and eleven in the main body. One vehicle mounted weapon." I could barely understand him between the southern drawl and the dip in his mouth.

"I copy, be there in a second."

Everyone had heard the transmission and started scrambling to fighting positions inside the building. I headed up to the roof, followed by Ahmed. Along the way, I told Red to be ready to go out and do a meet and greet, and to bring Ziv as a bodyguard. We had done this before, encountered survivors and it could go three ways. One, they welcomed us with open arms and wanted our help. Two, they were indifferent and went their own way. Three, well, three was to be avoided at all costs.

Chapter 101

At my signal, Doc launched a flare from his 203. It burst into light directly over the main body of intruders and they immediately went to ground behind wrecked cars. It slowly drifted down and burned out as it lay on the pavement.

When it was out, Redshirt crept forward, followed by Ziv. Now the hard part. They knew we were here, the next move was up to them. We waited a few minutes but they did nothing.

Red stood up and yelled out "UNITED STATES ARMY!" at the top of his lungs. The response was a shot from one of the scouts. Red grabbed his chest just as Ziv tackled him and they both fell to the ground as the machine gun on the vehicle opened up, along with scattered rifle shots.

Rounds started skipping across the pavement where they had fallen and Ziv picked Red up in a fireman's carry, dashing back to the cover of some cars. Killeen and Ahmed started firing, trying to take out the machine gunner. The vehicle accelerated forward and the front of the building was shattered by dozens of rounds.

Doc placed a high explosive round directly onto the cab of the truck and it exploded with a muted crump. Flames burst out of the engine compartment and the truck swerved, crashed through a storefront.

Shots started coming at us on the roof, aimed at the muzzle flashes of the sniper rifles. Dust flew from the wall in front of us as several zipped past, making flat, cracking noises. I fired back a long burst, hitting one of the scouts who had risen to fire at Ziv. Beside me, Killeen grunted and fell back.

"Nick, they are pulling back!" yelled Ahmed. We fired a few more shots at them but I could see them running down the street, leaving a half dozen bodies and the burning pickup truck. I called for a cease fire over the radio. No need to waste ammo and there was going to be a shitload of zombies attracted to the noise of that firefight.

"Watch your sectors!" I yelled as I raced down the stairs, scrambling down the ladder to the first floor.

I waved at Brit to follow and told Doc to go check out Killeen. We headed out the door toward where Ziv was carrying Red back to the building and helped put him down on the ground.

Brit ripped open his body armor and started feeling for blood. "Ow, dammit, that hurts," grunted Red. She shone a flashlight onto his chest where a big purple bruise was spreading. A red mark showed where the ceramic front plate had been driven into his skin.

Brit kissed him on the cheek and yelled in his ear "Suck it up, you puss!"

"Ziv, Brit, get him inside." I started to run back but Docs' voice came over the radio.

"Nick, Killeen is dead."

Chapter 102

"Roger, understood. You want us to reconnoiter the approaches to the Verrazano Bridge, see if it is serviceable, Lost Boys out."

"Well now, ain't that just a bullshit mission." Brit said through a mouthful of#12 MRE, Penne pasta with vegetarian sauce.

Ziv stared at her. "How can you eat that crap? It tastes like cardboard."

"You should see what it tastes like when I poop it out. Same consistency, too."

"Maybe someday I will."

"Over my dead body, Troll." He did kind of resemble one as he sat there grinning with his bad European dental work and massive shoulders.

Doc laughed. "I think you've met your match, Brit." Then he noticed the black bag with Killeens' body in it. He sat for a moment watching Red digging a grave for him over by the fence, then got up to go back inside and check on the two unknown intruders whom we had found still breathing. One was barely alive and the other was babbling in a fever. We had no medicines for them. Or, more like none I wanted to spare for them.

"Obviously we aren't going to walk there. It's a few miles. We can take Highway 278 across the island but I'm afraid that even if we can get there, getting back again will be a problem. We've got the gangbangers to worry about and whatever Zulus get stirred up and traffic jams."

We had patrolled down the road about a quarter mile, checking out the buildings and looking for any hidden observers left behind by the intruders last night. The road got progressively more jammed as you got out to the highway and I was sure the eastern ramps to the Goethel's Bridge over to Jersey would be a massive cluster.

"So, we have a mission from higher up which can be done by us, take a day or so and likely get the team wiped out. Plus, we will have to leave two people behind with Desen. Doc and Red, probably, so that leaves me, Brit and Ziv to recon through 12 klicks of one of the most densely populated areas of the country."

"We're good but we ain't that good, Nick." said Brit. "Ever read Band of Brothers? We should do what Major Winters did when they wanted him to send out a useless patrol."

Ziv grunted and said, "Yes, he told his superior that he had done mission but not send patrol. We often do this in Serbian war when commanders are stupid."

"Wow, he can read, too!"

Ziv laughed at her. "I am from foreign country, not stupid, Little Girl."

"Great, now you two kiss." I held up my hand to Ziv as he looked at me with a shocked expression and said, "But she is your woman!" Brit made a gagging sound.

"It's just an expression. It means 'let's get on with what we were doing.'"

"You Americans with your slang."

As far as Mid-Atlantic Command knew, we rolled out bright and early the next morning, made it as far as the interchange for I-278 and U.S. 440 and had to turn back due to blocked roads. We actually used the time to clean our weapons and get some sleep. The last of the unknown shooters died just as the first Marine Osprey came thundering in and a squad rushed out the back.

Doc packed up his aid bag and stripped off his gloves. Before he had slipped into unconsciousness, the man had bragged about being a Crip, how they ruled the island, motherfuckers were going to pay, yadda, yadda.

I had seen it before. Gangs were often the only organized, well-enough armed and ruthless enough group to cope with the zombie outbreaks in an urban environment. They took what they needed to survive, from whoever had it. They often kept slaves and we had been seeing more and more of them turn cannibal as food got scarce. We negotiated with them when they were stronger than us, until we came back with more firepower. Sometimes they actually welcomed us.Either way, it was the Marines' problem now. I met their company commander as he walked across the container yard.

"Nick, I relieve you!"

"I stand relieved, Bob." Another one of my buddies from our vacation in Bermuda.

"Looks like you had some trouble. Sorry we couldn't get here sooner, Team Four was getting hammered in Philly."

"We handled it. Local gang bangers running the show here on the Island. Looks like they had done a pretty good job of cleaning out the zombie problem but I bet they will come back here with more firepower than that probe last night."

"We can handle it. I've got a reinforced rifle company. We are going to hunt this place clean over the next month, zombies and scumbags alike."

"Yeah, well there might be some regular civilians holding out, too. Seen it all before."

"Agreed. Heard you lost a man. Sorry about that."

"Yeah, well, random gunfire is random and doesn't care who it hits. It was quick, he took a round though his head. Never felt a thing." In my mind, I could still see Killeen lying next to his rifle, staring up at the sky where Doc had flipped him over. A hole the size of a pencil eraser just above his eyebrow. I didn't want to think what the back of his head looked like. Chewing tobacco and blood had mixed in a puddle on the ground. Someone had gotten a lucky shot with their black-market AK.

We both turned towards the dock area, where a beautiful sight waited for us. A giant Roll On /Roll Off cargo ship was pulling up to the pier, pushed by a tug. Beyond it stood the knife-edge silhouette of the *U.S.S Reuben James*.

"My company is going to hunt Staten Island. That ship contains the entire vehicle complement of the 1st Brigade, 1st Armored Division. They're going to roll hot right over the

Verrazano Bridge and shoot the shit out of Brooklyn, all the way to Floyd Bennett Field. Rangers will be dropping in next week to secure the airport and the Old Ironsides tanks and Brads are going to roll up the Belt Parkway. Welcome to Forward Operating Base Killeen, Nick!"

I wanted to cry. I really did. My mind flashed back to the zombie hordes overrunning our position on the weekend of the plague, the madness of trying to survive alone those first months. I watched as the Marines set up a temporary flag pole and saluted as Old Glory was run up.

Brit came up to me as I stood there, watching them lower the ramp off the ship.

"Nick, check it out! New orders. WE'RE GOING BACK TO CIVILIZATION! HOORRRAAYYY!" She started dancing around me, chanting, "Clean sheets, bathtubs, clean sheets, bathtubs!" as I read the iPhone she handed me.

FROM: CDR@TFEMPIRE.MIDATLCOM.MIL
TO: LOSTBOYS6@ TFEMPIRE.MIDATLCOM.MIL
CC: LOSTBOYS5@ TFEMPIRE.MIDATLCOM.MIL; S3@ TFEMPIRE.MIDATLCOM.MIL; J3@JSOC,MIL; JFOPS@NAVY.MIDATLCOM.MIL
SUBJ:TDY of JSOC-IST1

Nick, you and your team are being assigned temporary duty at Joint Forces Base Lewis-McChord as train-the-trainer instructors for Basic Training Cadre. Expect to be out of the field for 2 to 4 weeks. Bring your whole team, including attached elements. You can also be expected to be debriefed by the people at the Center for Army Lessons Learned.

Orders will be waiting for you at Fort Orange in Albany, then C-17 back to SeaTac. Try not to burn down the entire city of Seattle.

Major John Flynn
Acting Commander
Task Force Empire Shield

Chapter 103

The interior of the C-17 Globemaster was packed to the limit, filled with reclaimed electronics, car parts, gold bars, all the loot of the modern world to keep the light of civilization burning. Reclamation teams followed the path of the Army, disassembling cars, recovering precious metals, siphoning gasoline. It was shipped to depots and sorted. The jewelry was melted down into ingots for easy transport, the gasoline and oil fed into fuel blivets.

We sat on either side, our gear piled at our feet. Taking off the pilot had performed a sharp, twisting climb to avoid random potshots, leaving my stomach somewhere behind. I tried to sleep but I was drawn to the small window as we chased the setting sun.

Below me the flat plains of the Midwest stretched out. The great rivers, the Ohio, the Mississippi, the Missouri, had all broken their banks and flooded great stretches of the countryside. Here and there in the darkness below gleamed one or two spreads of lights, fortress towns that somehow survived. Ship lights gleamed on the Great Lakes, moving to Buffalo from the railheads in Green Bay, carrying supplies and troops to New York. I remembered how it all looked, the great spread of lights where Chicago, Detroit, St. Louis had all been. Now they lay faintly shimmering in the moonlight, reflections of the billion shards of broken glass that lay like sand on the beach.

We approached the Columbia Federal District, once known as Washington State, with the bulk of Mount Rainier shouldering its way above the clouds and touched down in the light rain that always seemed to hang in the air. The pilot's voice came over the intercom. "Welcome to SeaTac airport. There is a shuttle bus to JBLM at the U.S.O desk. Please go through customs and declare all weapons. Thanks for flying Zombie Air!" Very frigging funny.

I lifted my Alice pack onto my back, picked up my duffle, followed the rest of the guys down the ramp and into the closest building, where an Airman stood with a clipboard. He took a copy of each of our orders and ran our CAC cards through a reader.

"I see you guys are coming from the Wild Wild East. When was the last time any of you were here?"

"Doc and Jonesy, I mean, Doc and I were here last year. I'm pretty sure SPC Redshirt was here pretty recently."

"I was just here for Basic Training, never saw anything outside the base," said Redshirt.

"OK, well, then you have to understand some things have changed. You are going to have to wait two days in quarantine and all personal weapons have to be left here to be reclaimed when you fly back out."

"What the hell? Since when?" I went everywhere armed. We all did.

"Well, bad riots last year in response to the government-forced resettlement plan. Under the Federal Emergency Mandate, personal firearms and weapons are not allowed in the Columbia Federal District unless you are part of a law enforcement agency. In addition, all personnel arriving from areas not under federal control must remain in quarantine for prevention of spreading reanimation virus."

He sounded like he was reading from a bad movie script and looked bored as hell. We were tired and suffering from jet lag so none of us argued with him about it. Just grumbled and bitched as we started pulling guns, knives, grenades and various bludgeons from holsters and pockets. The more stuff we dropped in the amnesty box, the bigger his eyes got. When we finally finished, the box was filled to the top.

"You know," one of the two Military Policemen standing there said, looking at all the hardware we carried, "you all think you're so badass rolling in here with all this. How freaking bad can it be out there? I think you're all so full of shit it isn't even funny."

I ignored them and kept dealing with the Air Force sergeant. He was about to lock the box and hand me the key and a hand receipt listing all the items when I heard a commotion behind me.

"Oh shit, she's turning!" yelled Doc and he swung Brit, who twitched and spasmed, screeching and howling at the top of her lungs, toward the MPs, who reacted like a grenade had been thrown at them. Brit sank her teeth into the hand of the one who had called us full of shit and he screamed like a little girl. His partner fumbled to load his pistol while the Air Force sergeant dove under the table, dropping his clipboard.

The scene was absolute chaos for a second, until Brit abruptly stood up and started laughing.

"Who's full of shit now, you pogues?"

"You freaking bit me!!"

"Didn't even break the skin. Wimp."

Ziv had stepped in front of the other MP, who had finally managed to load a magazine in his pistol but hadn't racked the slide. He stared him down, then sidled past and out the door. Brit passed them, laughing and the rest of us filed out.

Outside, Doc passed us each one of the weapons he had grabbed out of the lock box in the confusion. I took my .22 automatic and slipped into my coat pocket, feeling a lot better and we boarded the shuttle bus to Joint Base Lewis-McChord.

Chapter 104

Brit put Game of Thrones back in the DVD player and hit play, then started chowing down on popcorn again.

"How many times are you going to watch this?" Red, Doc, Ziv and I were playing spades and Doc and I were losing badly.

"As many times as it takes. Gotta see my girl burn shit up with her dragons. Plus I got the hots for Captain Tightpants."

I threw a spade down on diamonds but Red cut me with the Big Joker. That kid had all the luck and he put it to good use. "Play again? Make it a thousand."

Doc threw his cards down. "No, I'm tired. Gonna hit the rack."

"I'm going to head over to the front desk, see if we can get out of here any sooner."

We had been in quarantine for more than a day now and it was getting boring. I could see Mount Rainier in the west and I knew that Seattle, with all its civilization, was only an hour away. After being out in the wilds for a year, we all wanted to get to it.

The Specialist at the desk was playing Call of Duty and ignored me for a minute. I stood patiently until his match ended.

"SPC Esposito," I read off his name tag, "how the hell do we get out of this place early?"

"You really want to get out of here early?"

"Sure do. You know none of us has the plague. We've been out in the wild for two years and I want an effing steak."

"Simple. Take me with you. I'm a clerk now but I've got a tour in Iraq as an 11B and a tour in Afghanistan as an MP."

I looked him over. A little heavy-set from sitting and playing Xbox all day but a few months in the wild would take care of that. We could use another shooter and anyone who wanted to go with us might be crazy enough to fit in.

"OK, when we head back to the Wild, if your command OKs it, you can join our merry little band."

"Cool beans!" He turned to his laptop, printed out a release paper and signed it.

"There you go. Cleared of quarantine. Go over to north Fort and draw quarters and you're expected at Building 4387 at 0700 Monday morning for an inbrief. Have fun and stay off the MP blotter."

I banged open the door to the Quarantine Block. "PACK IT UP! TIME TO ROLL! E.R. Rogers, here we come!"

Steak. I wanted some serious steak and the best place to get it was in Steilacoom. I had drawn a GSA van and we piled in. I called ahead and made a reservation for five. Ahmed went his own way, wanting to go to a mosque for Friday prayers.

The steakhouse was in a large, converted Victorian-era house. We made our way upstairs, Red peeled off to hit the bar and we headed to our table. "Stay away from the real firewater, Red!" I called after him.

"Well, look who came in out of the rain! How nice to see you, Sergeant Agostine, Sergeant Hamilton, Ms. O'Neill. And who is this gentleman?"

I stopped short. Dr. Morano sat at a table by the window, laptop in front of her. Her two bodyguards sat at another table a few feet away.

"Where is that young lady, Specialist Mya? Ohhhhh, that's right, I read the report. Such a tragedy." The smile on her face didn't reach her eyes.

I wasn't fast enough. I shot out my arm to grab Brit but she launched herself at Dr. Morano, catching her in a headlock and trying to bang her head into the table. The two fell to the floor and the bodyguards' table crashed over as they leapt up and drew their pistols. Ziv punched one in the back of the head with a set of brass knuckles that he had hid from the airport security guys. The other pressed his pistol against Brit's head. Doc and I had our guns out and pointed at him.

"TELL YOUR BITCH TO STAND DOWN!" yelled the bodyguard.

"DROP THE FUCKING GUN!" I yelled back at him.

Brit held dead still. She could feel the barrel of the pistol pressed against the nape of her neck. Beneath her, Dr. Morano spoke through smashed lips.

"Johanson, put it away."

He stood and holstered the pistol. Brit started to get up, then banged the doctor's head off the floor. The bodyguard started and Brit stood up and put her hands up in the air. "It's OK, you trained dog. I'm done." Then she hawked up some phlegm and spit on Dr. Morano's steak.

"Did you have to spit on her steak? That might not have been the best idea." We were driving north on I-5, having grabbed Redshirt from the bar and hightailed it out of there before the local cops showed up.

"Nick, I've done a lot of things that seemed like a good idea at the time. Spitting on her steak seemed like a good idea at the time."

"Yeah but I think somehow we're going to pay for that. I don't think the old Delta Force boy is happy with you punching him in the head, either."

Ziv snorted. "Some men, they need to be punched. It keeps them, what is the word? Humble."

*****

We were at a bar in downtown Seattle, far enough away from the bases so we weren't surrounded by uniforms while we knocked back a few beers. Brit went over to get herself a drink and lay a trap. Far enough away that if someone interesting came her way she could talk to him, close enough to us if she needed mutual support or extraction under heavy fire.

She didn't have long to wait. I could overhear the conversation but I pretended not to notice. A guy in uniform, badges piled high on his chest, sidled up the bar and leaned in. He looked about twenty years old but was wearing Sergeant Major rank. Undead Airborne wings with a star, Air Assault, Pathfinder, Combat infantry Badge with a star, Ranger, Sapper and Special Forces Tab over an Airborne Z Combat Command patch. He had more stuff on his uniform than our whole team put together, and I caught a glimpse of a familiar black and gold scroll. Oh boy.

"Hey Good-Looking, is heaven missing an angel? Because I want to turn you in for the reward!"

Brit laughed. "You're retarded." He looked crestfallen but waded in for another try.

"Hey, cut me a break, I just got in from the wild East Coast!" Doc choked on his beer and sprayed some out on the table. I shot him a look that said, shut it! This was going to be good.

Brit rolled with it, making her eyes open wide. "Really? Oh, my gosh! You were actually out in the Wild?" She rolled the neck of her beer between her breasts. His eyes never left the beer.

"Yeah, you might have seen us in the news, couple of weeks ago. Of course, our faces were blacked out, you know, Special Forces. We were the ones up at West Point. You know, that picture that was in 'Merika Today."

She leaned over and put a hand on his arm. "Oh, I bet that was some pretty bad stuff. Did you see some action?" She flipped her hair back over her shoulder. You go, girl!

"Hell yeah! There were zombies all over the frigging place! We got overrun. I was the last man on the chopper. Held them off with the butt of my rifle. See this?" and he rolled up his sleeve to show a small scar on his forearm. "I got a Silver Star and three purple hearts for that action. Bad shit."

"Ohhh, what unit did you say you were in?" she breathed out in a husky voice.

"Well, I'm not supposed to say but you might have heard of us. I'm with the Irregular Scouts. We go where no one else will."

By this point, we were all trying hard not to burst out laughing. Doc actually got up from the table with his hand over his mouth and even Ziv had the ghost of a smile on his craggy face.

"Oh, that sounds dangerous! That's the kind of man I'm looking for!"

His eyes lit up and he leaned in further toward Brit. "Really?"

"Yeah, I got a thing for tough soldiers. Matter of fact, I wouldn't mind showing you a thing or two! You know, support the troops and everything." As Brit started to lift her shirt, the look on the guy's face was pure amazement at his luck.

"Hell yeah!" he started to say, then cut it off when he saw the still livid scar across Brit's abdomen.

"Yeah, I need a man who can take care of me. You know, when I come home tired and SHOT!"

His face had turned a bit green and we all burst out laughing. "Whoops, I forgot about that! You see, I got SHOT. In NEW YORK. Before we went to WEST POINT." She pulled her shirt down and pulled up the leg of her shorts.

"OMG, I totally forgot about this one! I got SHOT. In the LEG. When I was in NEW YORK. Before we went to WEST POINT!" We were all rolling on the floor, laughing our asses off. The guy turned and ran out of the bar as the whole place erupted in laughter.

I loved that woman.

Chapter 105

I stood in front of the auditorium, drinking coffee, trying to get the projector to work for our PowerPoint presentation. Doc sat at a desk, feet up on a chair, snoring loudly. We were both trying to get past our hangovers and get down to work.

Our job over the next few weeks was to pass along the lessons we had learned about fighting zombies to instructors at the Fort Lewis Basic Training unit. Since the plague, Fort Lewis had turned into a giant training ground and headquarters for the Army and there were now thousands of troops being cycled through every month. Knowledge from the field was passed on through the Center for Army Lessons Learned. We were being used to give firsthand experience the instructors would pass on to the recruits.

They filed in, a group of captains, lieutenants, staff sergeants, sergeants and corporals. Most of them had combat patches on their right sleeves but only a few of them had a red Zombie Combat Command patch. It was considered "cooler" to wear a patch earned by fighting in Iraq or Afghanistan. Anyone could fight zombies. They all had a patch, though. The Army had learned, finally, that you don't train your troops with inexperienced leaders.

We got past the standard introductions, all the wanker-measuring, all the street creds. Then, in answer to a question from one of the guys, I told them about our detachment.

"Well, you all know what a mess things are out there in the wild and how hard it is to get trained replacements on a regular basis. Anyone left out in the wild is obviously a survivor, or led by a survivor, used to living in areas that are infested. So, the Irregular Scout Teams are composed of Regular Army, Reservists and civilians." From the back of the auditorium Brit let out a yell. "That's me, sucking the taxpayer's tit!" The guys (and not a few ladies) laughed.

"Keep the comments from the peanut gallery down, please." I continued on.

"Currently there are six--"

"FIVE!" yelled Brit.

"Yes, sorry, five Irregular Scout Teams. Our business is a bit hazardous. We have had a roughly, um, three hundred percent casualty rate over the last year."

A Captain in the first row spoke up. "Three hundred percent? Is that a bit much?"

"Sir, we do a very dangerous job. We're out there all alone, trying to avoid zombies and people who would just as soon shoot us as welcome us. Last two missions, we lost, um, let's see …" I added them together in my head. Ski, Jacob, Jonesy, Mya, Killeen dead, Redshirt, Brit and Desen wounded. "We've had 5 KIA and 3 WIA. For an eight-man team, that's 100% casualties. IST-4 was wiped out to a man last week in Philadelphia."

I turned my attention to the rest of the crowd. "We're here today and for the next couple of weeks to help you understand a little more about fighting zombies, using the information that teams such as ours can bring you and help you pass the info along to your trainees. We're all volunteers, so whether we live or die, we will get you the information you need to do your jobs."

Redshirt started a PowerPoint briefing and a collective groan arose from the crowd. "Shit, not PowerPoint!" said someone in the back row. I grinned an evil grin and said, "Next slide, please!"

A picture of multiple undead appeared on the screen and I launched into the spiel I had been working on all night.

"First off, we're not here to talk about the "why," of the Zombie Apocalypse. It happened and no one knows why. Nor are we any closer to figuring out what a zombie actually is. Our job is to kill them. Actually, your job is to kill them. Ours is to scout areas you may be going into so that you don't get your asses handed to you.

"The very first thing your troops need to remember is that you are smarter than a zombie. Well, some of you. We'll leave the junior officers out of this for now." That brought a laugh from the crowd.

"The reason most people die out in the wild is they don't use their heads. If you just use some freaking common sense, you can live out there. My team members back there, the two civilians," I said, indicating Brit and Ziv, "did it for two years."

Then we got down to the serious business. How zombies found you. Where they concentrated. How to avoid them. How to kill them. How to avoid getting killed or turned by them.

"I see all of you are wearing the new multicam uniforms. Notice the heavy kevlar panels sewn into the sleeves. Yeah, they are annoying but if you cram your arm into a zombie's mouth and let him chew on that for a few seconds, it will give you time to shoot or smash their brains. Just don't inhale when it splatters back at you. Also, the hoods attached to the blouse can and will protect your head and necks from being bitten."

After a break, Doc moved onto a session about emergency battlefield medicine.

"The one thing I can tell you, the one thing you must get these kids to understand, is that an infected soldier will turn into a Z quickly and break your lines. Many of you have seen that. As leaders, don't be afraid to neutralize a former soldier of yours. There is no room for compassion."

That didn't sit well with the crowd. One of them raised a hand. "What if we, you know, cut off an arm or leg or something?"

"Are you willing to take that chance with the rest of your soldiers? In the middle of a zombie swarm? No. Just shoot him. You will be doing him and your soldiers a favor."

We finally broke for lunch. It was going to be a very long day.

Chapter 106

When I woke up it was pitch black. I tried to sit up but a strap was across my chest and another held down my legs. I lay back as the incredible stench of zombies hit me. Rotting putrid meat smell and I gagged, trying not to throw up.

I lay there for several minutes, trying to figure out what was going on. I heard nothing. If there were Zs close by, if I smelled them that strongly, I should have heard them by now. I did hear something. Someone was breathing regularly, the deep breathing of sleep.

Last thing I remembered, Brit and I had been eating dinner at the mess hall on north Fort Lewis. When you find yourself in a tough situation, the number one rule is to not panic.

"Damn," I muttered to myself. "No towel."

As I said that, I heard a door open in the darkness and bright lights flickered on, just as I closed my eyes. I blinked them open after giving myself time to adjust, then lifted my head to look around.

To my left, strapped to a table just like I was Brit, out cold. In front of me, accompanied by one of her goons, stood Dr. Morano.

"Nice shiner you got there, Bro. Can't say it helps your looks," I said to the Delta Operator. His right eye and jaw were black and green where Ziv had punched him at the restaurant. I figured two days ago. He started toward me but Morano put her hand up.

"Sergeant Agostine, so glad to see you're awake. Did you have a good sleep?" She smiled at me but I could still see the red marks around her neck where Brit had tried to choke her. She started washing her hands leisurely at the sink.

"I actually feel like crap. Nice place you have here." It was a lab, with several other tables and, over in one corner, a pile of severed body parts, including a head that kept snapping its jaws. The red eyes stared at me. "Actually, I think you need a new housekeeper."

"I do admire flippancy in the face of adverse conditions," she said casually, "but don't worry, Nick, I'm not going to kill you. Or Ms. O'Neill, either. We live in civilized times, do we not?" She walked over to a cart with several instruments loaded into it, picked up a needle and a bottle, examined the contents and withdrew some clear liquid into the needle.

She walked over to Brit. "For example, you've merely inconvenienced me. You haven't killed anyone I have regards for, or who works for me, so why should I kill you, or any of your associates? Your little girlfriend here, however, did embarrass me at the restaurant the other night," she said, wiping an alcohol swab around the corner of Brit's right eye.

"What about Specialist Mya? She's dead because of you."

"Ah yes. Well, the nerve agent wouldn't have worked on zombies anyway. It didn't in the lab but I thought it might in a field experiment. I can't help it if your troops have no discipline, Sergeant." She stood with her back to me and moved so I couldn't see what she was doing. I kept straining my neck but Brit was blocked from view. After a moment Morano stepped back and threw the needle into a disposal chute.

"Johanson, let's go. Nick, before you swear revenge, or whatever your stupid moronic code of honor demands, remember this: I can get to you anywhere, any time. The Army needs me and my program and they give me carte blanche to do whatever I want. I've arranged a nice little vacation for you and your friends in Denver. Please do have a good time."

"Revenge? For tying me and Brit up like this? This is all you've got?"

"Oh, no. She'll see what I've done. Or, should I say, she won't."

I said calmly as I could, "If you've hurt her, I'll kill

you."

She laughed and her bodyguard smirked. "Nick, never go up against a Sicilian when death is on the line!" Then she unstrapped my arms and stepped away. The whole time, her goon kept his .45 rock-steady on my face. I didn't move a muscle; I knew those Delta guys could shoot. She walked out and he gave me a shit-eating grin as he backed out the doorway. "See you later, Sucker. You should watch what you eat."

The door clicked shut just as Brit started to wake. She groaned as I sat up and unbuckled my legs, swung down from the table and unstrapped her, helping her sit up.

"Nick, what the hell? Where are we?"

"Dr. Morano's lab, I think. Are you OK?"

She nodded, went still, blinked a few times, put her hand over her right eye, moving it further away and then closer. Finally she turned to me. I could see the bright blue of her eye had become dull and the pupil was cloudy.

"Nick, I can't see out of my eye! She blinded me!"

Chapter 107

"You can't see anything?"

"I can see perfectly out of one eye but nothing out of the other."

"Does it hurt?"

"No, not at all. I am going to kill that bitch!" She started up off the table and I sat her back down.

"No, no you're not. Listen to me, Brit. She could have killed us any time she wanted to. Made us disappear. I've seen it happen. Look around you."

She did and took in the medical equipment, the pile of rotting body parts on the floor, the Zombie head still snapping at us. It looked like some kind of medieval torture chamber. On the wall hung one of those crappy inspirational posters.

I took her face in my hand and turned her good eye to me. She was furious and I had to stop her right here, right now. "Brit listen to me. We have to move very, very carefully from here on out. We are on her turf. As long as we are in Seattle and around the big Army, we can't do anything to her. Do you understand me?" Her one good eye glared at me, full of fury.

"Brit, you have got to understand. I swear to you, we will deal with her someday, in our own way but if we fight her here, we will die and I'm not losing anyone else if I can help it. Especially you."

A tear rolled out of her good eye. The other one sat blankly, staring and lifeless. "I'm going to kill her, Nick. Soon."

"Soon, Brit. I promise. Now let's get out of here."

We made our way out the door and down a long corridor. Several doors were set on each side, looking like cells, with an observation window set in each one. As we passed the first door, something crashed into it with a loud bang thump, making us jump back. I went over to the window and slid back the little covering. Inside, a zombie was backing up to rush at the door again. He was wearing shredded Army ACUs, with dried blood coating the pixelated surface. His lower jaw had been torn or cut off and a large hole gaped where his larynx had been. Brit pushed me aside to get a look, just as it crashed into the door again.

"She cut his voice out. He was a soldier. Look at his patch." I peered in again and saw what she was talking about. On his left sleeve was the Screaming Eagle of the 101st Airborne. The entire division has been wiped out to a man, after air assaulting into Washington, DC to evacuate critical government personnel. That was a year ago, in the middle of the chaos. Their Forward Arming and Refuel Point in Virginia had been overrun by panicked civilians trying to get onto the helicopters, stranding all three brigades at the barricades surrounding the Capitol. Doc had told me of being in the TOC in Manhattan, listening to the units drop off the net as they were overrun, one by one. When we went after Patient Zero in the spring we had flown across piles of bones where they had sold their lives in a running gunfight against the millions of zombies who swarmed out of the cities on the eastern seaboard. How Dr. Morano had gotten one of them out to the west coast, I didn't want to know.

"Nick, we have to kill it. He was one of us, not some goddamned freakshow experiment!" She started to open the door, gripping the handle tightly. I pulled her off and further down the corridor. She struggled and then finally let me pull her way.

It was the same at each of the doors we passed. The Zombie inside would charge the doorway as we went by. Each of them held a ragged, bloody, rotting form in the remains of an Army uniform, several of them with obvious wounds to their heads. Experiments.

The last door held the worst. Lying there, listlessly, were the remains of Specialist Mya, our medic who had been killed by nerve agent back at Firebase Castle in New York. Her body, which we had left on the island a few hours after she had been accidently killed, was bloated but still recognizable, pushing against the remains of her uniform. The Z which had been her crawled slowly across the floor toward the door, arms twitching and flailing as it dragged itself across the floor towards me.

"Holy fuck!" yelled Brit. This time I didn't stop her as she flung open the cell door. The thing which had been our teammate seemed weak, not in control of itself but its eyes still glowed that insane red. Brit walked over to it and stomped as hard as she could on the thing's head, cracking its skull. It twitched once or twice, then lay still.

"Oh Girl, I am so sorry we left you out there in the rain. We didn't know. We didn't know. We thought you were dead." Brit kneeled in front of the cooling corpse, ignoring the blood that soaked her jeans, crying.

"She *was* dead." We both started at the sound of Dr. Morano's voice from the just outside the cell.

"All soldiers now sign a release authorizing the Army to use their bodies to best effect in order to combat the zombie plague. Don't you know that? It's a small clause, buried very deep in their draft papers but oh, so useful to me." She had a little smile on her face. Such a beautiful woman and rotten to the core. "As a matter of fact, Ms. O'Neill, even your civilian contract with the Army has the clause. Do me a favor, leave your body whole when you do get killed. Nick, please don't shoot her in the head." She turned and walked out. Her bodyguards, who had been standing with guns drawn on us, followed her out and up the stairs.

When we got to the front of the building, Ahmed and Ziv were waiting, engaged in a staring match with an armed security detachment at the front doors. Ziv made a gun out of his hand and pointed it at Dr. Morano's bodyguard, who had stopped behind some plexiglass security doors to watch us go and mimed pulling the trigger. Morano smirked and bowed.

Chapter 108

We had to get out of town but I wasn't sure how to go about it. We were TDY here at Fort Lewis to provide instruction to the cadre but there was no way we were going to stick around in Morano's turf. She could reach out and touch us anytime she wanted and I didn't know how long I could hold the team from going after her.

We pulled back in through the gate at JBLM just as my cell rang. It was the duty officer at the training unit. I pulled over and talked to him for a minute, then spoke to the team.

"Listen up, guys, I have to go to a punishment enforcement over at the Basic Training Unit. Doc, see what you can do with Brit's eye. Ziv, you're coming with me. None of us are going alone anywhere until we can get out of this place."

I dropped them off at the Troop Medical Clinic, picked up my dress blues and drove over to the Basic Training Division on north Fort. I left my GSA car parked outside the Headquarters and went inside to find the duty officer who had called me.

"Nick, what is this punishment enforcement thing you speak of?"

"Well, I don't know how they handled disciplinary action in the Serbian Army but things are pretty strict here now."

"In Serbian Army, sergeants would beat you if you talk back to them. We take care of trouble ourselves."

"Yeah, well, you can do that in the U.S. Military now, especially out in the wild. It didn't use to be that way, before the Zombie Apocalypse. NCOs were pretty much stripped of their disciplinary power. Tell me, how did you handle sexual harassment?"

"Pah, no women in Serbian Army. Useless."

"Yeah, well, don't let Brit hear you say that."

He considered for a minute, then muttered something under his breath that sounded like "she-devil." I laughed and told him not to let her hear him say that, either. Then again, maybe she would take it as a compliment.

"Here on post, the Uniform Code of Military Justice is applied but it's not like the old one. They changed it a year ago to allow corporal punishment. Two senior noncoms and a junior officer are allowed to decide punishment for a variety of charges if the soldier is found guilty by a majority of NCOs in his unit by secret ballot. Charges are read, evidence given, guilt decided and punishment administered the same day. The ones who decide the punishment can never be from the convicted unit. I got called in to sit on a punishment enforcement."

"What did this soldier do?"

"Two of them. One for theft. Broke into a bunch of lockers at night, went through people's wallets stealing new dollars. He was found guilty. Another NCO, a drill sergeant, was found guilty of aggravated sexual harassment."

I changed into my dress blues and walked over to the table set up in the Company Orderly Room. A 2nd Lieutenant and a Master Sergeant were already sitting, going over the case notes. Introducing myself, I asked them what we had.

"OK, well, the private was found guilty of theft, breaking into soldiers' lockers at night while he was on Firewatch. Someone caught him in the act."

"So, no other witnesses? That's a tough one, one person's word against another."

"No, we have a witness. The whole thing was caught on a monitor. That and the soldier that caught him beat the crap out of him with a garbage can when he tried to run for it. Dumbass."

"Easy enough, then. Twenty lashes, reduction in rank, cut off of rations." Every soldier in the military was given an extra allowance of ration cards to send home to his family. It was a way of keeping them happy, knowing they were doing something to help out their families and provided them an extra enlistment bonus. Cutting them off would bring shame to his whole family, which was often more effective than physical punishment.

"Agreed. Now, about the drill sergeant. This is his second time but there was no proof the first time, or not enough, anyway. This time he was stupid enough to try his crap in front of two females. Actually put his hand on one of them, squeezed her ass. They reported him right away."

"He's gotta go," said the Master Sergeant.

I nodded my head. "Agreed. No room for that. We need every single gun we can get and this tool is going to ruin unit effectiveness and cohesion." I never understood that. You always get further with a woman by showing them respect than trying the old 'one out of a hundred likes it, so I'll try grab-ass on a hundred and one women'.

"OK," said the LT. He turned to the first sergeant of the Basic Training Company, who had been standing by. "Top, have the company fall in to witness punishment."

Outside was one of those constant drizzling rains that always seem to be happening at Ft. Lewis. The entire basic training company, some two hundred soldiers, had assembled in a box formation around a concrete pillar set in the pavement.

The first soldier was walked over to the post, had his cuffs attached to the post and his platoon sergeant gave him a quick twenty lashes to a measured drum beat. Though we NCOs have the power once again to administer punishment, it has to be us who give it, because, in a way, it was our failure that had brought the private to this point. After the tenth strike of the whip, blood started to run down the private's back but I'll give him credit, the kid didn't scream once. He would either turn into a great soldier or be out of the Army soon enough. Nobody likes a thief. He would be held back until his wounds had healed and he could be recycled into another class.

Next, the drill sergeant was brought out. He stood in front of the entire company and I walked over to him. He wouldn't look me in the eye. No combat patch on his sleeve, no Combat Action Badge. I wondered where he had been hiding out the last year and how he had slipped past the requirement that all Drill Instructors be combat veterans.

"Sergeant Dwayne Owens, you have been found guilty of two counts of aggravated sexual harassment by a group of your peers and you are a disgrace to the NCO Corps. Your punishment is to be the following." At this, I reached out and removed his drill sergeant hat from his head and handed it to the Master Sergeant who stood next to me. Owens didn't say anything, merely gave me a look that was more defiant than anything else.

"You are hereby discharged from the Military Forces of the United States of America. Your service record will be sealed and you will be barred from serving in any of said military forces. These soldiers are entrusted to your care and development and you have betrayed that trust. In addition, your file will be marked for any future employer as discharged for sexual offense." As I spoke, I used my knife to cut off his rank and unit patches and let them fall to the floor.

"Mister Owens, you have one hour to leave this military installation. You will be provided transportation back to your home of record."

I hated it but it had to be done. It was one thing to mutually joke and smoke with female soldiers of equal rank out in the field. It was a whole other thing to be in a basic training environment and use your authority to take advantage of impressionable young women who were scared of that authority.

The First Sergeant uncuffed him and he walked away, head hanging down, in the direction of the Headquarters Building. The entire company watched him go. Not a few of the female soldiers had a smile on their faces.

While I was on my way back to the billets to meet up with the rest of the team and plan our way out of JBLM and Dr. Morano's reach, my phone rang again. It was Doc. "Listen up, Nick. We got orders for the entire team to fly out to Denver and join in the big push that III Corps has on, trying to take back the Denver metro area."

"What the hell, that's a straight-up mechanized infantry push! What use would we be there?" Then I thought back to what Morano said to us in the lab, 'Have a nice vacation in Denver.'

"I know," replied my second in command but it does get us out of here. Either way, orders are orders."

Chapter 109

We rode a troop train out of Seattle, headed for the front lines outside of Denver. Like all soldiers, we slept, played cards, and got bored. I used the time to get to know our newest guy, Specialist Esposito.

"Not what you were expecting, was it? Heading to the front lines."

"I'm getting out of the office, that's all I give a crap about. I was turning into a zombie myself, doing admin shit all day. I spent half the time trying to get my stupid CAC reader to work. I mean, really, who is going to try to hack our networks now?"

"Nobody but you know how the Army is. Once something is in place, it will never be taken away, only added to." He seemed like a decent guy and it would help that he had combat experience in Iraq and Afghanistan. Different fight but experience was experience. We did the usual "where were you in `09, what FOB were you at, did you know so-and-so." It was military guys' way of sniffing each other's butts, like two strange dogs getting to know each other.

As the train clattered over the mountains of Idaho and down into the plains of Wyoming, I thought about our problem with Dr. Morano. One way or another, I was glad to be out of her immediate reach. Payback would have to come and it would be a showdown to the end. You can't leave enemies like that, ones who were willing to kill without conscience, alive and able to strike at you. We would have to be very careful, though. This wasn't some jumped-up jackass of an officer who had it coming and nobody around him gave a shit. I had read about some of her research and she was a big shot, a favorite of the powers that be. The fact we were on our way to the front lines was proof enough of that.

We rolled out onto the northern plains, sweltering in midsummer heat. Above us, regular flights of Kiowa Scout helicopters started to appear. One of the few things getting priority of manufacture was the small, lightweight observation copters. They could cover a lot of ground and ran regular patrols all over the countryside. Any figure or groups of figures that didn't respond to interrogation with some sort of signal showing they were human was immediately engaged, either through a lightweight chain gun mounted on the nose or rifle fire from the observer/sniper who rode alongside. They would land several hundred meters from the Z and hop out to take the headshot. Shooting accurately from a hovering helo was something you did in movies, not in real life. If it was a group and they were advancing quickly, the team would do what was called a "skip and shoot;" landing, shooting, pulling back several hundred meters, then landing again.

If things got out of hand, quick reaction rifle squads were scattered every seventy-five miles or so in remains of small towns and could be there within a half an hour by Blackhawk or two hours by truck. A real horde of several hundred or more would be led by the scout helo flashing lights and playing sound to attract them to a designated "kill zone," where troops had established permanent fighting positions and would be waiting for them. The kill zones were set up every hundred miles or so, depending on terrain features, and had pre-registered artillery, deep ditches and palisades.

They had been used a lot in the first year of the war to stabilize Montana, Idaho and the Dakotas and cut down on the number of hordes wandering about. Now we held the northern Great Plains north of the I-90 corridor. We had patrols as far south as Kansas and a mechanized infantry division sitting outside of Omaha shooting anything that stumbled out of that ruin. We also had four divisions getting ready for the push into Denver, one mechanized and three light infantry.

In California, we were massing wheeled infantry in the mountains, getting ready to try and take back the Imperial Valley with all of its agricultural potential, and the Navy wanted San Francisco Harbor back. They were tired of being holed up in San Diego and the Marines were itching to get into the fight, training constantly at their bases in Hawaii. The brief and bloody fight against the secessionists in Utah had devolved down to mopping up in the mountains and the sensible people in Salt Lake City had thrown out the "Emergency Council of Elders," after they had vowed to fight the government "to the last saint."

In the small picture, our picture, Third Corps (III Corps) had established a cordon around the greater Denver Metropolitan area and was preparing to take the city. The government needed the rail lines and transportation infrastructure as a forward base for taking back the rest of the country and there was talk of moving the capitol there after everything was cleaned out. For now, though, there were estimated to be close to a million undead gathered there. Our job was to first scout the airport.

"Why don't we just drop a neutron bomb on it?" asked Red, who had been looking over my shoulder as I read the intel updates. "You know, just fry their asses and leave the buildings standing and all that."

"Tried it already, in Los Angeles. Didn't work. Just left a bunch of pissed-off, radioactive zombies."

"Damn. Well, what about, you know, carpet bombing it or something? Blow the hell out of them, leave a lot less for the Army to clean up. I know you won't kill a lot of them that way but it will sure mess up a bunch."

"Won't leave the buildings intact and we need to take Denver so it can be reoccupied. The Air Force carpet bombed … where the hell was that?"

"Reno," chimed in Doc, who was pretending to sleep in the seat across from me.

"Yeah, Reno, Nevada. Pounded the whole place flat. Carpet bombs, fuel air explosives, Napalm, everything. All that, a small city and it STILL took three weeks for a full division of troops to declare the place a hundred percent secure."

"So, let me get this straight. We're still scouts, right?"

"As far as I know, yes."

"And we're going to scout an area we can't bomb and has a million Zs in it?"

"Something like that, yeah."

"Damn, White Man, I should have stayed on the reservation."

I laughed. "Red, don't worry, this will be a piece of cake compared to New York."

Just then, the train hit a rough patch in the rails and my coffee jumped in my hand, spilling the hot liquid on my uniform. Damn, what a way to start.

Chapter 110

Somewhere in Wyoming the train ground to a halt and an announcement came over the intercom.

"All troops, this is the train commander. Air scouts are leading a zombie horde, about one thousand strong, toward our position. All troops will mount rooftop firing positions and engage targets. Estimate contact time is ten minutes."

Brit let out a whoop. "Hell yeah, I was getting bored watching Red moon over all those buffalo. He's had a hard-on for the last two hundred miles."

"I'm a Navajo. We screw sheep, you stupid paleface squaw."

"OK, OK, quit it and gear up, you two." We checked weapons and ammo and moved into the aisle. Doc still pretended to sleep. I slapped his boot and he grunted, rolled over into a more comfortable position and started snoring. Esposito finished loading his rifle and then asked, "What's with him? Isn't he going to help?"

"He's just faking it. He'll be down here with his medkit in case someone gets injured."

A ladder had been pulled down from the roof and soldiers were climbing up through a hatch. We made our way up onto the flat roof of the train. I had wondered why the roof was so low and I saw that several feet had been sawn off the roof and a parapet placed around it. The car was still low enough to pass under tunnels and bridges but provided an elevated, protected firing platform. There was even an overhang to prevent Zs from climbing up.

As we crowded over to the southern side of the train car and took up firing positions, the helos thundered overhead. I looked out over the open plain, which was shimmering with heat waves. White stones stood at various intervals that I judged were every hundred meters or so and piles of picked-over bones lay around them. Hundreds of thousands of bones and the smell coming off them reminded me of a slaughterhouse.

"What's with the rocks and the bones?" I asked one of the regular train security personnel who was directing the placement troops along the parapet.

He laughed. "Those are for estimating range. You don't think we just stopped here at a random place, did you? This is a regular ambush. We do this about every fifth train ride." He leaned over the edge and pointed to the ground below.

"See that?" I leaned over myself and saw a deep ditch dug along the tracks, which approximated the entire length of the train. It too was filled with bones but it made it impossible for any Z to even get close to the train cars, much less climb them.

"Every couple of weeks the air scouts come across a wandering horde and lead them back to this place or a few others we have along the rail line. Then we just let the troops on board shoot the piss out of them. Plus, we got that," and he gestured towards the last rail car.

"Is that what it looks like?"

"Yep. 100 kilowatt FIRESTRIKE Laser. Made by Northrup –Grumman. We just start at the back of the horde and work our way forward, frying the crap out of them."

"I want one!" said Brit, who had been listening in.

"Fat chance, Lady. We have an extra diesel electric locomotive hooked to the train to provide power for that sucker. Still, it smells like a good old pork BBQ when we get done."

In a few minutes, I heard the zombie howl drifting over the wind. Brit looked over and gave me a thumbs-up. Ahmed settled more comfortably behind his scope. On my left, Red looked a little nervous. I couldn't blame him, after what he went through at West Point. Espo tapped a magazine against the rail, then seated his patrol cap a little further back on his head.

Ahmed shot first, a flat crack coming out of his rifle, unsuppressed for once. Damn, that was loud. I reached into my sleeve pocket, pulled out a set of foam plugs and squeezed them into my ears. I'd rather have my hearing than compensation from whatever agency managed to succeed the Veterans Administration.

I felt the engine powering up for the laser and toward the back of the horde, individual Zs started to burst into flame. Some only smoked as they moved out of the laser's aimpoint. I guess it took a second or two for the full heat effects to be felt. Thank God the wind was blowing away from us, or I think I would have puked from the smell of burned flesh.

The horde resolved itself out of the heat waves, running toward the train, drawn by the sound of the gunfire. At five hundred meters, the designated marksmen opened up, dropping them with every other shot. At three hundred, some of the guys joined in. At a hundred and fifty meters, everyone else opened up and at a hundred we started firing with our .22 magnums. At this point, there was a continuous roar coming through my ear plugs and the whole train deck was vibrating. I could barely see anything through my sites, just fired whenever I recognized the pattern of a face.

"CEASE FIRE! CEASE FIRE! STOP FIRING YOU STUPID JACKASSES! AMMO AIN'T CHEAP!" The train crewman kicked the back of our feet and we stopped pulling our triggers. The roar of shots dropped away. Spent brass cartridges lay all around us on the roof and I could smell the cordite. I loved that smell but killing was hot work. I took a very long drink from my camelback.

In front of us there was a pile of steaming, burning corpses. Some still crawled toward the train and a couple of snipers took individual shots. Every now and then one would pull itself upright and then it would drop in a spray of blood from its head. The nearest zombie corpse lay ten feet from the train tracks.

"OK, before you go back down, police up all the brass!"

"You have got to be shitting me," said one of the soldiers.

"You think brass grows on trees? There are ammo crates by the ladder, make sure you sort by caliber!" Damn. I pulled off my patrol cap and started putting .22 shells in.

As we filed back down, I asked the trainman what would happen to any stray Zs.

"A squad will be coming in by air in the next thirty mikes. They'll take care of any leakers."

Doc sat up as we took off our gear and stowed it overhead. "What did I miss?"

"We just whooped a whole buncha zombie ass!" said Brit. "I could get used to this big Army stuff."

"Don't," I said. "You know when we get to Denver it's going to just be us all out on our lonesome. The Lost Boys are who they call when they need to know but are too scared to find out."

"Hell, yeah!" Brit and Red exchanged high fives and she started to do a sexy dance in the aisle to the catcalls and hoots of the troopers around us. Then the train started up again with a lurch and she fell on her ass.

Chapter 111

Dust and mud. That's what being a soldier is about. Cold, too, usually but thankfully it was midsummer. Another thing that always bothered me about zombie TV shows. Being in a survival situation is, well, dirty. You never see the hero scratching his crotch because he hasn't showered in two months and has heat rash. You never see the hero reporting in to his commander and the commander's nose wrinkling up because the hero smells like a few weeks of rotten ass due to being on the run all the time. Or the zombie brains and blood and guts that are splattered all over his uniform, which smelled rank long before they got splashed.

Thankfully, this time, it was just dirt and mud. Dust first, then mud, after a thunderstorm had dropped an inch of rain on FOB Griffin, about twenty miles north of the front lines around Denver. The rain had turned the road in between the tents, already stripped of any vegetation by passing trucks, into a clay that gripped my boots. Every few meters I had to stop and scrape the mud off my boots onto whatever was handy. By the time I got back to the trucks I was covered in mud splatters up to my knees. Screw it, just something you get used to after a while in the field.

Our two gun trucks were sitting on the remains of a parking lot. Once we had signed for the trucks, Red had gone to work with a can of paint and a stencil, blocking out the old bumper numbers that said, "4 ID HHC-04" and, "4 ID HHC-13" and stenciling them with "JSOC-IST 1–06" on my truck and, "JSOC-IST 1–05" on Doc's. Brit, Red and Ahmed were welding a Z-catcher, an angled iron "V", on the frame of 06. Ziv and Espo worked on mounting a M-249 SAW in the turret of 05. I took a minute to review the operations order in my hand. It was short and to the point. Lengthy op-orders had gone out the window with the zombies.

1. SITUATION
Enemy forces.

Expect upwards of seven hundred thousand infected in the greater Denver Metro Area. Over flights of the airport show scattered activity. Significant hostile surviving population have been reported in outlying areas.

b. Friendly forces. JSOC-IST 1 will be operating in support of Task Force Bronco.

c. Attachments and detachments. None.

2. MISSION: On order, JSOC-IST 1 will conduct a tactical reconnaissance of the Denver International Airport to determine runway and facilities conditions.

3. EXECUTION

Intent:

a. Concept of operations.

(1) Maneuver: Conduct intelligence gathering at Denver Airport.

(2) Fires: TF Bronco will dedicate one battery of 155mm Paladin Howitzers in direct support.

(3) Reconnaissance and Surveillance: See attached aerial photographs.

(4) Intelligence: See attached aerial photographs

(5) Engineer: None

(6) Air Defense: N/A

(7) Information Operations: N/A

b. Tasks to maneuver units: Coordinate passage of lines with JSOC-IST 1

c. Tasks to combat support units.

(1) Intelligence: None

(2) Engineer: None

(3) Fire Support: Coordinate suppressive fires for ingress and egress.

(4) Air Defense: N/A

(5) Signal: See attached SOI

(6) NBC (Nuclear, Biological, Chemical): Possible radiation hot spots due to failed nuclear strike southwest of Denver Metro area. Radiation contamination at crater at site of Former Rocky Mountain Arsenal.

(7) Provost Marshal: N/A

(8) PSYOP: N/A

(9) Civil military: TF Bronco elements will make all efforts to rescue Survivor Civilian Populations (SCP).

(10) As required

d. Coordinating instructions.

(1) Time or condition when a plan or order becomes effective: 0001 Local

(2) CCIR (Commander's Critical Information Requirements): Suitability of Airport facilities for flight operations.

(3) Risk reduction control measures: None

(4) Rules of engagement: None

(5) Environmental considerations: None

(6) Force protection: None

(7) As required

4. SU.S.TAINMENT (formerly Service Support)

a. Support concept: JSOC –IST 1 will use organic TF Bronco assets.

b. Materiel and services. JSOC –IST 1 will use organic TF Bronco assets.

c. Medical evacuation and hospitalization: 934th Aero-Med Company will be on standby to support all combat operations.

d. Personnel: JSOC –ST 1 and attached Airforce elements.

e. Civil military: N/A

f. As required.

"Who wrote this shit? Some a first year ROTC cadet?" scoffed Doc.

Blah blah blah. Again, we were off on our own with little support. Not that a battery of Paladin 155mm howitzers were something to laugh at, but I had already spoken to the Task Force Fire Support Officer. The conversation went kinda like this:

Her: "Don't expect shit from me."

Me: "Roger, Ma'am, won't expect shit." She wasn't

being a jerk, just explained to me that she had literally hundreds of standard high explosive rounds but few if any of the new firecrackers, the ones that sprayed ball bearings all over their blast radius.

"The fighting down in Mexico in the oil fields took up a lot of the production priority and the chemicals used to produce the high explosive are in short supply. We can fire regular shrapnel rounds all day long but you know they don't do much against Zs."

So, as usual, off again on our own. We did have one attachment, an Air Force sergeant who specialized in Flight Operations. He walked up to the team as I was reading the Operations Order.

"Uh, hi, my name is Sergeant Ozturk. Call sign "Wizard." I'm looking for some Special Operations guys, uh, IST-1 or something. Have you seen them?"

He was talking to Brit, who had taken to wearing a red bandanna around her head. Said it made her look more like a pirate with her eye patch. I was ignoring it until we actually rolled out of the base.

"Well, looks like you found us!" she said, "Are you, some kinda general or something with all those stripes on your arm?"

"Uh, no, I'm just a Technical Sergeant."

"Well, OK, are you like one of those PJs? A parajumper? Air Force Special Forces?" He was getting a little red in the face, because as she questioned him, Brit poked him in his rather large stomach several times.

"Um, well, no. You see, I know how to run airports. I'm supposed to go with you guys to check out the tower."

She turned to face Red. "Hey Red, do we have a trailer we can use to haul Mister Dunkin Donuts here out to the airport?"

I stepped up and told Brit to cut the crap. "Welcome to the Lost Boys, Tech Sergeant. Soon as we get you checked out on the weapons on the turrets, you're free to stow your gear in the back."

"Uh, I dunno, I've never fired any kind of automatic weapon. I think I might just get in your way."

Brit rolled her eyes and I shot her a dirty look. The rest of the guys pretended to be busy. "Well, how about that M-4 you're carrying? Can you use it?"

"What, this?" he said and slung it off his shoulder, sweeping it around in a wide arc that flagged most of the team, holding it by the grip with his finger on the trigger. It had a magazine in, too. I smacked the weapon down toward the ground before Ziv could buttstroke him. He looked very embarrassed.

"Well, uh, I fired it a few times in Basic Training. At least a whole magazine. They don't give much ammo to us Air Force guys since the Army needs it."

"Don't worry about it!" I said, with a forced grin. After all, it wasn't this guy's fault. Like everyone else, he went where the military told him. "Tell you what, Brother Zoomie Guy. You just ride in back and let us do the shooting. I assume you know how to do your job?"

A look of relief passed over his face. "Yeah, sure, airports I know."

Chapter 112

I lay there on the hood of the HUMVEE, trying to get some sleep, wrapped up in my poncho liner. Tomorrow was going to be a big day and we had to get up at 0500. I stared up at the stars in the clear, high plains air and tried to force myself to sleep but it eluded me again. I could take the Ambien Doc kept in his medkit but I hated it. It never felt like sleep then, just like a period of blackness and I woke up even more tired.

When I finally did drift off to sleep, the dream started again. I was standing in the kitchen of my old house, dressed in full combat gear, my rifle slung over my shoulder. Outside the window I could see a horde of zombies pressing against the glass. There was no sound in the dream; there never was. It just happened over and over in the same way. I reached for my daughter, who was playing on the kitchen floor. Just as I did she crawled away from me. Always she crawled away and I could never pick her up. What happened next in the dream was almost a repeat of what really happened that day, except that day I never got to see my daughter.

I looked up and my wife stood there, blood dripping down her face, a large gash ripped open in her neck, blood splattered down her side. In her hand was our daughter's arm, fingers still clutching to her mothers'. She reached for me and in the dream, I wanted to go to her. It was such a powerful urge that I could never resist it and I always woke up with a jump as she bit down on my shoulder.

In reality, I had moved faster than that. I swung the stock of my M-16 as hard as I could at her head and kept swinging until her head was a bloody pulp and the plastic rifle had shattered apart in my hands.

Tonight was no different. I dreamed the dream again and woke with a start just as the predawn light was filtering into the sky. I looked at my watch, 04:23 and tried to wrap myself a little deeper in the poncho liner. Thirty-seven minutes of sleep was thirty-seven minutes of sleep, any old soldier knows that but I was afraid of drifting off into the nightmare again.

On the roof of the truck, Brit lay wrapped in the green half of a Gortex sleeping bag. I listened to her moving around restlessly. She probably had her own nightmares to deal with, too. Six months spent living on the deserted campus, dodging zombies, scrounging for food. I knew she had been an architecture and aerospace dual major, smart as hell and I wondered if she would ever shed her new, post-apocalypse persona of a "live life to the fullest, devil may care," hedonist. Probably not; there was no going back to our old lives. Still, I looked forward to the day when we could put our guns down, I could pick up a hammer and a saw again and maybe build a new life with her.

A muffled ripping sound came from the top of the truck and Red, who was lying on the other side of the turret, made a puking sound. "OH MY GOD, WHAT IS THAT SMELL?"

Brit laughed and said, "That, ladies and gentlemen, is why they call it a fart sack!"

Ziv, who was sitting watch on top of the other truck, laughed out of the fading darkness. "You are pig, Woman but I like you."

"OK, screw it," I said, looking at my watch again. 04:37. "Everyone up, thirty minutes to shit, shower and shave." Muffled groans sounded from inside the cab of the HUMVEE where Ahmed was curled around the doghouse radio mount. I have no idea how he slept like that. Esposito came back from his roving patrol. Ziv shook Doc in his sleeping bag on the other hood, then jumped down and kicked the little pup tent the Air Force guy had set up. "Time to make donuts, Fat Boy!" he yelled inside the tent flap and laughed at the cursing that came back at him.

Brit called across to the other truck as she brushed her red hair out and tied it up in a ponytail. "Time to make *the* donuts, you damn foreigner. Get it right."

Well, I guess morale was OK. As the sun came up, I

broke out the handy wipes and cleaned yesterday's dust and sweat off of my face, armpits and crotch. Then I shaved with cold water, using my canteen cup and the truck mirror. Through the cab of the truck I could see Redshirt applying camouflage to his face, making a series of vertical stripes from forehead to chin.

"Hey Red," I called through the window "putting your war paint on?"

"Yes I am, Sergeant. Today is going to be bad shit. I can feel it in my bones."

"OK but just don't get caught up in the irregular part of Irregular Scouts. You're still a part of the Army, unlike Brit, Ahmed or Ziv," I reminded him.

"I got you, Boss. I just have a bad feeling about today and I want to go to war properly, if you know what I'm saying."

"Just keep your coup stick in your rucksack, OK?"

"You got it. Coup don't count on zombies and I'm a Navajo, anyway. We ain't all the same, you know."

I looked around and the guys were acting pretty serious. Ahmed had unrolled his prayer mat and was kneeling east, in the direction of the radioactive crater that was Mecca. Ziv was sharpening the large knife he wore strapped across his back. Hell, it wasn't a knife, it was a small sword. Esposito worked on his new .22 magnum M4-A3, getting used to the action and practicing feeding the long stick magazine into the well. Doc was cleaning his shotgun and Brit sat on the roof of one of the trucks, staring at the sun coming up over the Great Plains. I watched her for a minute, a strand of her red hair gently moving in the faint morning breeze. She saw me looking and looked back at me, a small smile on her face. Her one good eye burned into me like a bolt of lightning, and I finally looked away before I lost my will to fight anymore.

"OK, let's go! SP in five mikes, lock and load once we get outside the gate. Brit, you're driving 06, with me as TC and Red on the gun. Tech Sergeant Ozturk, you will be riding on 05 with Ahmed driving, Doc as TC and Ziv on the gun.

Try not to touch anything. Espo, you are in 05 and you are Sergeant Ozturk's personal bodyguard."

Red climbed into the turret and I handed him up a can of ammo for the MK-19A2. He laid the belt of 40mm shotgun shells in the breech. The −A2 was a standard 40mm automatic grenade launcher. The shells, however, instead of being grenades, were oversized shotgun shells which fired about a hundred steel pellets in a killing range out about a hundred meters. It made the barrel useless for firing the grenades after a bunch of shells destroyed the rifling but who needed grenades against zombies anyway? I was happy to have the extra firepower for once.

"Ugh, this thing moves like a pig with all that extra armor and the steel zombie catcher on the front." Brit tested the brakes a few times, resulting in a jerky motion that threw Red around in the turret. He kicked her in the shoulder. "Hey, quit it, Squaw! That shit hurts!"

"Stop screwing around, let's go." I told her, then keyed the handset on the radio as we rolled through the gap in the concertina wire at the front lines.

"Griffin Main, this is Lost Boys Six, SP this time, mark, over." As I talked, I looked out the window. Hundreds of Abrams main battle tanks, their main guns replaced with short, stubby shotgun cannons, Bradley Scout armored personnel carriers and the troop carriers, the real killers. Bradley chassis with the turrets removed and even old M-113 APCs, all with a steel wall about three feet high welded around the top. The troops rode on them, firing over the sides, unreachable by any zombies and protected from potshots Reavers or other uncooperative civilians might take.

The radio crackled back right away. I appreciated a TOC that was awake at all hours. *"This is Griffin Main. Lost Boys, SP 0542. Happy hunting, over."*

"Lost Boys, Roger out."

Chapter 113

The highway was clear all the way to the airport. We occasionally caught a Z with our front bumper. OK, Brit occasionally swerved to catch a Z with the steel V on the front of the truck. By the time we pulled up to the airport fence, the front end was covered with dark splashes of zombie blood.

"You're cleaning that off at the wash rack when we get back." She stuck her tongue out at me as we bounced over a ditch and she wound up biting it. "Serves you right," I said.

We got onto the runway and hauled ass, pushing the trucks up as fast as they would go, braking to a hard stop in front of the tower facility. I had Brit drive into the front doors, smashing them aside, then pulling back. We parked one truck in front of the doors, blocking access.

"OK, you know the drill. Me, Doc, Brit and Donut and Espo, we're going in. Ahmed, you, Red and Ziv maintain the perimeter with the trucks. Keep 05 driving around so nothing sneaks up from behind the building." Ahmed for long range shots at random Zs, Ziv on the 249 for 'suppressive' fire and Red on the Mark 19 for close-in action.

The tower offices were dark, only illuminated by the morning sunlight filtering through the dirty windows. I didn't expect much Zombie activity in here because the airport would have shut down early in the collapse and the employees would have fled. I was right; we encountered nothing. Still, by the time we got to the tower stairs, I was soaked in sweat from adrenaline that flooded through me each time we kicked a door open. Brit and I took turns being the first one through each door and it got nerve racking. At one point, Brit actually fired at a life-sized safety poster pinned to a wall. Three rounds of .22, two of them hitting right in the posterized Flight Attendant's forehead.

"Great shot!" She looked sheepish. "You're starting to make this a habit, you know" said Doc, laughing at her.

"Hey, better alive and feeling stupid than dead," she shot

back.

I called back to Ahmed with all clear in answer to his query about the shots and we moved up the stairwell of the tower. When we got to the top, the Air Force Sergeant went to work. He pulled out a large, heavy box from his ruck.

"What's that?" asked Espo.

"Capacitor, with a built-in modulator. Gives me a few minutes of 120 volt AC. Allows me to check out the electronics, computers and stuff, see if they're still working."

"You mean like the radar and stuff?"

"No, the radar isn't here at the airport. That gets run by a FAA regional center, can't remember where the one is for this local area. No, all the info for the flight traffic controllers would be fed here by a data uplink from there. We'll have to set up a mobile radar unit to run this field."

Lights powered up around us, screens flickering to life. "Looking good, looking good," he muttered under his breath.

"Uh, Nick?"

"Yeah, Doc?"

He was standing at the tower windows, looking westward through a pair of binos. I raised mine to look.

"Oh, damn."

From around the terminal on the opposite side of the airport came several thousand zombies. Hundreds more streamed from around the edge of the building.

"I guess the recon flights missed that horde."

"I guess so."

Down below, Ahmed started firing at them but his hits were lost in the crowd. A long stream of tracers reached out and started slapping into the front, rounds skipping off the tarmac into them. A few fell but like all unaimed, automatic fire, the hits were mostly wasted. Blowing holes through the undead didn't stop them.

"Ahmed, get up here with those guys and blow the stairs!"

He didn't answer but the firing stopped. Then I heard one of the truck engines start again through the open tower window and 06 raced out onto the runway. It moved down the front of the horde and I heard the bang bang bang of the automatic shotgun.

"Ziv and Red took the truck, said they would buy us some time to rig explosives. I am coming up." I acknowledged but I knew what Zivcovic and Redshirt didn't. Zombie crowds didn't break in the face of heavy weapons. Red was too inexperienced and Ziv had been fighting a running, hiding battle for the last a year on his own. Never against a horde.

"06, get your ass back here!" I ordered over the radio.

"Little busy right now, Nick!" came back Red, over the firing of the gun. I did see the truck start back, though, as the crowd of undead flowed past it, despite the dozens mowed down by the gunfire and smashed under the truck. They quickly outdistanced the Z's and skidded to a stop in front of 05, adding a further blockage to the doorway. I couldn't see what happened after that but the gun started firing again.

"Nick, I need a few seconds more to set this charge!" yelled Ahmed up the stairway. Then Redshirt piled into the room and fell to the floor.

"Where the fuck is Ziv?" I yelled at him.

"He stayed to cover us!" He was out of breath and crying.

"Goddammit! Ziv, get your ass up here!" I yelled into my headset.

"My country. It is gone." And his next words were drowned out by the zombie howl and the firing of the gun. " ... will give you time. Ahmed, you heathen bastard, blow the stairs!" Then a long string of curses in Serbian and the gun fired nonstop.

Screw that, I wasn't going to lose another team member. I looked over the windowsill as the firing stopped and shifted to single shots from Ziv's 9 millimeter.

"Ziv, drop in the turret, now!" He had drawn his knife and was hacking at the arms reaching for him as he stood on the roof. They were climbing onto the hood and over the pile of parts from the Zs he had shot down already. He stood there swinging the knife with a mad look of battle rage on his face. As I watched, he kicked one more in the face as it lurched onto the roof, then dove face first into the turret opening.

I yelled to the team. "Grenades, on three!" On the count of three we threw them over the edge in front of the parked vehicles. Brit held hers a bit to cook it off. Five grenades went off, four on the ground, one in the air. The crowd of Zombies were knocked back by the shrapnel and concussion and the sharp explosions rocked the up-armored HUMVEES, bursting tires, knocking off a side view mirror and scoring the windows.

I yelled into the radio as we poured fire into the quickly recovering Zs. "Ziv, out of the turret, across to the other one and drop through, then out the side door into the building!" I saw him struggle out of the turret and crawl across the roof, then roll off into the gap between the trucks. I had hoped he would be able to jump it. Then I saw the side door open on 05 and he struggled in. Ahmed appeared on the other side of the truck, pulling open the door and grabbing Ziv by the strap on his body armor. He pulled him across the back seats and out the door. As he dragged him in, I saw a streak of blood left on the ground.

"Red, Espo, go get him, let Ahmed blow the stairs. Doc, get the kit, he's wounded." Doc was already opening up his medkit. The two others charged out the door and down the stairs. They returned with Ziv, blood running down his leg and onto the floor, just as the demo charge went off and wrecked the landing below. Doc set to work immediately, first checking for other wounds, then cutting open his pants leg.

I knelt next to him. "No more hero shit. We thought you were dead."

"I thought I was dead too. For a while I felt like it. Ah, dammit, that hurts!" Another Serbian curse as Doc pulled a piece of grenade shrapnel from his upper calf.

Brit jumped up. "That was mine! Mine went off in the air, how frigging cool! Must have gone through the turret opening and hit you in the leg! Can I keep that?"

Glaring at her he muttered, "If you were daughter I would beat you with belt. Impudent wench." He threw the bloody piece of metal to her.

"YES!" She took it off the floor and put it in the extra grenade pouch where she kept her "mission souvenirs."

I sat down, opened up an MRE and started to heat it. That whole episode had left me drained. "Sergeant Ozturk," I asked, "what's the deal with the equipment? Is the airport OK?"

He leaned over his laptop. "Well, the runway is in good enough shape for C-130 or C-17 operations. They have rough field capability but I wouldn't land a 757 or a C-5 on here. Too many cracks in the pavement. The electronics are good to go. We can set up a data link to a mobile radar unit and run flight ops from here. I already sent the report up to the Air Liaison at Corps."

"OK, great. At least something went right this time. Going to be a long night, People. Get some chow, start the watch rotation."

Brit leaned over and swiped the candy out of my MRE. She turned to Ziv, who was staring stonily at Doc as he bandaged his leg. Ripping open the packet of candy with her teeth, she poured it out onto Ziv's lap.

"Here, you grumpy old man. Skittles make everything better!"

Chapter 114

The sun rose over a horde that had grown to several thousand and they packed the stairwell and the bottom floor of the building. We didn't shoot them in the stairwell because we didn't want a pile to start that the Zs could climb and reach us. The stench, however, was bad enough to make us want to vomit and we were caught between the smell coming up from the stairs and the smell wafting in through the window. At first light I got on the radio to update the TOC on our situation:

"Griffin main, this is Lost Boys and we are still surrounded, over."

"Roger, lost boys. Is your position still secure, over?"

"Roger that, until we run out of food and water. Estimate three thousand plus in horde. Airfield status report being sent now, over."

"Understood, lost boys. Stand by for the cavalry, over, probably tomorrow, over."

"Garry Owen and glory, Lost Boys, out."

The Iraqis, when we fought them in the Gulf, called the Abrams tank "Whispering Death," on account of how quiet the turbine engines were. In any case, we would never have heard them over the sound of the zombies moaning below us.

What we did hear was the sound of the case shot being fired by the tank cannons, a rolling boom that echoed across the airfield first thing the next morning. When the first volley of tungsten pellets cut through the horde like the proverbial hot knife through butter, we jumped up and crowded around the window to watch. Hundreds of bodies fell, in four huge swaths. The next volley came twenty seconds later, aimed along a different axis, cutting apart more zombies. Then the Abrams charged across the field. They hit almost forty mph in the short stretch and plowed into the milling crowd of bodies, firing as they went. The drivers started spinning their tracks, knocking down Zs and grinding them into the airport tarmac. When they had gone completely through the horde, they spun on their treads and charged back in, the tank commanders firing their own MK-19A3s into individual clumps. I don't think anyone who has ever seen an Abrams tank charging full on into a crowd will ever forget the sight. We had been watching the fight and cheering the tanks on but we all ducked down beneath the sill of the window when a stray pellet came ricocheting into the tower, sixty feet above the ground, and pinged off Redshirt's Kevlar helmet, knocking him down. He gave a weak thumbs-up and an "I almost peed myself" look and we all laughed. When we looked back, after the cannon fire had stopped, a dozen armored personnel carriers had joined the fight, forming a circle with the tanks. Soldiers on top of the APCs fired individual shots as the Zs rushed at them. When the pile threatened to get high enough where the zombies might come over the top, the tracks peeled out and pulled backward fifty meters and the slaughter resumed. They had done this countless times in the battle for the northern plains and operated like a well-oiled machine. We would win this war.

I let the team join in, shooting from behind the horde. Wasting ammo but it had been a long day and they needed to blow off steam. Sometimes shooting things was the best way.

Half an hour later, a platoon of infantry was clearing the building below us. The rest of the dismounts in the mechanized infantry company were walking slowly through the pile of zombie bodies, firing individual headshots into any that showed movement. The guys downstairs advanced into each room behind plastic riot shields, forcing the zombies back and the line behind them fired with pistols at the zombies' heads.

"SERGEANT AGOSTINE, ALL CLEAR!!!" yelled the lead trooper as they reached the bottom of the stairs.

"COMING DOWN!"

Ziv refused a medical chopper, instead moving with our help into the truck where he climbed into the back seat. The rest of us loaded up and rolled out.

Red called down from the turret. "Sarge, this gun is

screwed. The feed tray mechanism is jammed all to hell."

"Don't worry about it. Just cover things with your rifle and keep your eyes open. There have got to be leakers from the infantry attack. We need a few minutes to change this tire anyway."

"Roger, Chief."

We rolled up the highway, back toward the forward line of TF Bronco. I was half dozing, listening to the road pass under the big treads of the truck tires and keeping my eyes open for any threat. I was tired and so was the rest of the crew but sleep would have to wait.

"Oh shit!" yelled Brit and I felt the vehicle start to tip off to one side. The road had crumbled underneath the heavy weight of the truck and we started to fall off the side down into a dry streambed. Flash floods over the past year, without maintenance crews fixing the back fill, had undermined the blacktop.

I reached back and grabbed Red's legs and pulled as hard as I could. We hadn't had time to practice rollover drills and I hoped Red remembered from Basic. He slid off the strap holding him up and fell inside just as we went completely over.

I don't remember what happened next. I woke up to Red cutting my seatbelt, letting me fall out of the door and onto him. The truck itself was lying on its roof, the wheels were still spinning, a cloud of dust settling around us.

Brit lay on the ground, unmoving. Red had pulled her out first. As he dragged me over next to her around the front of the truck, I screamed. My collar bone grated together and I felt like I was going to puke. The world swam in and out of my vision, going gray.

"Sarge, Brit seems OK, she's just out cold, still breathing. There are a bunch of Zs coming down the wash. I'm going to head them off. Doc is trying to rope down here but the road edge is really crumbly."

"O-OK. Something in my shoulder, it's messed up. Give, give me my pistol."

Red chambered a round and pressed my .22 into my left hand. Then he ran out of my field of vision and I heard him start to fire.

I think I passed out for a few seconds. When I woke up, three zombies were coming around the back end of the truck. Damn, damn, damn. I raised the pistol and started snapping off shots but it was hard to aim and my vision was blurry. I hit one in the head and it went down but the other two came closer. One made it to Brit and I emptied the magazine into it, just firing until my slide locked back. It fell backwards, away from her.

Then I felt an incredible pressure on my ankle and a hot, burning sensation. I looked down to see the last one, a little girl with her face rotted off, had bitten me just above the top of my boot. She kept biting, chewing her way into the muscle, her broken teeth sinking deeper.

I screamed and reached down, swatting at the creature with the empty pistol, feeling the infection burning into my leg. It was like a hot piece of steel, still glowing red, shoved into my calf.

The thing's head exploded and the round continued its flight to bury itself into the ground, carrying a trail of bloody red mist. I didn't look to see where the shot had come from, instead reaching across my shoulder and tearing the tourniquet off my body armor. Kicking the corpse of the zombie off me, I wrapped it tightly around my leg, just below the knee and a few inches above the wound, twisting it as hard as I could, feeling it cut into my leg. Then I ripped open the leg of my uniform.

A raw bite mark was in my calf, just above the top of my boot. Dammit all to Hell! It burned like someone was pouring raw alcohol on it. I let go of my leg and crawled over to Brit, who was still unconscious, and lay down with my head on her chest. Waves of nausea came over me and actually felt my eyes roll back into my head.

I woke up to a slap across my face. "Nick, come on, man," said Ahmed. He slapped me again and I threw a wild punch at him, making my shoulder blaze with agony. He sat back, easily avoiding it and keeping his pistol trained straight at my head.

"He is awake. Not a Z yet, either."

Doc leaned over me, blocking out the sun. "Nick, you got the TQ on in time but you know what we've gotta do. I'll make it as painless as possible. Here, bite on this."

Ahmed gently put a canvas strap into my mouth. "Go for it," I mumbled. How bad could it be? My leg felt numb already.

"OK, I can't give you anything for the pain."

I spit the canvas strap out and yelled, "Just shut the hell up and do it!" I looked over at Brit, who was awake, sitting up against the side of the rolled over HUMVEE. She looked back at me, tears streaming down her face. "It's just a flesh wound, babe," I said and reached for her hand as Ahmed put the strap back into my mouth.

Good thing he did, too. Doc cut into the muscle of my calf with a razor blade, in a neat circle around the bone, slicing through ligaments and blood vessels. I bit down hard on the canvas strap, so hard I felt like my teeth would break. I screamed into it, a soul-wrenching scream I tried to keep inside of me and squeezed Brit's hand so hard I thought I would crush the bones.

"Almost there, Nick." Doc reached a bloody hand out and Ahmed handed him a small, battery-powered Mikita grinding saw from his medkit. It whirred to life and I could feel the vibration as he cut into the bone. My leg was a dull, roaring throb that pounded up my body.

The last thing I saw was Doc lighting the torch he carried, bending over to cauterize the blood vessels. I felt the thud of the chopper blades as the MEDEVAC helo thundered down from overhead and smelled my burnt flesh. Before I passed out again, I heard Brit.

"Doc, tell me he's going to make it."

"He'll live, if he doesn't go into shock."

She squeezed my hand and whispered in my ear, "Live,

dammit."

The world fell away from me and I fell with it.

Chapter 115

Three months later

My leg hurt. Well, not really, because my leg wasn't there anymore. Instead, I was getting used to the prosthetic attached to the stump, just below my knee. It still hurt though, like a bitch. I had spent the last three months recuperating at the military hospital in Boise while the Team went back to NY to get some crops in and work on our new place. Now we were sitting in a briefing room at Joint Base Lewis-McCord, the massive combined Army – Air Force facility south of Seattle. Overhead, a C-17 thundered out towards Puget Sound. I watched it out the window as it turned and headed east, back towards the Wilds.

"Sergeant Agostine?" The briefer, major from the Corps S-2, had stopped his slideshow.

"Huh? Yeah, sorry. Leg was bothering me." He looked at me and then turned back to his presentation.

Brit leaned over and whispered in my ear "You're full of shit."

"Shhhh!" I said and tried to pay attention to what was going on.

"Intelligence assets have picked up rumors of a plot by unspecified groups which have plans to use a weapon of mass destruction in the Seattle area, directed against the United States."

He paused for a minute to let us think about it, apparently and then continued. "The intel is originating in the Tacoma FEMA Displaced Persons Camp. Your mission is to go into the camp, determine the validity of these rumors and take appropriate action as necessary."

We waited for him to provide more details. The officer stared back at us.

Ziv broke the silence. "In Serbia, we call this clusterfuck."

Specialist Redshirt chimed in. "Sir, with all due respect

but that's it?"

"Right now, that's all we have. I wish I could give you more but that's it."

I sat and waited for the team to get it out and Brit spoke up the loudest. "So, let me get this straight. You want us to do the government's dirty work, killing enemies of the regime and all that? And you can't tell us who, or what. What, exactly, does this have to do with killing zombies?"

"Nothing, Miss O'Neill and I remind you, you're a volunteer. You can walk away from this at any time."

"No, sweet cheeks," she said, making me inwardly groan "I got this. Can't let Doc here babysit Old Pegleg by himself."

Well, time to go all in. "Are you asking us to do this mission, or telling us?"

"Telling."

"Well that settles that, then. We'll need access to your intelligence sources inside the camp, civilian clothes, etc."

He seemed to have this already covered. "We pulled your records, all the appropriate clothing sizes will be available at the Central Issuing Facility. New ID cards, cover stories, pistols, communications equipment. We don't think that you'll need more than that, because the camps are weapons free zones."

Brit laughed. "Hey sucker, I got a bridge back in New York I want to sell you. Weapons free, my ass."

"What's our cover story?" said Doc.

"You're a salvage group, bringing in surplus from the San Francisco ruins. Your truck got impounded for use by the Army and you got put in the FEMA camp till something opens up. This way, you can stick together as a group and maybe develop some contacts."

I nodded. "We can use that." In my head, though, I figured things would go a different way. They always did.

*****

The FEMA camp sat miles south of Tacoma, which was itself overflowing with refugees. There were still large burnt-out areas of the city but things had attained some sort of order over the last year but unrest was rising again. People were getting tired of the permanent "state of emergency," and there had been riots the last time we were here, a few months ago.

Now the Army patrolled the streets in force and travel between the camps was severely limited. Every few days a new round of riots would break out, spread by some accident or by design. Rumors were flying about armed groups that were plotting against the government and sniper fire occasionally hit Army convoys traveling on I-5. The day before, an Improvised Explosive Device had been detonated south of Olympia and two trucks had been destroyed. The Predator drone on overwatch had left the attackers a smoking hole in the ground. Yeah, it was a sticky place. This was the situation that we were being dumped into and none of us trusted the Army, even JSOC, to have a good plan. We needed to come up with our own.

"Anyone got any ideas?"

Redshirt spoke up first. "How about we contact the guys providing the intel and see what they say?"

Doc answered, "Yeah, well, kid, times like this you learn to trust your gut and things are too unsettled for us to just go walking in there and associating with known rats. They'll make us in a second."

He was right along with my thinking. "Doc, I know you used to run with some of the motorcycle gangs."

"Clubs," he corrected me.

"OK, clubs. I know you were an East Coast guy but you might know some of them in the camps. No bikes anymore but I'm sure they stick together. I need you to get in touch with them, see what you can find out."

"Not a problem. I know three guys who made it back alive from upstate, been in touch with them through email before. They were thinking of going back east, now that we cleared out the Mohawk Valley. I'll see what info I can get from them in return for a way out of the camps."

Brit chimed in. "Oh, wait, I know, you want me to be a stripper! See what info I can wheedle out of some Johns, maybe make some New Dollars!" Sarcasm dripped from every pore.

"Um, no. I know deep down in your heart you want to be taking your clothes off for fat sweaty men but, too bad, so sad. You're going to stay wherever we set up our base of operations."

She was pissed. "What the hell, Nick? Should I just sit back in the kitchen and make sandwiches? Maybe shine your frigging boots?"

Ziv laughed his low rumble. "Watch out, Nick, she is, how you say, catching fire? Don't get burned." He was right, her pale face was almost as red as her hair and her eyes were blazing.

I sighed. "No, Brit, it's not like that. Once we get settled, they are going to come to us. The good Major might think that we can go all incognito but I'm sure they'll figure us out soon enough. These camps have been in existence for a year. It will be like walking into a small town, where everyone knows everyone else and there are powers that be. I need you there to watch our backs and listen to the powers that aren't here in the camp. The little people who try to stay out of the way but know what's going on."

I looked at the team. We were hard. A year of living out in the wild, marching hundreds of miles, dozens of firefights and hundreds of encounters with the undead. Ziv with his cruel, scarred face. Doc with his bald head, huge arms covered with biker tattoos. Red with his thousand-meter stare. Brit with her gunshot wounds. Esposito's lean, lethal frame. Ahmed's calm, neutral sniper eyes.

Yeah, we were going to fit in with these FEMA camp sheep like a bunch of wolves. I'm sure the other wolves would sniff us out pretty damn quickly.

"OK, then, let's roll out."

Chapter 116

I have served in some pretty nasty places, all over the world before the Zombie Apocalypse but I never thought I would see things like this back home in America.

The camp was a disaster. A riot had gone through it the day before and armed guards stood just outside the perimeter but not inside the camp. As we stood at the in-processing center an infantry squad climbed into two HUMVEES and started through the gate. There was a long queue waiting in the rain for food rations and as we watched, a fight broke out down the line.

We had seen the camps as we drove down I-5 last time we were here, before I lost my leg outside Denver. Each one held about ten thousand people, the size of a large town. Some were well organized, others were a seething mess. It wasn't rare to see one of the plywood and canvas tent structures blaze up, either from an accident or arson. Political unrest, unhappiness with the government, lack of movement on the resettlement; all made for a tinderbox. Travel between the camps was limited and you had to apply for a pass, which was rarely given.

The Chain of Command had given us a briefing on the current situation on this camp, Bravo Two Zero. It was located just outside Tacoma, in between JBLM and the city proper. Buses left each day to shuttle workers between the camps and the armament factories in Tacoma and Seattle but this particular camp had been on lockdown since yesterdays' riot. Rations had also been cut in half, as punishment. The S-2 suspected that the riot had been organized by a group calling themselves "Free Americans," dedicated to overthrowing the current emergency powers government but had a lot of ties to white supremacist gangs. They had been fighting to control the drugs that were smuggled into the camp from Tacoma. Marijuana had been legalized; it kept the population sedated but there was an outfit up in the mountains that had been growing poppies and coca plants in hot houses and selling heroin and crack for gold. Meth was making a new appearance too, as looters smuggled industrial supplies in from the ruined cities and set up labs back in the woods.

There was an ongoing race war inside this camp, too, apparently. The "Free Americans," were battling it out with the remains of the black gangs from Tacoma and apparently they were winning. Throw in all the different tensions that come from having thousands of shell-shocked civilians, many of whom had lost their families in the zombie attacks, and you had a recipe for disaster. Most of the fighting age males were out on the front line, serving with the Army in the Midwest or with the Marines on the East Coast, or down in Mexico securing the oil fields. That left policing the camps to older men and women. Their opponents were felons who had too much of a record to serve in the army and that had to be pretty damn bad. As a result, some of the camps were running wild, including this one. To be honest, I didn't care about all that crap; let them fight it out. We wanted whoever was running a big picture op.

The patrol rolled past, manned by older guys with worn out, lined faces. Instead of mounting machine guns, they had an Active Denial System, which fired a non-lethal microwave. Someone messing with them was going to get a serious sunburn and be slightly cooked. Brit blew them a kiss as they drove past.

We carried our duffle bags down through the rows of tents. The gravel crunched under our boots and the ever-present rain started to run off the front of my Gore Tex hood. Sullen faces stared out at us from under rolled up sides of the tents. Even the kids, usually curious about strangers, hung back. This place had some very bad juju.

"Nick. I got a bad feeling about this." Brit eyed a tent that was burned down to the ground, only blackened concrete pilings still standing. The tent next to it had been shredded by heavy machine gun fire. I was sure that the rounds had continued through whoever had been inside, out the other side and through a few more tents and anyone who got in the way of their immutable laws of physics. Rivulets of blood had stained the bottom of the tent.

Ziv barked out a short laugh. "This is nothing. You are not pussing out on us now, you silly woman."

"I ain't pussing out on shit, you communist prick. Maybe there will be some Muslims for you to slaughter here."

He laughed again and fingered the hilt of his big combat knife "I hope so. My trophy ears are starting to rot in this rain."

I ignored them, looking at tents on the left side of the street. Doc checked the ones on the right, looking at the chalk marks showing what was what.

"This isn't right," said Doc. "Backup."

We turned back. Through the shreds of the shot-up tent I could see the numbers given to us by the JSOC Major.

"Bullshit," said Red and I agreed. "What do we do now?"

I turned to the tent behind us. A couple of biker looking guys sat on a makeshift porch, eyeing us. "Well, we're supposed to be some hard ass crew. Let's go be hard ass."

Chapter 117

"I got this."

"Be my guest." Brit walked past me and walked up to the closest, a big bellied guy with a long beard. He eyed her suspiciously and scratched at his beard.

"What the hell do you want, little girl? Need your diaper changed? Maybe your bottom spanked?" His friends found this uproariously funny.

"I'm here to steal your soul, Duck Dynasty." He had one second to let out a quizzical "Huh?" then Brit hit him right behind the jaw with an extendable graphite baton. He fell like an ox that had been poleaxed.

The others, four of them in all, jumped up and started to rush her. I stood still as the rest of the team went past me. Brit kicked the fat man hard in the head and a general melee erupted. I couldn't move very fast on the still healing stump of my leg, so I waited for what I knew would happen.

Out of the doorway came a guy with a sawed off double barrel shotgun. I drew and fired in one smooth motion, just like I had learned reading Shane. Aim like you're pointing your finger. The .45 round caught him in the right hip and spun him around and the shotgun went off into the next guy coming out of the door and punched through his gut. Everything stopped and the fighting figures came to a halt.

"Out! All of you!" The gut shot man was staring wide eyed, trying to stuff his intestines back into his abdomen. "Take your trash with you." I walked past the two wounded, picked up the shotgun and headed into the tent. The bikers picked up their wounded friends and carried them off, cursing us.

Inside was a pigsty. In the corner was a still, dripping out moonshine from copper coils. Filth was piled high, empty MRE bags, water bottles full of piss. It never pays to underestimate the opposition but if this was the local thugs, well then, I'd take it.

"Nice," said Esposito. "I've seen zombies take better

care of their places. What's next, Nick?"

"Well, we clean up. And we wait. I'm sure whoever is creating the mayhem and whoever is behind this supposed terrorist plot, will show up sooner or later."

We settled down to wait. There was power run to the tent, so Red got to work hooking up a SINCGARS, a medium short-range FM radio, with a communications security device to scramble our calls. He made a quick radio check with higher, then shut back down. Outside the base, a Quick Reaction Force sat waiting to back us up if we needed help, or to extract us if things went really bad. A UH-60 with a squad of Army Rangers was kept five-minute alert but I hoped we wouldn't need them. The firepower that a Ranger squad could bring would lead to massacre of the civilian population. All the world had gone to hell but this was still America and I didn't want that to happen.

*****

We waited until dark but nothing happened. The lights of the camp came on but shadows sprung up around the tents, lending a sinister gloom to the whole surroundings.

I stood up and walked back into the tent. Time for some action, time to stir the hornet's nest. If they wouldn't come to us, time for us to go to them.

"Ziv, Doc, time for a little entertainment. Somewhere, there has got to be something going on in this camp."

Brit stood up and Ziv put his hand on her shoulder and pushed her back down. She collapsed down with an "ooff" and shot daggers with her eyes at him. "What the hell, you jerk!"

He laughed. "This is mans' work, little girl."

"Nick, what the hell!"

"He's right, Brit. We're going to some rough places tonight and you would be more of a distraction than a help."

She was pissed but there was nothing I could do about it. I knew I would pay for it later but honestly, I didn't want to have to worry about her shooting her mouth off at the wrong time. That, or get sexually assaulted and stick or shoot one of her attackers.

"Fine! I'll just stay here and sweep, do some dishes, make you some sammiches." Oh yes, she was pissed.

I went outside and walked out into the darkness. Doc and Ziv were waiting for me. We went down the muddy street, heading into the middle of the camp. Like a spider web, that was where the action would be.

When we got there, there was an open area and on one side, a large, low tent. Sounds of a crowd were coming out as a muted rumble, punctuated every now and then with a cheer. As we approached a shaft of light flashed out as a flap was opened and a body was thrown out, to land heavily in the mud.

"I think we found the place, Nick," said Doc.

"You up for this, Ziv?" He didn't answer, just pulled his knife out a half inch, then pushed it back in and grunted.

We went inside and pushed our way through the crowd until we reached an open space. A wooden ring went around the dirt floor, about twenty feet in diameter. On the far side of the ring sat a man on a camp stool, dressed in black jeans, work boots and a black jacket. The action swirled around him but didn't seem to touch him. He was the center of the tent, no doubt and he confirmed it by raising his hand. The noise immediately stopped.

"Well, what have we here? More challengers for our entertainment?" The crowd broke into a cheer. He let them go for a minute, then waved his hand for quiet again, standing up and striding across the ring to us, holding out his hand.

"Welcome to the Thunderdome! Here for a fight?"

I ignored his outstretched hand. "You gotta be shitting me. The Thunderdome? Really?"

He dropped his hand and a big grin spread across his face. "Well, I do admit, it's a bit cheesy but we don't get satellite TV in the camps. Gotta keep the masses entertained somehow. "

"Uh, OK. We're here looking for work, really."

"Work? Well, we'll see about work. But first, well, first comes entertainment. Randall Flag, at your service," and he bowed low.

This guy was a loon but he was holding all the cards. Behind us, the crowd had closed in and three guys with baseball bats stood in front of the exit. In for the penny, in for the pound.

"Nick." I nodded to my left and right "Rob and Ziv."

"Pleased to meet you. Though, I think," and he stared hard at Ziv "I think I know this man. Yes, yes, I do. A long way from home, are we not?"

Ziv cursed low under his breath, then spoke up. "Yes, I know you. You were the butcher of Srebrenica."

"What's that expression? One death is a murder, a million is a statistic? I fell somewhat short but oh my, it doesn't matter now, does it? With the whole world in ruins?" He laughed uproariously.

I waited for the laughter to die out, then asked. "So, what's the deal?"

I knew what he would say even before he opened his mouth to say it.

"The deal? Well, it's easy. Two men enter, one man leaves."

Chapter 118

Well, if that was the in, that that was the in. I started to step forward but Doc put his hand on my shoulder and Ziv stepped past me. "Nick, as your doctor, I say no frigging way. Besides, he's better than you ever were."

I stepped back, grumbling and sat down at a low bench, one hand inside my jacket on the butt of my pistol. I didn't care, if it looked like Ziv was going to lose, I would drop his opponent and we would shoot our way out.

Ziv handed Doc his jacket, then his shirt. He was muscled like a bear and old scars zigzagged across his torso. Low down, just under his ribcage, a horrific line of stitches showed on his back. In front was the angry red pucker of a large caliber bullet entry wound. Old white scars from shrapnel and knife wounds told of a lifetime of fighting and there was a harsh burn mark on one shoulder.

He balanced his double edged, foot long knife low, point down but held rock still, sizing up his opponent, who had just stepped into the ring. I had been expecting a giant, some muscle-bound redneck but this guy was medium height, whipcord thin and all hard wire and bone. He had almost as many scars as Ziv did.

"Shit," said Doc and I echoed him. Ziv was a hard man to like and I didn't ask him too much about what he did when he was in the Serbian Special Forces, because, honestly, I didn't want to know. However, we had been through some tough times together in the last year and I respected him. We each owed the other our lives, many times over. I was wondering if he had met his match. This guy wasn't some brawler, he was a knife fighter and a killer.

The crowd broke into cheers as the other guy held up his knife, a long stiletto of cold steel and did a slow strut around the ring. He grinned, showing a mouthful of broken teeth. Dried blood from his last fight still coated his arms and the ragged jeans he wore and matted his dirty blonde hair, which hung down his back in a ponytail. Prison tattoos were inked up and down his torso, mingling with the scars. As he strutted, the crowd started chanting "SWEDE! SWEDE!"

Doc leaned over to Ziv and started talking. "He's going to be fast, real fast, Ziv and he's going to try and get inside your guard, going for a low stab in your gut, or maybe cut your Femoral artery inside your leg. He'll take a cut across the back to give you a fatal cut on the inside. Don't let him get inside you."

In answer, Ziv spit on the ground. A girl stepped into the ring, dressed in Daisy Dukes and a bikini top, carrying a sign with a big "1" on it, meaning, I guess, round one. She followed 'Swede' around the ring as he pranced. The first time around, Swede gave Ziv the finger. The big Serb just stared back, impassive and immobile. The second time around, as the crowds' roar was getting even louder, he reached out to give Ziv the finger again and Flagg stepped into the ring, holding a megaphone.

Ziv grabbed the other fighters' outstretched arm and pulled towards him. The man stumbled, off balance and Ziv drove the top of his knife down through the point where his neck met his shoulder. Once, twice, faster than I could see it, then he spun the man single handedly across the ring to land at the feet of the girl carrying the sign. A jet of blood spurted from the wounds, spraying across the girl and her sign. She dropped it, put her hands to her mouth and screamed. The crowd fell silent, cutoff in mid chant. The Swede, grabbing at his neck, choked once and spat up a gob of blood, then collapsed into the sand.

The only sound was of Flagg laughing.

******

I jumped into the ring, pistol out, hammer cocked back and stood next to Ziv. Doc did the same, facing the opposite direction. We stared down a half dozen guns on either side. I figured in the next ten seconds, we were probably dead. My heart was racing and my hand shook slightly as I sighted down on Flagg.

Instead of ordering us killed, he stepped out and started clapping his hands. "Bravo, bravo, bravo! Now THAT is what I call entertainment! Something unexpected! Put your guns, down and we will talk business." He waved at the crowd, motioning for them to put their weapons away. The man casually stepped over the body of Swede and ran his hand across the face of the girl holding the sign, smearing the blood that had splattered her. Then he licked the blood off his fingers.

"One hundred percent, grade A wacko," I muttered and holstered my gun. We followed him through the crowd and out of the tent, crossing the open ground to a smaller tent and heading inside.

Flagg's personal bodyguard stood just inside the tent flap, a huge guy leaning on an actual frigging sword. He had his head shaved and beard twisted into a braid and black steel and kevlar body armor covered him from his neck to his feet. This guy would be hell to fight in the confined spaces of the camp. As we came in, the guy stepped in front of us and put the point of the sword to my neck, making me stop short.

"Taylor, let them in. We have a business deal to discuss." The giant grunted and lowered the sword, stepping aside. We walked past and Ziv patted his cheek. "I will see you later" he growled. The two of them stared each other down for what seemed like an eternity, until Ziv barked a short, harsh laugh and turned away.

Flagg sat down on the edge of a cot and I sat across from him. "So what's this business?"

"First, tell me about yourself and your crew. Why are only three of you here and not all seven?"

He was telling me that he had good info on us already. Time to play our hand and see if he would bite.

"Guarding our stuff. We've lived rough for years and we don't trust anyone."

He sat and pondered for a minute, making a great show of thinking. Then it looked as if a light bulb went off in his head.

"YES! I know you! I know you all. You were in the newspaper last year. That scout team in New York, up at West Point!" Busted. Things were going to get ugly real quick and we balanced on the knife edge of violence.

"That was some pretty awesome stuff! I followed you in the paper. How many zombies did you snuff? Where is the big black guy? Is the redhead in the tent the same woman you had with you? She is frigging HOT!"

I let out my breath slowly. Great, a frigging fanboy. Doctor Evil had a crush on Brit. "He's dead. Died right after that, on the exfil. One of the reasons we don't work for the Army anymore. Gave it up to freelance."

"One of the reasons? You have more?" Great, this guy was buying the whole thing. I rolled up my pants leg to show the crappy wooden leg I had strapped on.

"This is the other one. I lost my leg and all I got was this."

"Screwed by the government. Happens every time." He leaned back on the cot. "What would you say if I told you that I've got a plan to bring the whole thing crashing down?"

Jackpot! "I'd like to hear that very much."

Chapter 119

Flagg leaned forward again. "I assume you know your way around Zombies?"

"A bit."

"Do you think you could handle one? Move it from place to place?"

Where was he going with this? "Probably. Fighting zombies isn't hard if you're smart about it."

"So I understand. You wouldn't think so, with the number of people who died in the recent collapse." He had a huge grin on his face. This guy actually seemed to be getting off on thinking about all the death.

"Well, we didn't go all the way under."

"More's the pity. But back to business. Handling zombies."

"Sure, we could handle a Z. But there isn't one within five hundred miles of here. The quarantine is pretty damn solid."

He waved his hand in the air. "Never mind that. I have some friends who are infuriated that the Great Satan is still standing, even as their own country is a radioactive dust bowl. Jihad, they call it. They have managed to acquire some undead for me."

Great. The Middle East had been hammered in a short, sharp exchange of nuclear weapons between Iran and Israel. After the plague broke out and things broke dow, terrorists had detonated a bomb in Tel Aviv and then a couple of missiles had hit Israel's other cities, fired from Iran. The Israeli military had hammered Tehran and the other Arab capitals flat and then the Chinese had launched their disabling cyberattack against our nuclear forces. Then they had nuked Mecca, Jerusalem, Riyadh, Baghdad, Cairo, just to get them out of the way.

"So, where do we fit into this plan?" I could kill him right here and now, in fact, I wanted to but then we would lose the lead to his contacts. "What, exactly, IS your plan?"

"How many people are in this camp?"

I thought quickly. "Maybe five thousand."

"And what do you think would happen if five thousand undead suddenly scattered across the inside of the quarantine zone?"

My blood went cold and I heard a sharp intake of breath from behind me where Doc stood. "Well, at a minimum, the Federal Government would fall. All their forces are oriented outwards."

A look of glee came across his face. "EXACTLY! Riot and mayhem, death and destruction and the cycle turns again!"

This guy was absolutely crazy. Completely over the line. I also knew something that he didn't. Orbiting in a racetrack pattern, twenty-four hours a day, seven days a week, a B-52 from Fairchild Air Force Base circled the sky over the Federal Zone, armed with nuclear weapons. At the first hint of an outbreak, they would drop one, or two, or three, or however many the authorities thought they would need to contain an outbreak. Regardless of who was in the camps or village or city at the time. Nuke it from orbit, it was the only way to be sure.

"So, what do you need us to do and what's in it for us?"

"What do you want?"

"Gold. As much as we can carry."

He reached under the cot and dragged a heavy chest out, then flipped the lid open. In the light of the Coleman gas lantern, a pile of gold jewelry gleamed, looking like Smaug's hoard in The Hobbit.

"Looks good. So what do you need us to do?"

"We need security and help moving the undead from the drop off point into the camp."

I thought about it for a minute. "How many and where?"

"Three and you don't know need to know where. Just be at the south east corner of the camp tomorrow at breakfast."

"Early morning? That takes some balls, in broad daylight."

He nodded to the Viking. "Taylor, do you have that diversion planned?"

"All set, boss," he said, never stopping his staring game with Ziv.

I probed him for more information. "Are you just going to let them into the camp? Let them run loose?"

"That is the general idea. In the confusion, I'm sure you and your people will be able to get out, easy enough. We just need you to keep any military patrols away from the transfer point, if they come around, and then get the Zs into the most crowded area."

I pretended to think about it, then leaned forward and offered my hand. "Tomorrow at sunrise, then." He took my hand in his and his grip felt like ice in my hand. I let go as quickly as I could and stood.

We filed out of the tent, Ziv backing out with his eye on Taylor. As he left, he drew his finger across his throat. Taylor raised his sword to his face, then lowered it.

"Ziv, do you have to piss off the big guy in the armor?"

I could almost see his grin in the darkness. "Because some people are just asking to die. You can see it in their eyes."

"You, or him?" asked Doc.

"That remains to be seen."

Chapter 120

We made our way back to our tent, avoiding the open area. As we passed the remains of the burnt out tent I saw a half dozen figures coming up the street in the opposite direction. They stopped in front of our tent.

"Heads up, company."

I pulled the Motorola radio out and keyed it. "Brit, company outside. You tracking?"

"*Roger. Ahmed and Espo are out and about. We're going outside to meet-*"

She was cut off in mid sentence. Simultaneously, in front of us, bright flashes shattered the night and the flat CRACK CRACK of pistols firing. We all hit the dirt, right where we stood and drew our guns but held fire. The attackers were in between us and our tent and in the dark we couldn't be sure of our targets.

Beside us, in the destroyed tent, a stab of flame ruined my night vision and a loud BANG ruined my hearing. One of the attackers dropped and I heard over the ringing in my ear the sound of Ahmed racking the bolt of the Mosin rifle he had hidden just outside the fence the night before. He fired again, dropping another one. At the same time, off to one side of our tent, from under the wooden floorboards came a low ripping sound and more muzzle flashes. Red emptied a full thirty round magazine from a MAC-10 machine pistol into them. From the other side, Brit fired the sawed-off shotgun we had taken earlier in the day. The last of the attackers fell to the ground.

"CEASE FIRE!" I yelled and stood up. Beside me, so did Doc and Ziv; Espo and Ahmed crawled out from the ruined tent. We advanced cautiously and Brit and Red came out to us, shining flashlights on the bodies. They were more of the crew that we had taken this tent from earlier in the day. One was crawling away and Brit shot him in the back of the head. Doc checked the pulses of each of the others and when he found one still breathing, he quickly cut his throat.

I sat down on a crate after holstering my pistol. My hands started to shake and I jammed them hard into my pockets. It took a minute for my heart to stop pounding and when they stopped shaking, I stood back up. There was the smell of cordite, blood and dead meat in the air.

"OK, let's get out of here. We don't want to be anywhere near this in the morning when the patrols come by. Grab your stuff, time to roll."

We were ready to move in a few minutes; the radio was the only thing that needed to be broken down. Red stowed it in his pack and Ahmed hid the rifle under the burned out tent, pulling the bolt and putting it in his pocket. We moved out through the night, hunting for a new place to grab a few hours of sleep before tomorrow.

The further we got from the shootout, the more faces we saw peeking out from tent flaps. As we passed they slid back inside. No one wanted to get involved when the wolves were chewing on each other.

We found an empty tent and instituted a sleep plan. It was past midnight and I was exhausted. I tossed and turned and tried closing my eyes but every time I did, I saw the exchange of pistol shots like afterimages from camera flashes. I finally got up, unable to sleep and not wanting to take any of the drugs the VA had given me. Picking up my crutch, I hopped out and sat down on the wooden steps in the front. Espo was sitting there, smoking a cigarette. I knew Red was somewhere hidden in line of sight.

"Put that out." A cigarette was well and good but it ruined your night vision and gave an aiming point for a sniper. Shouldn't be a problem in the camp but a bad habit to take back outside the wire.

Esposito grounded it out on his boot, then put the stump back in his pocket. Tobacco was expensive, now that the fields in Virginia were just a mass of weeds and scrub brush.

"Sorry, Chief. Having a hard time sleeping again?"

"Yeah. Bad shit keeps coming back. Had the shakes again today."

"Maybe you need a vacation." We both laughed. A vacation, ha, right. "No, seriously, Nick. Look at all the shit you've been through in the last year. Lost your leg, lost a couple of friends, house blowed up."

"Blown up," I automatically corrected.

"Whatever, point is, you have been through a lot of shite. You gotta destress. Why don't you go try to take a poke at Brit? You know she's crazy about you."

"Old man like me? That will be the day."

"Just go talk to her, you dumbass. With all due respect, Sarge."

I sat and thought for a minute, then put my hand on Espos' shoulder and used him to lever myself up. I stumped back inside, sat on my cot, opened my team book and started writing notes on today's events. I heard a sigh as Brit sat up and fixed her eye patch over her ruined right eye.

"Can't sleep either, huh?" I asked quietly.

She nodded and came over to sit next to me. "Whatcha doin?"

"Putting down an account of todays' action. For posterities' sake. Who knows, maybe I'll write a book someday about all this."

"Am I in there?" She moved closer to me, trying to get a look at my notebook.

"Ever since we met, way back in Syracuse. Almost a year now."

"You remember pulling me out of the water in West Point?"

I thought back to that. She had kissed me after saving her life but we had put a stop to that real quickly. Teams don't work well when there is that kind of dynamic going on. "Yeah, I remember."

She moved even closer, putting her arm around my shoulders. "Remember what we talked about?"

"Yep, remember that too. Still the same. Nothing between team members."

"I know that but I want to ask you a favor." She leaned

her head on my shoulder.

"Go ahead." I had an idea of what was coming.

"Promise me something."

"We owe each other our lives, a couple times over. You can ask me anything."

"Promise me that when we head back east, we go back to Stillwater, farm some land. Quit all this crazy stuff."

I thought hard about it. I HAD been thinking hard about it, ever since I lost my leg. Even before that, when Brit lost her eye. Maybe even before that, the first time Brit got shot.

"I'll be honest," I said, "my patriotism meter is running pretty low. I've been thinking about it for a while. That shit with Doctor Morano."

Brit squeezed my shoulder. "Yeah, I'll deal with her. Someday soon. But, Nick. Listen. I'm not your typical woman. I'm not going to beat around the bush. I love you, you're my best friend and…"

She was interrupted by a loud, raucous snore from Ziv's cot. Picking up my prosthetic from beside the cot, she reached over and wacked him in the chest. He woke up with a snort. "What the hell was that for, you devil woman?"

"Stop fucking snoring. I'm trying to seduce Nick."

He rolled over and pulled the blanket up over his head. "About goddamn time. Stupid idiot Americans."

She turned back to me. "Like I was saying. Let's quit. Start a farm. Make babies. Make a new world." She leaned over, kissed me long and gently on the lips, then sat back.

"OK. After this, we're done. Just … can I keep my soul, Miss one-eyed, crazy redhead?"

"Too late, I've already got it. And your balls too. In a jar."

Chapter 121

The sun rose on, hopefully, our last day in the camp. For once, bright sunshine silhouetted Mount Rainier in the distance. At first light, we had called Special Operations Command and filled them in on what was going on. While Doc called it in, I sat on the steps and shaved with cold water. Brit sat next to me, picking through a Pasta MRE meal.

"Hey. About last night..." I started to say.

Between mouthfuls of pasta she said, "Shut your piehole. No idea what you're talking about."

OK, that's how she wanted to play it. Women.

Around us, the camp was coming to life. People were moving about, heading for the mess tents at the end of each street. A two-truck patrol, the same guys as yesterday, passed us. The gunner in the front truck, crouching behind an M-249 SAW, spinning the turret to track us as they passed. People looked away as the trucks went by but we didn't and that marked us. A difference in the pattern. A good combat veteran, a survivor, identified a break in the pattern. Stayed alive.

Next came a quick weapons and ammo check, ran through the plan, then moved out through the muddy streets. We made our way through the tents to the area Flagg had told us about, drifting against the crowd in twos and threes. As we moved, I started kicking myself. I was walking with Doc next to me. Brit, Ziv and Espo were moving parallel to us the next row over. Ahmed and Red had left earlier.

I was beating myself up for bringing the whole team in at the same time. We should have infiltrated in over a day or two, kept some of the team incognito. Ace in the hole. Now, we had no backup. Dumbass amateur mistake. Sure, the Rangers were on call but fifteen minutes could be a lifetime in combat. Screw it, we would just have to take what came.

On the southwest corner stood a gate, used for bringing in supplies. Kellogg, Brown, and Root, also known as KBR, my old buddies from Iraq, ran the mess halls and cleaned the shitters out. They were bringing the pre-cooked meals into the camp in 5 Ton trucks. The contractors would set the food out on long tables each meal time, twice a day, with MRE's for lunch. The truckers themselves were hired from even more wretched refugee camps, out on the Alaskan islands, where boat people from fallen countries had been settled by Coast Guard patrols.

I stood and watched for a minute or two, scoping out the area. Flagg stood by the gate, with his bodyguard next to him, the big guy named Taylor. He wore a long black coat and I was sure that underneath he still wore his armor and had his sword. As I watched, Brit came up next to us.

"Is that the Viking dude? What's with the armor? And a freaking sword?"

"There's going to be a riot today. Ever been in one?" I asked her.

"No."

Doc whistled. "Well, aren't you in for a treat. The reason old Taylor is wearing armor is to keep from being trampled in the dust, or getting a knife stuck in him. The sword is for killing people in close quarters."

"How do you know there's going to be a riot?"

"Just watch," said Doc.

We didn't have long to wait. Flagg strolled over to us and Taylor moved off into the camp "Good morning, gentlemen. Miss O'Neill. I'm a big fan of yours." He nodded to us and then leered at Brit.

She stuck her finger in her mouth and made a gagging motion "Creeper. Ugh."

A look of anger flashed across Flagg's face and for a moment, I saw something dark and evil blazing out of his eyes.

I stepped in front of her. "OK, Flagg. We're here. What do you need us to do?"

The look faded from his face and he calmed down. "In a few minutes, there will be a distraction. I need your team," and here he glanced around. "Where is the rest of your crew?"

"Here and there."

"I see. Well, I need your team to make sure one of these trucks gets to the middle of the camp. After that, you are free to go. The gold is in my tent."

"OK. Sounds like a plan. How will we know which truck?"

"You'll know. Ohh, this is going to be GREAT! Goodbye, America! As for you, Ms. O'Neill, just be glad I'm busy right now. I doubt you would be immune to my charms." He walked away, around the corner of a tent.

Doc spoke up. "Can I kill him? Pretty please? Twist his head off?"

"No. Like he said, we have our own work to do. One of those trucks will be carrying Zombies on it. Maybe more than one, if Flagg is smart."

At that moment, all hell broke loose. A burning object flew in a high arc and shattered on the cab of the second truck through the gate. Flames splashed over the truck and the canvas over the bed quickly caught fire. The crowd around the closest mess tent turned into a milling, shoving mass, trying to get away from the burning truck, which had rolled towards them as the driver jumped out of the cab.

The first truck pulled over to the side and started to head towards us, then turned into an alley between the tents and stopped, mostly out of sight. I saw Red and Ahmed across the open space and pointed two fingers at my eyes, then at the truck. Ahmed nodded and grabbed Red's arm and they moved out.

Burning fiercely, the first truck crashed into the mess tent and that quickly caught fire. This was a hell of a distraction and people were streaming in from all around to watch. The two HUMVEEs from the morning patrol pulled up, trying to insert themselves between the crowd and the burning truck. From the lead vehicle an amplified voice ordered the crowd to disperse.

"RETURN TO YOUR TENTS!" boomed out from the speakers mounted on the roof. The crowd ignored the orders, getting pressed in from behind. That's where the trouble makers would be, out of danger and egging the crowd on. Sure enough, rocks started bouncing off the trucks.

The Area Denial System mounted on the second truck spun in a slow arc and the crowd began to move back away, people in the front starting to shout and scream. Even from a hundred meters away, I felt my skin start to burn as it moved past me. The ADS was pumping out microwaves, putting a punishing radiating heat into people's bodies. I had been on the wrong end of one of these before and I knew that those closest to the system would be feeling sick and wanting to get out of the way as fast as they could.

Another burning arc through the sky and a Molotov Cocktail, a bottle filled with gasoline and a burning wick, shattered on the HUMVEE. The soldier in the turret dropped down inside the truck and...

"OH SHIT!" Doc and I both said at the same time. We each grabbed one of Brit's arms and pulled her flat on the ground just as the gunner in the first truck opened up with his mounted M-249. Tracer rounds flew overhead, then answering shots, flat pistol cracks. The crowd started running towards us and the machine gunner dropped his elevation and fired directly into them. People stepped onto us and Doc and I shoved them off our backs.

Doc leaned over and yelled in my ear "We gotta get the hell out of here!" I nodded my head, then grunted as a body fell on top of me. I pushed the woman off, then stuck my fingers to her neck, checking for a pulse. They came back bloody, my fingers finding a throat torn out by a bullet.

The firing stopped and there was a momentary break in the crowd. We both jumped up and half carried, half dragged a protesting Brit towards where the second cargo truck was hidden, knocking people down when they got in our way, stepping over fallen people and bodies. The square was a screaming, pushing mob, fighting each other to get away from the gunfire. We scrambled around the back of the truck and ran smack into Red and Ahmed, weapons drawn. Ziv and Espo stood at the front of the truck and Flagg was between them, a look of mad glee on his face. Next to him stood Taylor, hulking in his coat over his armor.

"This is GREAT!" Flagg shouted. He walked over to me and clapped his hand on my shoulder. "Don't you think? Madness and chaos is the natural order of things." His dark face was flushed, a bright gleam in his eye.

"Yeah, great," I said, sarcasm dripping from my voice. If he heard it, he ignored it.

"OK, on to business. This truck," and he slapped the side "needs to get to the center of camp. Once there, the driver will take care of things. I need you to make sure it gets there. The patrols are distracted but there will be people who get in the way."

"Where are the people who supplied the zombies? How many are there?"

"Oh, there was only one. By now, I expect, there are three or so. I locked up the terrorists in there with them this morning. After all, it's every Americans' patriotic duty to fight the War on Terror, isn't it?" and he laughed that maniacal cackle, making my skin crawl.

"So that's it, then? All the terrorists are locked up in there?"

"Yes, why?"

"Randall Flag, under the authority of the Federal Emergency Powers Act of 2015, you're under–" and my words were cut short by Taylor whipping his sword out and swinging it at my head.

"Son of a BITCH!" I fell backwards and twisted to one side. As his sword whistled over my head, I felt something go POP and a wrenching pain shot through my lower back. He swung again, downward and I tried to roll to one side but couldn't move.

Ziv hit him broadside in a football tackle. They both crashed down in the dirt and started rolling around. From my position on the ground, I could see Ziv's knife skidding across Taylors' armor. I tried to stand but I couldn't raise myself any higher than one knee. "Doc! My fucking back! I can't move!"

I heard Brit yelling "I can't get a shot! I can't shoot!" and saw her aiming her pistol at Ziv and Taylor. Doc grabbed me by the shoulders, wrapped me in a bear hug and lifted. My back went POP again and I could move. He set me down on my feet and I looked around for Flagg. Espo, Red and Ahmed had moved around to the back of the truck and were working the pins, ready to put down the things inside rather than let them escape. Three would be easy work for them and the threat ended.

I heard a loud CLANG and the tailgate of the truck fell open. Two dozen undead started piling out, scrambling down, screaming their zombie howls. They streamed past the guys, heading straight for the melee in the square. Taylor and Ziv had gotten to their feet and were facing each other. Ziv held up one hand to Brit, waving her off, ignoring the Z's. Brit was ignoring him in turn, firing as fast as she could into the crowd of zombies. I drew my own pistol and started firing just as fast but several of the Z's ran around the corner and disappeared, chasing the crowd of rioters.

"GET FLAGG!" I yelled at Espo and they took off after him.

"Would you just cut that shit out!" I strode over to Ziv and Taylor, who were trading knife and sword strokes, faster than I could see. Doc fired at the last Zombie coming at us and it fell at our feet. Taylor stood back as shots and screams broke out in the camp, mixed in with the howling of the Undead. He stood with an uncertain look on his face but not taking his eyes off of Ziv.

Red and Ahmed, followed by Espo, reappeared around the far corner. "We lost him, boss!" said Espo.

"Forget it, this place is blown." I loked at the big guy, trying to decide if I should shoot him. No, there had been enough death. "Taylor, get the hell out if you can. You were just doing your job." He nodded to Ziv, lifted his sword to his face and saluted us all, then walked off, sword still drawn. I grabbed the radio handset out of Red's backpack and the guys formed a defensive circle around me.

"Iron Mike, this is Lost Boys, SHOPPING BAG, I say again, SHOPPING BAG, Camp Bravo Two Zero, over."

It took a second but then the voice came back, loud and strong.

"LOST BOYS, THIS IS IRON MIKE. CONFIRM SHOPPING BAG BRAVO TWO ZERO."

"I say again, I confirm, SHOPPING BAG."

"ROGER, EXTRACT FIVE, I SAY AGAIN, FIVE MINUTES."

"Five minutes, Lost Boys out!"

I stuffed the handset back in Red's pack and took my place in the circle. Doc crouched next to me.

"Shopping Bag? Who the hell comes up with these code words?"

"Some dipshit staff officer in the New Pentagon. Thinks that if anyone overhears it, it won't start a panic."

Doc nodded. "Are they going to pull us out?"

I thought about it. "Fifty Fifty. They might scrag the whole camp just for shits and giggles. If you'll excuse me."

I got up and moved next to Brit. "Hey Brit. We might bite the big one on this. I just want you to know…"

"I know, Nick. Even if it all ends right now, I know."

Around us, the howls, gunshots and screams grew louder and fires leapt up, smoke blotting out the morning sun. Red handed me the handset to the radio. In the distance, we watched the surviving HUMVEE from the patrol charge across the square, mowing running people down and bumping over bodies. They knew what was going to happen and were trying to get out. It seemed like they would but a steel barrier shot out of the ground, closing the gate. They hit it at about forty miles per hour and stopped dead. As a horde of Zs came howling after and them the gunner let loose a wild burst from his machine gun, blowing bloody holes in bodies but they still came on. The gun jammed and he pulled out his pistol, firing until the slide locked back. He might as well have been spitting into a wave. They swarmed him and tore him apart. None of us moved; our survival now depended on staying out of the way.

"Lost Boys, this is Warbird, thirty seconds out."

"Roger, Warbird, be advised, LZ may be hot."

"Understood, Lost Boys. Macguire rig extraction. Mark smoke, over."

Ziv pulled the pin in a red smoke grenade, flipped off the spoon and tossed it between us and the horde. It started billowing out, blocking the massacre in the square from view. An MH-60 Special Operations helo popped over the fence, the rotor wash sucking up the smoke into a giant swirl and held at a hover thirty feet up. Two rope bundles fell out, one from each side. Machine gun fire started raking the crowds on the other side of the smoke. The pilot wasn't going to risk his rare, multimillion dollar aircraft by setting it down into chaos.

"HOOK UP!" yelled Doc. On each rope were four slings that clipped around a person's chest. I slung mine under my arms and turned to check Red's sling, making sure it was tight. He checked Ziv's and Ziv checked mine. On the other sling, the rest of the team did the same. The crew chief leaned out, saw that we were ready to go and the rope tightened and heaved us up in the air.

Below us the camp was a madhouse. Tents were burning and people ran in every direction, being chased by undead. Gunshots echoed and a mob was pressing at the front gate. Steel barriers had blocked their exit and they were trying to knock down a section of fence. As we rose, I closed my eyes. Thousands of men, women and children. All dead because of me. We spun in our harnesses as the chopper turned east, dipped its nose and poured on the power.

Chapter 122

As we flew, twisting in the wind, I could faintly hear Brit screaming and yelling over the thud of the rotor blades. I craned my neck to try and see what was wrong but the wind tore at my vision and I could only get occasional glimpses of her. Nothing I could do about it till we hit the ground.

We flew steady on for ten minutes, then swung around a road cut. The pilot set the ropes down on the ground and we unsnapped as he landed and powered down. The crew ran past us, pointing to a ditch on the side of the road, with the hill between us and the camp, forty kilometers away. I put my hands over my ears, opened my mouth and squeezed my eyes shut.

The flash, even that far away, burned through my eyelids like a giant flashbulb, even though the hill was in the way. When the first shockwave hit, it came through the ground. We were bounced two feet up into the air. Then the blast wave came thundering over the hill, first rushing past us as a hot wind, then coming back the other way as the mushroom cloud sucked in air to feed itself.

The nukes were set for low yield and low airbursts to maximize the heat scorching everything. The only way to be sure was to kill it with fire. The camps themselves were downwind and miles from any kind of civilization. Any Zs that escaped and made their way into the countryside would be hunted down by air patrols with radiation detectors. They would be glowing white hot on any scanner.

When the wind had died down, I crawled over to Brit. I was worried that she had caught a stray round as we were leaving the camp and in our rush to seek cover I hadn't had time to check on her. I put my hand on her shoulder as she sat up, covered in muck from the drainage ditch.

"Hey, are you OK? What was all the screaming about? Are you hit anywhere?" I started to look her over for bleeding but she pushed my hands away and started rubbing her chest.

"My goddamned boob got caught in the sling and it was pinching the whole fucking way here. Mother of God, that shit hurt!"

The team laughed, as behind us, the face of Shiva, the Destroyer, lifted itself into the skies.

******

Spring, Year Two.

We stood on the shoreline of our island in the Hudson River, thirty miles north of Albany. Canoes were tied up the dock and the team was loading them, lashing gear and extra ammo into them. There was a cool crispness in the air but winter had finally broken.

Doc shouldered his aide bag and his second in command, Staff Sergeant Toshi, handed him his M-4. "Sure you don't want to go with us? Just a quick trip up river to Burlington. Easy vacation."

I shook my head. "Nope. We're done, Doc. Gonna dig some dirt, grow some corn."

"And make babies!" said Brit.

"Well, practice, at least," I said.

It was true. I was done. The nightmares still came but at least my hands had stopped shaking. I needed peace and quiet. I had been fighting for more than a year, first in survival mode, then by order of that fickle parent, the military. We needed to settle down, to start over. I would miss it, though. These were my friends, my brothers, going in harms' way and I felt guilty. Had I really done enough? I felt the phantom pain where my leg used to be, that itch that I could never scratch. Yeah, it was never enough but sometimes you just had to call it quits.

"If you need anything, call us and we WILL come and get you. It might take some time but you know we'll be there. Even if it's just to pop you in the head after you've turned Z."

"I expect nothing less, brother." He picked me up in a bear hug and squeezed the breath out of me.

"Put me down, you moronic biker retard."

Brit slapped the back of my head. "That's not politically correct, Nick! You can't say retard."

Doc laughed and followed Toshi out to the last canoe. They shoved off and started paddling upstream, cutting a wake through the sheen of oil on it.

"Well, let's go plant some corn."

Part II

Chapter 123

It never failed.

Specialist Redshirt felt the rumbling in his guts about ten minutes after he had eaten his lunch MRE. Could be the water, could be the food itself. Good water and unspoiled food were getting hard to come by, almost two years after the Zombie Apocalypse had pretty much trounced Western Civilization.

The rest of the team sat finishing their meal. Doc and Ziv picked idly at their MREs, the springtime heat making it hard to eat. Red was standing watch, along with Ahmed but he had to go. He motioned to Sergeant Toshi, who was stretching her legs.

"Sarge, I gotta hit the tree line. Take over for me."

She grunted and climbed to her feet, tossing her rucksack onto her back and shouldering her rifle. Beside her, the big Swedish guy, Svenson, levered himself up off the ground. No one went anywhere alone.

They were taking a break in a small clearing, just off the remains of Route 9, north of Ticonderoga. To the east, Lake Champlain stretched out, a broad sheet of water reflecting the summer sun. Their canoes lay drawn up on the shore where they had stopped at sunrise. The team was heading north to see what remained of the Air National Guard unit at Burlington Airport/ After that to check the locks at the end of the lake where the Richelieu River wound its way down to the Saint Lawrence. They had stopped for the day just north of Port Henry on the New York side of the river.

"Oh crap," muttered Red under his breath and he dashed for the trees, setting his rifle down, dropping his pants and barely making it before his guts exploded. Coming up behind him, he heard Svenson starting to laugh.

"That's what you get for picking a number eleven MRE, Red!" he started laughing again but it was cut off with a choking sound. Red saw the feathers of an arrow sprout from the big man's neck, just above his body armor. He fell to his knees, grabbing at the shaft. A stunned look lay on his face as he spilled forward, choking.

Red scrambled to pull up his pants, yelling "AMBU.S.H!" at the top of his lungs and dove for his rifle. He grabbed it just as a burst of shots dug into the ground where he had been squatting. Recovering his footing he ran as hard as he could through the woods, away from the gunfire that had erupted between him and the rest of the team. He dove over a fallen tree and then started to scramble around to the right, trying to get back in the clearing where the team was.

After a few minutes, he could see through the trees. Two dozen figures in a haphazard collection of camouflage and carrying an assortment of weapons, everything from M-4's to shotguns, had rushed the area. and a squad of them was moving towards where Svenson lay. He noted that they moved in covering fire teams, cautiously advancing.

Sergeant Toshi lay out in the open, an arrow sticking out of her face, her feet drumming on the ground. Ziv was in the middle of a brawl, swinging his big combat knife. As Red watched, someone hit the Serb on the back of the head with the butt of a rifle and he fell to the ground. Ahmed was nowhere to be seen and one man stood with a pistol to Doc's head. Even as he watched, Doc let out a yell.

"Red, RUN!"

Specialist Eugene Redshirt, Irregular Scout Team One, United States Army, ran. Before he did, though, he fired a long burst from his suppressed carbine at the squad moving towards Svenson's body. He saw one fall before he turned and ran deeper into the woods, deeper into the mountains surrounding the lake. Deeper into Zombie Territory. As he did he heard gunfire behind him and then a red-hot poker zipped through his leg, making him stumble and fall heavily forward. His rifle flew out of his hands as he tried to stop his fall. Behind him he heard yelling as the ambushers started off in pursuit.

Redshirt got up again, holding onto his thigh, squeezing

it tight to try and stop the blood flow. It hurt but it felt numb more than anything else as he limped deeper into the forest. The sounds of pursuit died off and then he heard one voice calling to him.

"Hey, you're gonna die out there and I ain't wastin' none of my men comin' to get you. I knows yer wounded and unarmed. I hope you got enough sense to kill yourself before you get eaten!"

He risked a look back and saw the squad heading back to the ambush site. One of them held his rifle in his hands. Damn. His pack, all his extra ammo, food, everything was back at the site, as well as the rest of his team.

First things first, his leg. The smell of blood and the sound of gunshots would draw any zombies, even though they had stopped at a deserted stretch of shoreline. He ripped open the leg of his pants and looked at the wound. A shot had creased the muscle, tearing out a bunch of skin and flesh. It hurt like hell but he wasn't going to bleed to death. He pulled out a field dressing and wrapped it around his leg.

Redshirt started crawling back to the campsite but flanked around to the left, where he could get a good view. A big motor boat had pulled up the shore and the team was being hustled onto the boat. He counted more than twenty of the reavers. They had stripped Sergeant Toshi's body but it didn't seem like they were going to eat her. Not cannibals, then. As he watched, one put his boot on her head and pulled out the arrow. Doc was already on the boat. Ziv must have been unconscious, because they threw him into the bow like a sack of potatoes. The boat backed out of the shore after about half of the Reavers had climbed aboard, then headed north up the lake. The rest melted into the woods, moving as a disciplined squad, headed north.

He climbed slowly onto a high rock and waited. One hour. Two. Three. The whole morning passed before he saw the stay-behind ambush. Three of them walked out of the trees and used an ax to smash holes in the canoes drawn up on shore. Then they walked back into the woods, following a trail that ran northwards along the shoreline.

His leg was starting to hurt and he was hungry. The nearest safety he knew of was a hundred miles south, through wrecked civilization and hordes of zombies. Redshirt checked over his inventory. A silenced .22 automatic, 450 rounds of .22 Magnum ammo in his Load Bearing Vest and his survival kit strapped around his waist. It contained a hammock, 50 feet of paracord, lighter, some spare food, Poncho, extra five shot .22 revolver, 20 rounds of ammo, signal mirror, water purification tablets and a multi-tool.

He slid slowly down the rock, pistol in hand, favoring his wounded leg and made his way to the campsite, carefully skirting the perimeter, trying to make sure no one else was around. Finding none, he made his way in, careful to avoid the naked body of Sergeant Toshi. There was nothing left on the ground except some expended brass and some MRE wrappers. He quickly ripped them completely open and licked off whatever food was remaining inside.

"Got you! Knew you were somewhere out there!" He heard the safety flicking off a weapon and raised his hands, then slowly turned around. In front of him stood a figure camouflaged in a set of old Army BDUs, wearing body armor and holding a pump shotgun pointed at him from about fifteen feet away.

"Drop the weapon and start walking!" The reaver motioned with the shotgun barrel. "Hell yeah, I knew I right! Captain is going to be happ—"

As he started to swing the barrel back towards him, Red dropped his hands and dove to one side, firing his pistol as fast as he could. The shotgun boomed and his left arm stung but he kept firing until the slide locked back. Standing up, walked over to the man lying on the ground, grabbing at his face and screaming. Red watched as the man coughed blood out of his mouth, then shuddered and went still. Red kicked the shotgun aside and started stripping the body of everything usable. Then he picked up the shotgun, ejecting the spent shell.

He looked the corpse over one last time. "You white people … you talk too much."

Chapter 124

The tractor caught on another rock, heaved up by the winter frosts. I jumped down, careful to land on my good leg, and stumped over to it. The prosthetic on my right leg, a blade of carbon fiber, was good but the stump was still raw and painful sometimes and I didn't want to irritate it.

Joe had already brought the four-wheeler up and I helped him lift the rock into the small trailer. It joined the others that would be dumped at the edge of the field, helping fix the rock wall built by farmers around two hundred years ago. We were raising it high enough that a random zombie couldn't tumble into the field. Almost two years later they were still thick on the ground in the ruins of the towns up and down this stretch of the Hudson River, despite our "clearing," trips we went on once a week. The field I was working was east of our little island fortress and I was desperate to get some honest-to-God corn and wheat growing. Brit was doing pretty well with the garden but we need trade crops.

"OK, Joe, let's call it quits for the day." He grunted in agreement and waited until I had secured my rifle on the ATV and hopped on. A twist of the throttle and we headed back to the bridge. Joe was an extra hand who I had hired, a guy who had had enough of the FEMA camp in Albany. Didn't say much, worked hard and lived in a room in the old farmhouse. He was saving his New Dollars pay so that he could homestead somewhere properly, with a new wife. Hopefully somewhere close by. He was a good man to have around.

We pulled up to the gate on the bridge and I got down to open the heavy barrier. As I did, out of habit I looked over to the canal, just checking to see what might have washed down the river. Occasionally there were zombies, starting to rot once the water immersion killed the parasite. More often it was live ones who had just fallen in and were still snapping and trying to climb out. Those I shot once in the head.

This time, I stopped and looked hard. Drawn up on shore, next to the ruins of our old house, was a canoe. Someone was onshore. I tapped Joe on the shoulder and he jumped down next to me, readying his old lever action Winchester. I called quietly to Brit over the radio, keying the mike in a two-tap alarm. Back at the house, her Motorola would beep twice, giving her the "come quick, be armed," signal. Not that Brit went anywhere unarmed anyway.

I sent Joe off to the left, to flank anyone who might be moving up the other side of the small island. I moved down shore, toward the canoe, first tightening the straps that held my leg in place. Approaching steadily, looking over the sight of my M-4, ready to fire a quick burst. Out of the corner of my eye I saw Joe come around the side of the old house foundation and he gave me a quick "all clear" sign. We moved together towards the canoe.

On the other side of it lay a figure, clad in the rags of an Army Multicam uniform. Rough bandages were around his leg and his arm and he lay sprawled face down in the mud. I dropped my rifle in its sling and ran to him, rolling him over.

Specialist Redshirt was dirty, bloody and chewed to hell. His ammunition pouches were empty and his .22 pistol lay on the ground next to him, slide locked back. I checked his pulse and breathing. He was alive but barely.

"Brit, this is Nick. Red is here, I found him next to a canoe on the old island. He's wounded." I checked his forehead; it was burning hot.

"*Do you need me there?*"

"Negative, we'll bring him in on the 4-wheeler. He's got a bad fever, looks like multiple gunshot wounds, infected bites. Get the Medkit out, antibiotics, IV, everything."

Red's eyes opened a little and tried to focus on me. "Red, it's me. It's Nick. You're safe."

He whispered and I had to lean forward to catch it. "Doc, Ziv, Ahmed, team captured."

"It's OK, brother, we got you. We'll take care of it. Just hang on." He squeezed my hand, then fell limp in my arms. I lifted him onto the trailer and we started back. I left Joe to close the gate.

Chapter 125

I sat looking at a map of Lake Champlain, lit by the kerosene lantern hanging in the kitchen. Brit sat across from me, cleaning her rifle. Joe was out in the tower, pulling first watch, keeping an eye open for any zombies or raiders that might be approaching under cover of the darkness. On the kitchen counter, a SINCGARS radio was tuned to the Fire Support Net at Firebase Horse, just outside Saratoga. Through long practice I had learned to keep half an ear out for our call sign. It had been quite a while since anyone had called, "Lost Boys," on the radio. I was out of the scouting business; for good, I had thought.

Red's team, consisting of him, Master Sergeant "Doc," Hamilton, Sergeant Toshi and a couple of civilian scouts, including our old friends Ziv and Ahmed, had stopped by the farm last week on their way north. Doc had filled me in on what was happening, Army-wise. We had a satellite dish that fed us the news through the internet and I had kept in regular touch with them on Facebook, while I recuperated from getting my foot pretty much hacked off.

"Well," said Doc, after he had checked on my stump, "Task Force Empire has been held up just south of Poughkeepsie, pretty much at the I-84 line. I think they've run out of fuel and manpower and are consolidating. The radiation from Indian Point has pretty much held off operating on the east side of the river, anyway. They took a LOT of casualties in Newburgh and Pough-town. The Marines cleared Staten Island and are turning it into a giant Jarhead/Squid base."

Apparently, the consolidation had freed up the team to go north and check out the canal links to Montreal. They had only stayed one night, pulling out in their canoes early the next morning under cover of darkness. Almost the same mission we had last year, except further north.

As I looked over the map I reached down and idly scratched between Rocket's ears. He got up, stuck his head out the small flap cut in the door, smelled the wind for zombies, then came back to sit on my foot. Brit finished assembling her rifle, snapping it shut and then doing a functions check. Then she pulled out her pistol and started breaking that down. I could tell something was bothering her, so I asked.

"Are you sure you're up for this?" she said. "Red mentioned Port Henry when he woke up before. That's a lot of travel on that leg."

"First off, we're not going anywhere until Red is up for it. Give him four or five days, I think he'll be back on his feet. The kid is tough." She nodded in agreement but I could see her starting to object again. I held up my hand.

"Brit, I'm not an action adventure hero. My leg is gone and my stump hurts like a bitch sometimes. We live forty miles from the nearest medical care and I know an infection can be the death of me. I'm not friggin' Superman."

"Well, you're Superman in bed." She placed her hands over her face and made an "OM NOM NOM," sound.

I laughed. "You're still a pig, Honey."

"There is a reason I won't let you keep sheep here on the farm, Nick. I don't want you to stray."

I threw an oily gun rag at her. "Seriously, though, I'm going to call in a favor. If we walked or canoed it, it would take us a week to get up there. We need that time for Red to recuperate. I'm going to call FOB Orange and see if we can get a ride." Last I knew, Major McHale was still commanding the Aeromedical UH-60 company at the Forward Operating Base. Hopefully he could help us out.

"That and we need intel. Someone in the S-2 might be able to give us some information on groups operating out of the Lake Champlain area. I know that they've picked up radio traffic and done overflights. It doesn't do us any good to go in blind. Plus, we need to know if there are any zombie hordes moving around there."

She got up and came around to give me a kiss on the forehead. "Only because it's our friends."

"Of course." I wanted out of the game as much as she did.

Chapter 126

One thing about the Army, you never know when it was going to throw you a curveball. I wasn't expecting the one we got an hour later.

"Lost Boys, this is Orange Main, over."

I got up from the table, where I had been cleaning my own weapons. Brit was upstairs checking on Red and I was about to pack it in for the night. The call from the Operations TOC at Fort Orange came as a complete surprise. It was being relayed through the retrans station at Firebase Horse.

"Lost Boys, this is Orange Main, priority, over," the caller repeated. Dammit.

"Orange Main, this is Lost Boys, over."

"Lost Boys, this is Empire Actual, over"

Damn. The Task Force Empire commander was on the horn.

"This is Lost Boys Six, send your traffic, over."

"Nick, I am recalling you to active duty, along with any other inactive members of your team."

I stared at the handset. *WTF, over? Recalled to active duty?* "Empire Main, this is Lost Boys Six. Say again, over."

"You heard me, Nick. Get your shit together, get Brit, and get every goddamned settler you can. All hell has broken loose along the line. A Chinook will be at your place at 1900 hours tomorrow. Bring enough gear for a week."

"Roger, be advised. India Sierra Tango One is missing, believed captured outside Burlington. We have one WIA from the team here, over."

"Understood. Figured as much when they dropped off the net. Bring him along; he'll get medical care at the CSH. See you tomorrow. Empire Actual out."

Damn, what the hell was that all about? I called upstairs to Brit, asking her to come down, then got on the radio again and switched over to what we called the "local" band.

Within a ten-mile radius, up and down the river, people who were tired of living on government handouts and

---

working the fields around Albany for FEMA had struck a deal with the Army. They were given radios, guns, ammo, seeds and equipment and one day's assistance from a platoon of Combat Engineers setting up a defensible position, preferably at a usable farm. In return, they were on call to assist against any attacks and provide manpower to the Army when asked. So far, there were an even dozen loners and two families who had taken up the offer and we often hooked up with them to "clear" the local area of zombies. Our place acted as a trading post for them. Most were ex-military who didn't care to deal with the government any more than they had to. We also acted as an early warning network for our friends in Schaghticoke and regularly traded with them.

Everyone was supposed to tune in for a net call at 2100 hours each night to check in. Two weeks ago, one of them, a tough old guy named Salk, had missed his call. Several of us had made for his place at first light, moving up the river to an old farmstead just south of Schuylerville. We had found a pile of dead zombies around the farm but one had gotten him in the end and Brit shot him through the eye as he stumbled towards us, dragging his half-eaten leg, snapping his jaws. You rolled the dice and you took your chances. We went and hunted down the rest of the Zs, a small group of a dozen that were stumbling down Route 4.

At 20:59, I keyed the handset, waited a second, then initiated the netcall. When everyone had answered in order, I got down to business.

"All stations, the Army is calling in their chips. I need you all here no later than 1700 tomorrow with a week's worth of gear and ammo. "

A chorus of curses broke out over the radio, most along the line of, *"Fuck the Army."* I waited them out, then got back on.

"They helped you when you needed it. Now it's payback time and your fields can wait a week, break." I keyed the mic again. "Jablonski and Smith, you are excused. I know you have families that need taking care of. See you all at 17:00

tomorrow."

I wasn't going to break up any families again but if Task Force Empire was calling in the Reserves, it was serious. I flicked on Fox News as Brit came down the stairs. We caught the tail end of the hourly newscast and I recognized the location on the video. Thousands of reanimated corpses were streaming up Route 9, overwhelming the barricades at I-84. As I watched, the footage switched over to a shot of a cruise missile slamming into the center span of the Tappan Zee Bridge, twenty miles north of New York City. Hundreds of bodies fell into the middle of the river.

"Damn!" said Brit.

"Damn." I agreed with her.

Chapter 127

The news wasn't any better the next morning. I had powered up the generator to supplement our batteries and left the TV on all night. I tried to pick apart details on what was happening but all that I got out of it was that there was a shit storm of zombies heading north out of NYC. Apparently, something had stirred them up but the Army wasn't saying. As I watched, the Verrazano Bridge fell into Lower New York Harbor, dropped by the Marines defending Staten Island. Another couple of billion New Dollars down the drain and something that wouldn't be rebuilt in my lifetime. Dumbasses could have just knocked a hole in both decks instead of dropping the whole span. Stupid Jarheads.

Red was still knocked out, helped along I'm pretty sure by something Brit had given him. We had carried the kid downstairs and he lay strapped to a folding stretcher. Our packs were sitting by the door, weapons sitting on top of them and I was adjusting the straps on my leg when we heard Joe call out. It was obviously someone he knew, or he would have challenged them. This sounded more like a greeting than a warning.

The first one I saw was the last one I wanted to see. I actually didn't see him at first, I smelled him. Donny the Butcher. We never could find out his last name. The guy stunk to high heaven and never, ever washed. He claimed that the smell kept the zombies off of him and he was still crusted with blood from the last clearing trip we had been on.

"OUT!" yelled Brit. "Get your nasty ass out of my house. Go jump in the river, before I throw you in. I'm not riding or fighting next to your nasty ass." He stopped dead in the doorway and beat a hasty retreat. Donny was terrified of Brit for some reason. I sighed, got up and shot Brit a look. She shrugged her shoulders and made a "what?" gesture with her hands. I shook my head and walked out.

Donny, who had actually jumped into the river, was soon joined by a couple of others and I looked them over as we did checks on our equipment. There were twelve all told. Tough-looking men, even two women, who had spent the last winter hacking out a living in an area that was rapidly turning back into a wilderness of ruined buildings and deserted fields. The biggest group was a crew of five, all ex-military, who were slowly looting Mechanicville of gold and silver. The rest, like Donny, were loners who enjoyed being away from society. The leader of the Mechanicville crew, a burly former Marine named Jim Lock, came over to me, asking what was going on.

"Best I can tell, Jim, is that the lines are breached somewhere south of Poughkeepsie and the Army is shitting a brick. Apparently, all the Zs in NYC have gone apeshit."

He nodded and scratched his chin. "Think that is going to cause any problems here?"

"Dunno. It seems to be only the NYC area and between your crew and the rest of us, we've cleared everything out on this side of the river, up to the Saratoga radiation zone. That and patrols from Firebase Horse have pretty much tagged every Z in the local area."

I knew what he was worried about. Brit, Joe and I had worked hard getting a crop in and building the farm up into a defensible position. It could hold its own for a week or two but more than that, we might have some surprises when we came home. If we came home.

"Well, if none of us make it back, here's the grid coordinates of our haul. You're welcome to it. Got about fifteen pounds of gold and almost forty-five of silver. Ton of diamonds and other jewelry, too."

What they did was tough work but they banked on it being rewarding, too. They went house to house, killing zombies and looting for jewelry to melt down into ingots, breaking into banks and pawn shops. Their plan was to get enough to buy a ticket to England. Problem was, they had already lost three guys to zombie bites and one to some guy holed up in his house with a ton of canned food and a shotgun. They had methodically cleared each house in

Mechanicville and planned to keep at it up and down the river.

"Much appreciated, Jim."

He laughed and said, "Just don't shoot me in the back to get it! If you miss I'll beat you to death with that fake leg of yours, Army puke."

"As if."

The helo dropped down out of the sky into a cornfield that was slowly growing, knocking down the young plants in a blast of wash from the two rotors. Dammit, I thought, another crop wasted. Stupid pilot had completely ignored the orange panels laid in the empty field next to it.

The crew chief hopped out and waved at us to board. First in was Red on his stretcher. He was awake and pissed off that he was strapped into the stretcher.

"Untie me, Nick!"

"Sorry, Kid. We're dropping you off at the Combat Support Hospital in Albany. We'll see you in a week or less. Get better so we can go rescue the team when we get back."

He looked at the rest of the guys filing in. They were loaded for bear, extra ammo, two heavy machine guns, the tube of an M-224 60-millimeter mortar strapped to the back of one guy's pack, the baseplate to another. "What's going on, Nick? Is this the militia? You guys look like you're going to fight World War Five or something."

"Or something. Lines are breached north of the City. They need all the help they can get." Brit strapped in next to his stretcher and reached out and squeezed his hand.

"Don't worry, Red. The guys on the team are either dead, or they're not. We'll go get them as soon as we kick some zombie ass."

The turbine engines whined and we started to lift, spinning around and racing south, following the river. I climbed up front and yelled into the crew chief's ear, asking what the hell was going on.

"I don't know much!" he yelled back. CH-47s are incredibly loud. "Someone from U.S.AMRIID sprayed something by airplane all over the city, supposed to kill the zombies. They went batshit crazy instead, crashed right into the T-barriers along the Cross Bronx and overwhelmed the pickets. That was two days ago and there are like a couple million moving up Route 9 and all the other routes out of the city."

"So where are we going?"

"Drop off your casualty at the FOB, hot refuel, then we're supposed to leave you off somewhere in Putnam County so you can interdict the horde and call artillery fire. Then we turn around and go get more militia." When they did a hot refuel, the rotors would still be turning. That's how short on time we were.

"You're dropping us off BEHIND the battlelines?" Infuckingcredible.

"Don't worry, we'll find you a nice high place to fight from."

"I need twenty minutes at the FOB to get more ammo."

"We can give you fifteen and that's it. That's how long it will take us to gas up."

I nodded to him and went to sit next to Brit.

"What's the deal?" she yelled into my ear.

"We're screwed, Brit and not in a good way."

Chapter 128

We flew south down the Hudson River, jammed packed with soldiers. Troops sleeping in the glow of the red lights, trying to get some rest before the eternal sleep. I had done this a hundred times but I couldn't help thinking of the last one down to New York City. Killeen was dead and what was the name of the guy who broke his leg? Dresden, something like that. Different faces but the same faces. So many gone.

We had picked up Specialist Esposito at Fort Orange, to round out the team. He was the only Regular Army soldier on the ride. After I had lost my leg in Denver, he had gone on a few missions with the team but then had met a girl at the FEMA camp and had quit. Meeting us at the LZ and throwning his gear on board without saying a word. He saw me looking at him and held up his hand to show off a wedding ring.

"Dumbass!" I shouted to him over the road of the turbines. He smiled, flipped me the bird and went back to reading a paperback copy of A Soldier of The Great War that I had lent to him last year.

We were being dropped on a hilltop just south of Interstate 84. I plotted the position on a 1:50,000 map I had grabbed at the FOB, marking Target Registration Points. If I could work it out, the Z horde would be channeled into a fire sack by the terrain, steep valley walls rising up from a flat plain. The first waves had broken through and Bradleys and Abrams were chewing through them. A second wave, far larger, coming up from the Bronx, was working its way up Route 9. Timing would be the key. If we could get into position before the horde left the valley and got a chance to disperse outside the Hudson Highlands, then we could use Firecracker rounds to devastate them.

It had been tried at the start of the apocalypse, artillery barrages on top of hordes, fired by the lone National Guard artillery battalion stationed in New York City. The shrapnel had ripped holes in their bodies but usually failed to score a hit on Z's brains and the howitzers quickly ran out of ammunition. Things were different now. There were four times as many guns, seventy-two 155mm Howitzers and a battalion of Multiple Launch Rocket Systems. Each gun had a thousand Firecracker rounds, each containing a thousand steel ball bearings, pre-stocked and a U.S. Navy cargo ship had been docked in Poughkeepsie, preparing for the clearing of New York City, with thousands of tons of munitions. On top of that, the Ready Brigade from the 82nd Airborne was being dropped to reinforce the lines of Task Force Empire.

We dropped off the infantry company in Poughkeepsie and then lifted again, a short flight. The crew chief came around and gave me a five-minute warning and we shook ourselves awake, checking on our gear and chambering rounds in our weapons. At the FOB, a pallet of ammunition, MREs, empty sandbags and water had been rolled on board and we would move that out as soon as we had secured the Landing Zone. The rear ramp dropped down and we flared in for a landing. Prior to our being dropped off on the hilltop, an artillery battery had dropped White Phosphorus onto it, burning off the trees and undergrowth. As we pulled in, the rotor wash sucked up the ashes and created a blinding swirl of dust and cinders. I stepped off the ramp and fell into space. The crew chief had misjudged the pitch of the hill and the tail ramp was a good two feet off the ground.

I fell flat on my face, my pack with the radio in it rode up and hit me in the back of the head and I blacked out. When I came too, I was being half carried, half dragged across the LZ. The taste of ashes was in my mouth and stars danced crazily in my vision. They dumped me on the ground and someone shone a flashlight in my face.

"No concussion. Pupils are OK. Wakey-wakey, Nick," said Brit and she slapped me across the face, then kissed me. Then she spat. "Ugh, you taste like shit."

Sitting up, I rubbed my face where my Night Vision Goggles had smashed me. I was bleeding slightly but I flipped them back down and turned them on again. The darkness was replaced by the usual grainy green picture. I wished again for one of the monoculars I had worn in Afghanistan but the newer stuff was reserved for the Regular Army troopers.

I started to get to my feet but Brit pushed me back down. I watched the team fan outward as the helo faded into the sky. They walked the entire hilltop, scanning for any zombies that might have been missed by the fires. Shouts of "CLEAR" rang out over the hill and the team immediately got to work.

As we had discussed while waiting for the pickup in Stillwater, the very first thing to be done was to dig two-man fighting positions in a tight circle, with overhead cover. We were on a spur off the hilltop, almost a crag, with a high mountain behind us and an open, steep slope leading down to the highway, several hundred meters away. Hopefully we wouldn't need the covered fighting positions but if the Zs got too close, I would be calling artillery fire directly on top of us. Like they said, though, hope is not a plan. Whoever THEY were.

An hour passed, then two. My hands were getting raw from the shovel and I was tired. My shoulders ached and my head was hurting. Filling sandbags was a monotonous, mind-numbing task and I was grateful when my turn came up on watch. I watched the road in the light of the predawn and saw figures shambling through the fog, ghostly figures. I motioned for Jim to come up.

"You have two suppressed rifles, right?" He nodded.

"Well, time to start a little interdiction."

He spit a long stream of tobacco juice out of his mouth. 'Well, I dunno. We've got, how many, a couple tens of thousands of zombies coming up this way, right? I don't think wasting a couple here with rifle shots is going to make much of a difference."

I thought about it and then agreed with him. "Finish the fighting positions and then try to get some sleep. In about two hours I'm going to register the arty. Brit and I will stay on watch."

"Can do, Chief."

He went back and in a few minutes Brit came to sit beside me.

"You know, Nick, this could go really, really bad, really, really quick."

"Yeah, I know."

"I've got some ropes rigged on the back face, we can climb up and evade if we have to."

"Brit, if they notice us, this entire hill is going to be overrun."

"Well, if that happens, don't let them get me."

"You didn't have to come, you know," I said to her and took her hand.

"As if I would let you screw this up all by yourself, Captain Dumbass."

We both sat and watched the sun rise over the hills in the east. Below us, hidden in a mist in the valley, the zombie moan carried faintly up to us.

Chapter 129

Four days. Sunrise on the fourth day. I was so tired that everything seemed to exist in slow motion and my eyes were raw from the caustic smoke caused by high explosive. Our sleep plan had gone to hell because the stream of zombies coming up the valley was nonstop. We had already beaten back six waves of undead that had made it past the artillery and were running low on ammo. I had slept only a few hours over those past four days and I felt shaky. When I held the binos to my face to adjust another volley, I had a hard time keeping them steady. I finally got them to focus onto a group of zombies climbing over stinking mounds of body parts and shattered corpses

"Alys, come over here and take the radio." The kid was a homesteader from up river and the only one of us who had never done a tour overseas, besides Brit. He had done his three years of active duty after the war had run down and didn't want to go back again. Just farm the land. Pretty steady in a fight so far, though. He got up from the parapet we had thrown up thirty meters down the hill. I handed the pack over to him and sat back down on the stump of a burned-out tree, took a canteen from Brit and swished some around in my mouth then spit it out. Next some toothpaste and a brush and I tried to scrub the foul taste out of my mouth. Ashes, dirt, the stink of rotting zombie flesh. I was so tired my body felt numb and hurting all over at the same time, too exhausted to even stand. I had to rest a while. A cold MRE for breakfast, tuna with noodles. Ugh, this one hadn't been on the menu for ten years. They must be getting seriously low on pre-war supply stocks to be dragging out this old stuff. I poured a whole bottle of Tabasco on it, trying to wake myself up and put some taste into it. I actually dozed off with the spoon in my hand and a mouthful of noodles and woke with a start as a stray pellet from one of the artillery rounds zinged off the dirt next to me but then kept on chewing.

A few feet away rose three mounds of dirt. We had taken casualties the night before when a zombie came down on us from behind, over the mountain. Our rear guard had fallen asleep and it was inside the fighting position before either of them could react. One man had died instantly, the zombie tearing his head off. The other was bitten on the neck and had turned in a few seconds, coming raging at us in the dark with the other Z. Donny had seen them first and lit out at them with a yell, swinging his heavy sledgehammer handle. Another one of Jim's crew had stumbled as he came at them and both the Zs went after him in a pile. Donny smashed all three, fast and hard. Good for them they had died, because I would have shot one of them for falling asleep on guard. I had done it before.

We had buried our three and tossed the body of the first Z over the side of the cliff. Now I sat and looked at the graves, staring at them and trying to make my mind work. Brit sat next to me, put her head on my shoulder and fell instantly asleep. I eased her to the ground and let her sleep, then got up to look at the perimeter. In front of me, about thirty meters down the hill, the squad kept up a steady firing, knocking down Zs that were trying to climb the slope towards us. The closest corpse was lying across the rough rock wall we had built. Resupply came in yesterday, dropping water and ammo and taking off one of the guys who had been throwing up and running a fever and another who had dropped a rock while building the wall, smashing the small bones in his foot. Probably on purpose.

As I approached, Alys stood and fired a 40mm smoke grenade towards the road. It landed halfway between us and the mile-long smear of dead bodies and parts lining Route 9. Another wave of zombies, several thousand, had backed up against the ruins of the shopping center and was scrambling to get over the rubble. Alys was talking an Air Force F-15E Strike Eagle onto the target, using the smoke as a marker.

"Roger, target is two hundred meters two seven zero degrees from smoke."

The pilot's voice came back over the radio. *"I copy, two hundred meters, two seven zero degrees. Stand by."* As I watched, the gray twin engine fighter jet flew over the valley from the north at about a thousand feet, getting eyes on the target. He banked around, disappearing over the hills, then started his run. They had been dropping five hundred pound Joint Direct Attack Munitions for us to cover while the artillery resupplied.

Staring at the plane coming in, something itched at the back of my mind. I was so tired that a cloud seemed to hang over my mind and I couldn't think straight. What was wrong? I looked down at Alys as he talked the pilot in.

Two hundred seventy degrees. I looked down at the smoke burning in the valley and held up my hand to block the rising sun. Rising in the east, over the hills.

East. Ninety degrees from our position. The zombies were east of the smoke grenade. Ninety degrees. From the smoke. I tried to figure it out and the truth burst on me like a flare.

"WAVE HIM OFF, WAVE HIM OFF!!" I screamed it at Alys and he turned toward me, a puzzled look on his face.

"What?" he yelled over the firing. We were all half-deaf from four days of constant gunfire and explosions. I could see the guys on the firing line, twenty meters away down slope, looking away from me. Only Esposito seemed to have heard. He looked at the plane and then he started to dive behind the wall.

"EVERYBODY DOWN!" I yelled as loudly as I could and threw myself backwards over a tree.

******

My ears were ringing from the blast and I felt blood pouring out of my nose. I sat up and then fell back down when everything swam in circles in front of me. I took a minute to catch my breath and let things steady, then slowly raised myself up again, pulling on the tree trunk to help myself back to a sitting position. I looked down at the firing line.

The bodies of four, no, five people were visible, not moving. Alys crawled towards me, away from a smoking crater, the radio on his back a ruin. The wall we had built from logs was smashed flat where it wasn't upended. I saw another soldier, I think it was Esposito, though it was hard to tell, trying to stuff his guts back into his stomach. They lay scattered around him and both his legs were gone. I couldn't hear him but I could see his mouth opening in a scream. I drew my pistol, held it balanced on the tree trunk and shot him. Twice, in the head, from behind. He fell limp.

Next to me I could feel the concussion from gunshots. THUMP THUMP THUMP. I still couldn't hear anything. I raised my rifle and pointed it drunkenly downhill, trying to focus on a target. Any target. I knew the zombies were still down there and they would be attracted to the explosion.

A hand grabbed me by the carry strap on the back of my armor and started pulling me up the hill, dragging my legs in the dirt. I still felt too wobbly to stand up and I passed out again.

When I woke, Brit was again shining a flashlight in my eyes.

"Damn, Nick, you gotta stop beating up your head. Twice in four days. I think you have a concussion this time. Not that there is anything to hurt up there. Good thing you had your vest on." She held up a jagged piece of shrapnel which had apparently torn its way through several layers of kevlar before glancing off the ceramic plate on my back. Her voice, which I could barely hear, sounded tinny and robotic and she was shouting.

"What, what about the squad?" She shook her head.

"Seven dead, one wounded. We have four effectives, not counting you."

"Zombies. Coming." I wanted to vomit. Not a good sign.

"Final Protective Fire, the arty is beating the shit out of them and making a wall of steel in front of us. Evac will be here in fifteen mikes. We're being relieved by a platoon from the 82nd. Maybe I can get a phone number from one of those cheesedicks, what do you think?"

She smiled at me but I could tell she was worried. The smile didn't reach her eyes and she kept waving away pieces of her red hair that slipped out of her helmet.

"Esposito. I shot him."

"Good thing, too. The Zs made it to the wall, he would have been torn up by them. He was dead anyway, Nick."

"Help me up."

She did and I looked downhill. I could barely hear the artillery but I felt it through the earth, a continuous vibration. As I watched, rounds continued to burst like clockwork, one every thirty seconds, walking their way back and forth across the foot of the hill. Jim Lock sat with our spare radio, calling corrections for the arty hitting the valley floor. He gave me a thumbs-up and turned back to the radio. Behind him, seven bodies were laid out in a row, covered by poncho liners. I stared at them, wishing them to move but they never would.

Dear Mrs. Esposito,

I know you and your husband John were only married for a few days and I'm sorry that the time you had with him was so short. I was against him going on this mission but he was a good soldier and he knew the risks involved. I don't think I could have stopped him if I tried.

I was his leader on this and many other dangerous operations and his death is my responsibility. I don't know if I could have done anything differently but I wish that he were alive and home with you. He was my soldier, my friend and my brother. He saved my life in Denver and if I could trade mine for his, I would have. Your husband fought for four days straight, through numerous attacks and died on the firing line. His death was quick and merciful, if there can be such a thing. He was never turned into an Undead.

I know these words are small comfort but he will be missed by all of his teammates. If you ever need anything, please do not hesitate to ask.

Sincerely,

Sergeant First Class Nicholas F. Agostine
JSOC (Z) – Irregular Scout Team One

Chapter 130

They say the only thing that drops from the sky is birdshit and assholes but I could have kissed the assholes that were falling from it now. Well, almost. OK, I wouldn't have kissed them but I WAS happy to see them.

The artillery fire had stopped for a few minutes, clearing the airspace, and a C-130 roared overhead, the familiar red tail markings of the guys from Scotia. Two sticks of paratroopers exited out of the side doors, ten in each, jumping low to stay concentrated on the drop zone, an open field off to the north of our hill. One figure fell quickly, his static line failing to open his main chute. The falling soldier tried to get his reserve chute open but hit the ground in a sickening, bone-crunching cloud of dust.

"Damn," said Brit. "They better start making new equipment, 'cause those chutes are wearing out. Lotta other stuff, too."

The Airborne formed a square, raised shields and advanced up the hill, smashing down the several zombies who stood in their path, saving ammo. As they made their way into our position, their platoon sergeant ambled over to me and sat down with an exhausted sigh.

"Hey Nick. Don't get up."

"I won't, Cody. Saw your guy eat dirt. He a loss?" The grizzled NCO looked like he hadn't shaved in a week and his uniform was crusted with dried blood and brains.

"Yeah. Happens almost every dozen drops now. Too many jumps, worn out chutes. Tired guys, inexperienced kids packing their own chutes. That was our Lieutenant. No big loss." He spat a stream of tobacco juice on the dirt and leered at Brit.

She threw out her hip and stood at parade pretty. "Not if you were the last pervert on earth, Cody."

"I'm pretty sure YOU'LL be the last pervert on earth, Brit." She blew him a kiss.

I could barely hear what they were saying but their

gestures amused me. I rolled my eyes and ordered, "Get a room, you two. Before you do, tell me what's going on."

He sat down on an ammo crate and started picking at his nails with a bayonet, trying to get the blood out from under his fingernails, watching his squad leaders directing the troopers, who were shoring up the defenses.

"Well. As you can see," and he gestured to the grime on his WWII style paratrooper jumpsuit, "we have been a little bit busy. That there twenty—"

"Nineteen," interjected Brit.

He glared at her. "Nineteen. Shut it, Pucker Lips. Like I said, NINETEEN fine airborne troopers are the remains of the company that parachuted onto the Interstate -84/Taconic State Parkway interchange a week ago when this shit sandwich started. Three hours ago we were relieved by a company of M1A5 tanks who went charging right up the Taconic, grinding their way over the mass of bodies we had piled up, including our own dead." A thoughtful looked passed over his face, then he started laughing.

"What's so funny?"

"Well, you know the Taconic Parkway right there, right? Where it heads into the hills, going south to the city? Real narrow, two lanes on each side, steep drop offs?"

I nodded. "Yeah, been that way many times."

"So this cavalry captain goes charging past riding out the hatch, yelling GET OUT OF THE WAY CRUNCHIES, firing that 120mm shotgun round, BOOM BOOM BOOM and letting his fifty cal rip, screaming GARRY OWEN AND GLORY and, get this, his driver can't see the edge of the road bed and throws a track and the whole thing spins around and rolls off down the embankment, must have fell about thirty feet. Last I saw of him they were using an M-88 to try and lift one side of the tank enough to let the crew climb out of the loader's hatch. I could hear him yelling at them from inside to hurry the hell up. The rest of his company just kept charging down the road."

We all laughed. Every branch of the services had its

heroes and idiots. It seemed like the new crop of jackasses were alive and growing well. I had thought the Zombie Apocalypse would have put an end to that but I guess human nature had prevailed.

He put the stock of his M-14 on the ground and used it to lever himself off the ammo crate. "Your evac is coming in. Pulling your wounded out, only. They're bringing wounded off an Observation Post over by Bear Mountain Bridge. We need the rest of your effectives. Brit, you go too."

"No shit, Sherlock. As if I would want to be stuck on this hill with you uneducated philistines."

"How you put up with her, Nick, I dunno."

"I hit the jackpot with this one, Cody. Maybe someday I'll have Doctor Morano clone her and send you one. Brit 2.0. Maybe some bigger boobs."

He made a two fingered, "avert evil" sign at me and shuddered. "No thanks, keep that demon away from me. You know this was her fault, right?"

"What do you mean? Morano?"

"Yeah, her crew sprayed some kind of chemical all over the City. It was supposed to sedate the Zombies, make it easier for us to sweep in and take them out. My unit was waiting at Stewart to drop into Central Park. Instead, well…" and he made a sweeping gesture to the valley floor. Another horde was moving up the valley, thousands of rotted voices howling blood red rage.

His second in command, a female Staff Sergeant, came hustling over.

"Sarge, ammo is redistributed, everyone has water and we're ready to go."

I looked at her closely. She couldn't have stood more than five foot three in her jump boots.

"Aren't you a little short to be a paratrooper, Staff Sergeant Sparks?"

She shot me a dirty look, fingering the bayonet she wore strapped to her soldier. "Get bent, you fat old man."

Cody laughed. He knew Sparky and I had been jousting

like this since way before the war. "Gotta go, got some Z-killing to do." Then he turned, cupped his hands around his mouth and yelled at his men.

"HEY YOU APES, YOU WANNA LIVE FOREVER? GET DOWN THERE AND KILL SOME ZOMBIES! AIRBORNE, ADVANCE!"

They slung their M-4s over their backs, pulled out pistols with high capacity magazines, locked shields and advanced downhill to meet the horde, chanting "MER-IK-A! MER-IK-A!" as they advanced in lockstep. Cody winked at me, slapped Brit's ass, ducked under her return punch and ran downhill to join his men.

******

The ride back to Combat Outpost Thor took about twenty minutes and the thudding of the rotor blades didn't do my head any good. I closed my eyes and tried to sleep but every time I nodded off, Brit reached over and pinched the inside of my leg, hard.

"Not 'til you get checked out by the doctors, no sleepy time for you!" she yelled in my ear. Then she would go back to swinging her legs out the open door of the helo. After the fifth time she pinched me I gave up and watched the landscape pass beneath me.

The highways, both lanes, were jam packed solid with car wreckage heading north, out of the city. Two years of weather had flattened tires and started weeds growing through cracks in the pavement. Sooner rather than later, the road itself would be unusable to anything except four-wheel drive. Down the center lane the engineers had cleared a path, using a crane welded onto a wrecker to make way for supply trucks. Lone figures wandered on the side of the roadway, random zombies who couldn't leave the place where they had died. The supply convoys made sport of shooting at them as they drove past.

Occasional columns of smoke rose from deserted

villages, showing where salvage teams were burning off contaminated oil supplies to prevent them from leaching into the groundwater. The teams went through and stripped every piece of electronics, precious metals and manufactured items that were still usable. Then they burned everything that might cause havoc in the environment.

The helo flared onto the pad at COP Thor and we stumbled out while they hot-refueled, rotors still turning. We headed over to the Combat Support Hospital, following the stretchers carrying the other wounded. Despite Brits' protests, I was checked out as OK for limited duty and released.

"Where to now, Oh Fearless Leader?"

"Showers, then hot food, then the S-2 for some intel on the northern end of Lake Champlain." Nothing beats a hot shower after being in the field, let me tell you. About halfway through, Brit pulled me into the shower trailer, locked the door, and none of your damned business.

On the way down last week, I had shot a quick request to the Task Force Empire intelligence officer. I needed all the information that he had in Northern Vermont/New York and Lake Champlain. He delivered it to me in a slim folder, with the added comment of "not much."

INTSUM
NORTHERN LAKE CHAMPLAIN AREA OF OPERATIONS

Signals Intelligence has indicated surviving human populations in the area of Grand Isle, showing a level of organization of 5M on the survivor index, meaning some official government agency remaining, suspected military. No response to repeated radio query.

Two authorized over flights of local area and limited satellite reconnaissance have indicated substantive fortification of Isle La Motte and Grand Isle. Most bridges in the area have been destroyed. Heat sources indicate active

motor vehicle traffic and a population of 400 and 1000,
respective. Powered Maritime traffic has been observed in
the form of small boats in satellite reconnaissance.

JSOC (Z) – IST ONE was dispatched on XXXXXXXX to
attempt contact and assessment of survivors. Contact was
lost with the team on D + 5. No further attempt has been
made to contact due to insufficient personnel and assets.

I handed it to Brit and she read it quickly, then handed it
back.

"So, not much to go on. It does tally with what Red told
us."

"Yeah and I'm going to have to call in some favors to
get support for us going up there. We need a helo to get us
close and I'll be damned if we're going to operate so far out
in the wild without some kind of fire support."

I gave the report back to the S-2 and asked him to
forward anything else he came up with. Then we went to get
some sleep. I fell deep, despite the cannons firing a hundred
meters away.

Chapter 131

"BATTLE STATIONS!"

Brit yelled it full in my ear, the alert word we used for "get your armor on, grab your weapon and MOVE!" I rolled off my cot, slid my boots on, grabbed my armor in one hand and my rifle in the other and ran out of the tent as fast as I could.

I stopped, now at least half awake, in the middle of the dusty street, holding onto my rifle and armor, one boot falling off, wearing a t-shirt and boxers, blinking in the bright sun, looking for a threat. Support soldiers walked past, giving me strange looks.

Turning around, I saw Brit standing in the doorway of the tent, one hand clapped over her mouth, trying not to laugh out loud. She gave up and fell to the ground, holding her stomach and laughing so hard that her eye was watering.

"Very fucking funny, hardy har har. Payback is a bitch and so are you." I stepped over her and back into the darkness of the tent to get fully dressed.

"I think I peed myself."

"Serves you right."

Later that day we droned northward on a C-130. The canvas seats along the sides were, as usual, uncomfortable and I was happy it was a short ride. The cargo bay was filled with stretchers but there weren't a lot of wounded, all told, from the operation. When you were fighting zombies, you either avoided getting wounded or you were dead. Several of the guys on the plane had gunshot wounds but most were burned. In a battle, especially one against a raving horde of Zs that have breached your line, friendly fire isn't always, like the old saying goes. It happens more than people want to admit and the Army had been pretty liberal with using napalm this time. When the Apocalypse happened, weapons that tended to cause a lot of destruction, like napalm or cluster bombs, weren't used for fear of "damaging civilian infrastructure." That all changed, of course but by then it was too late. I remember that Boston took a nuke, right around Day 10 of the plague. Too much, too late. Not that I minded Fenway and the Red Sox getting nuked.

The first thing I had to do was tell Mrs. Esposito she was a widow. She handled it better than I thought she would. I had done casualty assistance during the Iraq War and I hated it. As a Senior NCO, it wasn't up to us to tell the families. That was a job for an officer. I worked with them, helped them deal with the Army paperwork, the funeral arrangements, the shock that finally hit when reality settled in. In some ways it was worse. The families were always so damn nice to me and I was wearing the uniform of an organization which had, for better or worse, sent someone they loved to get killed. Mrs. Esposito was different, though. I handed her the letter I had written but she just shook her head, squared her shoulders and turned away from me. I guess we had all seen too much death in the last two years for it to shock anyone anymore.

Next we went to the hospital to pick up Red. He didn't say much, just climbed into the HUMVEE Brit had borrowed and rode back to the JSOC liaison office with us.

The officer on duty, a Special Forces Captain who I knew from way back, rolled his eyes when he saw me come in and muttered, "oh, shit," under his breath.

"I'm going to cut to the chase, Captain Mueller. My team is missing and we're going to go find them. I need transportation and supplies for the three of us."

"Nick, you know that the ISTs are expendable."

"Maybe to you but not to me. Besides, you owe Doc your life." He didn't like being reminded of that. Along the side of his neck was a jagged scar where a knife in the hand of a refugee had ripped through the skin, nicking his jugular at the evacuation of Manhattan. Doc had sewn it up before it completely ruptured.

"I can get you supplies, ammo but there are no birds heading north. We can't afford to spare any aircraft until the fighting is done in the City."

"That could take weeks." He shrugged his shoulders and I knew that we weren't going to get anywhere else with him.

"Brit, you and Red go draw enough supplies for two weeks in the field. Make sure you pick up a laser designator, too. I have to go see someone."

That someone was our old friend, Major McHale. I had seen a MedEvac UH-60 sitting on the runway when we came in, being worked on at the old National Guard Aviation Facility. I was hoping he would be there, making sure it got back into the fight as soon as possible. He liked to fly the broken ones, bringing them back up to get fixed. I guess he figured that the best pilot could handle the worst aircraft. I found him hunkered down inside the engine compartment, alongside a crusty old warrant who looked like he had been fixing helos since Korea.

"Well, this bird will be back up by tonight. I was planning on taking it straight back but I suppose I could get disoriented and fly north instead of south. No one will notice anyway. It's not like there is a war going on here at Fort Orange or anything."

"Great, we'll meet you here around 2300."

Chapter 132

The helo set us down in a clearing two miles south of where the team had been ambushed, just as dawn was breaking. In addition to Brit, Red and myself, we had three good guys from IST-7, the Dark Knights. They had been refitting after a scout into Northeastern Pennsylvania, heading down the I-88 corridor to see if there were any coal mines still in working condition and had lost half their team just outside Scranton to a bridge collapse under their HUMVEE, sending three of them down into a river.

Their team leader, Captain Buswarry, was a good friend but I wasn't going to miss his NCO, Master Sergeant Collins. I was actually glad it had been him that took a seventy-foot drop into the Susquehanna. He had always been a dick and we had gotten into a fist fight in a bar in Bermuda when he wouldn't leave Brit alone. Too bad about the other guys, though. Buswarry was an immigrant from Nigeria who had made good in the U.S., going Special Forces. He was on one of the last flights out of Ghana, where his SF team had been training locals in a nasty fight against Islamist extremists, had joined the Irregular Scouts when we were recruiting up in Maine at the Navy base. His two contractors were both civilians I didn't know but he assured me they were good in a fight. A redheaded guy named McCross and a woman I first took to be a man. She was built like a brick shithouse.

When we had met them at the OPS center, Brit had kneeled in front of her and called her "Lady Brienne." The woman, whose real name was Hart, looked at her like she was an idiot.

"Ignore her. She thinks you're some character from Game of Thrones."

The look she gave Brit wasn't exactly friendly. I'm sure she was a bit touchy about her size. "Get up, you little twit, before I squeeze your head so hard it pops."

"Nick, I think I love her. Can I keep her?"

She called her Lady Brienne until later that day, as we

were loading magazines. Hart put a friendly arm around Brit's neck, then proceeded to put her in a choke hold that Brit almost passed out from. Brit gasped out "Uncle!" and the woman let her drop to the floor like a sack of potatoes. Red was laughing his ass off. When she had recovered her breath, Brit started to complain to me but I told her that if she couldn't take it, she shouldn't dish it out. "Maybe you should apologize to her, too."

Since then, she had ignored the big blonde woman, though I did notice that Red spent an inordinate amount of time talking to her. Good for him. McCross was a quiet guy who did his job without saying much.

Now he was walking point, along with Red, who was trying to recognize landmarks. Soon enough, we came to the site of the ambush. A canoe was still sitting on the shore, half swamped, and spent cartridge brass gleamed in the morning sun. While the team pulled security, Brit and I scoured the site, looking for something in particular. I quickly found the bones of Sergeant Toshi, mauled and scattered by wild animals, but that wasn't what I was looking for.

We found it after ten minutes, tied to a tree. A strip of brown uniform T-shirt, unnoticeable unless you knew to look for it. On the end was one knot.

"Red, you saw Ziv and Doc after the ambush, right?"

He thought hard about it. "Yeah, both were in the boats but I thought maybe Ahmed was down or unconscious."

"Nope." I showed him the strip of T-shirt and called Captain Buswarry over.

"Hey Glen, one of my guys is alive, or was after the ambush. You remember Ahmed?"

"Yeah, that sneaky Pashtun on your team. Hell of a shot."

"This is a message from him. He knew we would come after them."

"So how do we find him?"

"We don't. He finds us."

He did, just as the sun set. We had pulled back outside

the clearing and set up a perimeter on a small knoll, the same one from where Red had watched the campsite.

I was watching the site, wishing for full dark so I could turn my NVGs on. I heard a slight rustle off to my left and I turned to look in that direction. I found myself staring down the barrel of Ahmed's Dragonov. He had slipped past our rear security and gotten within five feet of me before I heard anything and then probably because he wanted me to. Then we both heard the quiet "snick" of a weapon being taken off safe. Ahmed whispered to the figure that stood over him.

"Godless American whore, at least let me pray to Allah before you kill me."

"OH MY GOD AHMED!" she whispered back loudly and body tackled him. At least she had the presence of mind to put the safety back on before she did it.

"GET OFF ME, WOMAN! COVER YOURSELF!"

When Brit helped him up to a kneeling position, Captain Buswarry had come over, leaving Red and his two others to pull security. A quick, quiet conversation followed.

"Nick," said Ahmed, through a mouthful of MRE, "there is a squad sized element advancing down the trail from the north. I am assuming they heard the sound of your helicopter and are hoping to ambush you as they did to our team last month. I have been following them since this morning and I moved ahead of them to warn you. We have about twenty minutes before they get here."

I quickly thought about it. Our forces would be about equal size but they knew the terrain and could move faster. We had the advantage of surprise, though, because we knew about them and they only suspected us.

"How good are they?"

"Nick, they are infantry. American infantry. Mountain soldiers, from the Vermont National Guard. Many combat veterans and survivors of the Zombie Apocalypse. They are good. I did not see any night vision equipment, though, and their weapons are a mix. One squad automatic weapon but I think they are short on ammunition. The gunner only had M-

4 magazines on him, no 200 round boxes and there was a 30 round magazine inserted."

I didn't ask him how he knew who they were, just assumed that one of their soldiers had disappeared in the prior month while Ahmed was living in the forest. We trumped them on firepower, too, since we had armed ourselves heavily based on the initial ambush. McCross carried an M-240B machine gun and we had two 40mm grenade launchers.

"Shit. I don't want to kill our own. Until we get this sorted out, though, I guess we're going to have to do what we have to do. If they ask for surrender, though, we give it. I want prisoners. Besides, I have a plan. Here's what we're going to do."

*****

I sat in the darkness, watching their lead scout approach through my NVGs. This was going to be tricky, a pretty slick piece of timing.

In the center of the clearing sat a military issue flashlight, turned on. It was shining on an American flag Brit had stuffed in her pack, suspended from a stick in the ground. I knew Ziv and Doc had talked, they had no reason not to. So the Vermonters, for want of a better name, had to know the U.S. Army was back in town. I'm sure whoever was running the show was thinking long and hard about what to do now. They had ignored repeated radio calls for survivors but real live soldiers were a different story.

As I watched the point man stop outside the circle of light, he held up a hand and his squad fanned out in a line behind him. A figure rose up from the ground beside him where Ahmed had lain in wait and a brief struggle ensued, followed by Ahmed getting up and moving away. The scout lay on the ground for a minute and crawled back towards his squad.

Captain Buswarry watched with me. "So, now we wait."

"Yep, the hardest part." We sat for about fifteen minutes, then I took off the NVGs, slung my rifle behind my back and walked forward into the light. I was freaking out. In the next few seconds, my life could be over. If they rejected our terms, I would get shot.

"I just want to talk," I yelled into the darkness. "Send out your senior man!" I held my hands palms up, in a gesture of peace.

Stepping into the circle of light, a man clad in old style BDUs slowly walked forward, dropping down his M-4 as he approached.

"Son of a bitch. Nick Agostine."

"Danny Westbrook. I'll be damned."

I held out my hand and he pulled me into a bear hug. "Damn," I said. "I haven't seen you since you got blown out of your HUMVEE in Mosul!" He stepped back and held up his left hand, showing me that it was missing three fingers.

"Cool!" I said. "Check this out, zombie bite!" and I rolled up my pants leg to show him the carbon fiber leg.

We both turned and waved our teams in and they eyed each other warily in the dim light, pointedly not aiming at each other. I wondered which one of them had killed Svenson and Toshi but I had to put that aside if we were to have a chance in hell of pulling this off.

Danny pulled up a log to sit on while we talked and he gave us the down low on what was happening on this end of the lake. "Well, first off, let me tell you, I wasn't in charge of the patrol that ambushed your guys. Not that I would have done anything differently, I just don't want you to hold that against me." I nodded. "Your two guys are in the lockup on Grand Isle. That's all I'm going to say until you understand the situation there."

"Go ahead. We all have a story to tell."

"It's like this. You guys are the first ones we've seen in what, two years from the federal government?"

"So far as I know, but there is satellite news and the Internet is still up in some places. You HAD to know there was still a functioning government in Seattle."

"Yeah, well, Seattle is a long way from here and us Green Mountain Boys have always been an independent lot. The Regular Army cut and ran once things fell apart in New York and we had to deal with a horde that came down from Quebec and Montreal. The Vermont Guard, well, we blew the bridges to Grand Isle and hunkered down."

I told him how we had done something similar in New York, with the creation of the giant base at Seneca Army Depot in the Finger Lakes. It only made sense.

"Well, that first winter was an ever-loving bitch. We had maybe ten thousand refugees crammed onto that island. The Adjutant General, Major General Allen, declared martial law on the Island. That went over like yelling fire in a theater. We killed a LOT of civilians, Nick. Ain't something I'm proud of. We ran out of food around March the following year."

"So, then what happened? Did you…" I left the question about cannibalism unspoken.

"No, none of us military guys did. The General made sure the military got fed first. The civilians, well we told them they could like it or leave. Most of them left. We're down to about eight hundred civilians and about two hundred military all told."

"Why are you telling me all this? Giving me all your numbers?"

"Because I don't like the way things are run there. The General, well, a decent guy at the start but all this power stuff has gone to his head. You know me, I don't have much patience for being bossed around. Never did. That's why I was still an E-6 when I got blown out of the service. That and he's got some real nasty types backing him up."

I thought about it for a minute. "Still, I don't see what business it is of ours. I have to tell you, Danny, we just came back this way to get our people. The U.S. Cavalry isn't going to come galloping in here to save anyone anytime soon. We have enough problems with NYC."

"I know that, Nick. Listen, you and I both know the

zombie threat is way down and the time for martial law is done. Last month, though, some civilians got together a delegation, asking General Allen to step down and hand political control of things back to civilians and concentrate on military matters."

"Sounds like a plan."

"Yeah, well, the thing is, I guess the General and some of the people around him disagree. He hung four of them for sedition, as he called it."

"So?"

"What do you mean, so?"

"I mean, what does this have to do with us?"

"Listen, Nick. We swore an oath. You did. I did. Against all enemies, foreign and domestic."

"Seems like I've been keeping my oath. What about you?"

"Well, his hanging of the civilians was the last straw for me. Yes, we killed civies when they tried to storm the food warehouse. Times were tough. It was either that or everyone went under. Now, though? Some of the guys have been talking to your two we captured and now they KNOW that things have to change."

I glanced around at the half dozen Guardsmen who were on the other side of the light. "What about them?"

"Do you really think I would be stupid enough to go out on a patrol with people that weren't loyal to me?"

Chapter 133

We had left Danny and his guys to make their way back to Grand Isle and returned to where we had ditched our zodiac boat. As I worked with Red to set up the outboard motor and Buswarry and Hart loaded our extra supplies, Brit talked with me.

"Do you trust him? Believe his BS story?"

"What makes you think it's BS?"

"Come on, Nick, I wasn't born yesterday and you get all teary-eyed around your old Army buddies. It's like this big blind spot you run into."

Locking down the engine, I hooked up the gas line feed and then turned to her. "Look, Brit, all I want to do is get Doc and Ziv back."

She laughed at me. "Bullshit, Nick. I know you. Deep down inside, there is this little guy running around in a Captain America outfit, screaming to get let out. You WANT to rescue those civilians. Power-hungry jerks are like your archnemesis. I could draw a freaking comic strip about you."

Red chimed in. "Yeah, Kemosabe, maybe you'll get your own action-adventure series someday."

"Stupid racist Indian."

"Native American. Get it right, Paleface."

Hart looked at all of us like we were crazy. "Do you all always act like this?"

Brit turned to her and yelled, "Look out, it's Jamie Lanister! The Kingslayer! Run, Lady Brienne!"

"I told you to knock that shit off, twerp."

"Yeah, Brit, lay off her." Red flushed but he stood up and squared off with Brit.

"Wait. Oh my God. Red, Lady Brienne, OH MY GOD I'MSOHAPPYFORYOU!" He took a swing at her and Brit ran away, laughing. "I'm going to give you a step stool as a wedding gift!"

"I'm going to kill her," said Hart but she was blushing, too.

Right then, everything went to shit. Like it always does. We had gotten so wrapped up in the details of dealing with the Vermonters that we had forgotten about what the real war was, fighting zombies. We were reminded in a harsh way.

It was a small horde, about thirty or so. Nothing we couldn't have handled on a good day, but today was not a good day. McCross was on guard but he was distracted by the conversation between Brit and Hart. The first zombie latched onto his leg as he stepped around a wrecked minivan, looking back towards us. It shouldn't have happened. McCross was an experienced scout, had been on dozens of missions and there was no reason for him to die but he did. So did Captain Buswarry, trying to come to his rescue, charging directly into the horde.

It was a madhouse and we wound up getting away by running full tilt in the opposite direction while the Z's scrabbled around McCross and Buswarry. They tore them apart, eating their intestines while they were alive, trying to rip open their heads to get at the brains. We didn't even have time to kill them ourselves. Red had to drag Hart away and she screamed as her friends died horribly.

"RALLY AT THE END OF THE BRIDGE!" I yelled as we crossed over a set of train tracks being held out of the water by a causeway, maybe five feet off the water. I reached the end and spun, firing into the horde as fast as I could aim, barely missing the others as they ran past me. Red, who had been carrying the 240B, flopped down beside me, extended the bipod legs, and yelled, "FEED ME!" Brit crashed down beside him and started passing linked ammo into the gun. It started barking in short, controlled sweeps, arching through head height about fifty meters away, blowing holes through the zombies, catching some in their heads, knocking others down by severing limbs.

Ahmed kneeled beside them, emptying the magazine of the Dragunov, one aimed round per second. Two out of three dropped zombies with headshots, a regular, steady rhythm. Once I had caught my breath and the red dot on my sight stopped jumping around, I started to add to the carnage. In the end, it came down to one last Z falling onto the water, shot through the head by Hart with her pistol. We were left with the smell of cordite and rotting flesh.

It was over in less than two minutes but it should have never happened in the first place. I stood over what remained of McCross and Buswarry, the latter crawling towards me with that red glare in his eyes, one arm dragging slowly in an effort to get at living flesh and eat. The sight of him made me want to scream and vomit at the same time. I reached over my shoulder, drew my mace, and smashed his head in.

We got back to the boat, secured the area and I sat down looking over the water. My hands were shaking and I held them between my legs to make them stop. Brit sat down next to me and watched me for a second.

"Brit, I don't know that I can do this anymore." I held up my hand to show her. She grabbed it and squeezed it hard and let go.

"Nick, you can quit. Anytime. I love Doc and, well, I sorta like Ziv but I am NOT going to lose you."

I knew what she meant. An American general in World War II supposed that a man only had so much courage to draw from. I wondered if I was reaching mine. Even before more than two years of zombie warfare I had pulled three combat tours overseas. I had killed my wife after she was bitten by a zombie and had eaten our daughter. My leg had been severed below the knee.

"Brit, I'm not going to let the guys down. We HAVE to go get them. I swear to you, though, that this is it. I'm done. I'm not leaving the farm again."

She nodded, looking off into the distance with her good eye. "Well, no, Nick. There is one more thing we are going to have to do."

"Kill Doctor Morano."

"Kill Doctor Morano." I looked over where Hart was crying while Red stood watch over her, one hand on her shoulder, watching the woods for more zombies. "But I'm not going to lose any more people. Swear to God."

"Nick, Baby, you can't control that. This is war. People die. Our friends, families, buddies. They die. I might die. You might. Meanwhile, we have got to LIVE. Snap out of it, Fearless Leader." She reached over and caressed my cheek gently, then slapped me hard on the inside of my leg. It stung like hell and I got her message.

"OK, let's saddle up!" We piled our rucksacks into the bottom of the zodiac, started the motor and headed out across the lake. Across the water, the Green Mountains of Vermont looked down on us; just another war party, like a thousand others they watched impassively in the last eleven thousand years.

Chapter 134

"So how do we do this?" asked Red.

"We go in, flag flying. We're the U.S. Army and I'm betting they won't shoot at us if we're representing the Federal Government."

Red shook his head. "I think your reasoning is wrong, Nick. I think if you go in there flag flying, some of these rednecks are going to shoot at you just because they think you're a jack-booted federal gubbermint thug who is gonna take their guns."

"Seriously? Why would I do that? Take their guns after surviving the Zombie Apocalypse?"

"There ain't no explaining crazy, Nick."

Brit was trailing her hand in the wake of the boat but she watched Hart, who was sitting up in the bow. I knew she was watching to see if she the new kid was going to break. Ahmed steered the boat, keeping the throttle low. We were in no rush to get there and there were some small waves we hopped over. I just sat back and enjoyed being out on the lake, a chance to let my guard down a bit.

Red was right. Any way we played it, we were outsiders who were going to upset whatever power balance existed on the island. In my experience dealing with survivors, they tended to resent us showing up. Anger that the federal government had failed them in the Zombie Apocalypse, or just a tendency to resent authority anyway. This was the first time, though, that we had dealt with such a large group and one that had somewhat legitimate authority.

We heard them long before we saw them. A long causeway extended from the mainland to the island, probably part of an old railway. I had been this way before, on a fishing trip and I knew there was a break in the causeway that you could run your boat through. Well, there used to be a break. Now there was a bridge and just before that, a large wall extending thirty feet up in the air, completely blocking the road.

Trailing off southward down the causeway were zombies. Thousands. Tens of thousands. Seemingly as one, they turned to the sound of our motor. All howling in symphony but staying away from the water. Ahmed cut the engine and we drifted slowly about a hundred feet off shore.

"Holy crap," said Ahmed. "That must be every single zombie in the Burlington area."

"Ya think? Frigging rocket scientist, this one," muttered Brit.

Hart scanned the barrier and the bridge behind it with a pair of binoculars. I saw her stop and then lean forward, trying to get a better look.

"Ahmed, can you bring us around the back side of the barrier?" she asked.

"Paddles, everyone. No need to get them any more worked up than they are already." We broke out the oars and started pulling around.

"Yep, I thought so." Hart handed me the binos.

"What am I looking for?"

"Look at the base of the barrier. There are charges set around the whole thing. Looks like construction demolitions, the kind used to take down derelict buildings."

"Are they set to blow the bridge?"

"Nope, if they go, they'll take down the barrier only."

Brit couldn't resist. "And how do you know all this, Lady Brianne?"

"Because, Little Miss Wiseass, while you were getting stoned and laid in college, I was defusing IEDs in Iraq and Afghanistan."

For once, Brit was speechless. I almost laughed at her. Hart, for her part, ignored Brit and went back to studying the barrier. She finally put the binos down. "I can't figure it. Blowing the charges would eliminate the barrier completely. I can see if they wired the bridge but the barrier …"

"It's a threat," said Ahmed. "The General is holding this over his people's heads. Maybe not overtly but if push came to shove, he could always use the threat of these zombies to justify martial law. If you look closely, you will find a radio receiver hooked to a detonator. His military forces probably have a fortress that can resist even the whole horde, with high walls. In the event of revolt by the civilians, they hole up, blow the barrier, and the civilians are done. Probably have an escape route too. Boats, most likely."

I nodded. "So much for the job of the military being to protect and defend civilians."

Hart turned to me. "Do you want me to disable it?"

"Can you do it without setting it off, one hundred percent guaranteed?"

She thought about it for a minute, studying it again with the binos. Finally she answered with a flat, "No, odds are, it's rigged. Not to blow but there are probably anti-personnel mines all over the place."

"OK, well, that settles that. Let's get away from here and go talk to the mad man."

*****

"OK, Ahmed, you're out. Red, you're his spotter. Lay low and watch for my signal. This could go bad pretty quick." We slowed the boat and they slipped over the side into the water, weapons and packs balanced on two inflated inner tubes.

We had left them on the empty, northern part of the causeway. Hopefully the watchers on the shore hadn't noticed us slow down. It left them no avenue of retreat, which I wasn't comfortable with but they both took inflatable life vests so they could take to the water if necessary.

"If we're not back in twenty-four hours, then Hart will come get you with the boat. Do hourly radio checks with Empire Main and call in the hammer if things go bad. Level that." I pointed to a building which crouched on the shore, surrounded by T-barriers, ten-foot-high slabs of concrete. From it flew the Vermont state flag and underneath that flew the yellow Gadsden "Don't Tread On Me," flag. Through the binoculars I had counted three guards standing on a platform inside the wall.

"Time to poke the dragon," said Brit and she, Hart, and I headed out in the Zodiac, towards a dock that stretched out into the water. The half mile passed quickly and as we pulled up, we could see a reception committee waiting for us. A half dozen soldiers, backed by a .50 caliber heavy machine gun. Hart kept her MK-19, mounted on a pintle in the boat, trained on the machine gun crew. They tracked us all the way in until we pulled up to the dock. I climbed up the ladder onto the dock and Brit backed the boat away, idling about a hundred meters offshore.

I stepped forward and saluted the two-star Major General standing in front of me. He was a short, compact man, wearing full battle rattle and he had an intense, blue-eyed stare. He glared at me for a moment and then quickly returned my salute, seemingly out of habit more than anything. Behind him, four bodies hung from a makeshift gibbet, swaying gently in the breeze. No quick deaths, those. Instead of dropping them and breaking their necks, these scumbags had pulled them up, leaving them up to strangle. I tried hard to hide the look of disgust on my face but the man standing in front of me saw it. His expression hardened.

"Sergeant, desperate times call for desperate measures and for men with hearts of iron."

"Save me the speech, General. Next you're going to give me a some moto bullshit you're a sheepdog, guarding the flock from wolves."

We stood that way for what seemed like an eternity and was probably no more than fifteen seconds. Behind him was a man wearing full colonel rank and two guys from what I figured were his brute squad. They were both over six feet and muscle-bound. I ignored them and looked at Danny Westbrook, who brought up the rear. He nodded to me.

The general broke the silence. "Staff Sergeant Westbrook here tells me that you are with the Regular Army, some kind of scout team. I'd like to see some credentials, please. And a copy of your orders."

Seriously? Orders? What planet was this guy living on? "Ah, general, the only thing I can show you is my old ID card. In case you haven't noticed, things have been a bit squirrely over the last few years. I have no written orders. In fact, I'm just here to get my men. I understand they have been your guests over the last few weeks."

"Um, guests, no, not actually. They are prisoners, on trial for murdering several of my men." He waved his hand and Ziv and Doc were escorted out of the gate of the fortress. Actually, Ziv walked out under his own power, in handcuffs, but Doc was dragged out by two men and dumped at my feet. The guards went back inside the gate and I knelt down to him.

"Hey, Nick," Doc managed to whisper. "You're late." His face was a mass of bruises and there were cigarette burns on his arms. No fingernails on his right hand. "I never said shit."

I looked up at the General. "Am I supposed to be impressed? I've seen worse in Afghanistan. What, exactly, is your point?"

"My point is, Sergeant, that I am the law here. This is the Sovereign State of Vermont and we are no longer a part of the United States. If there even is such a thing, which I doubt."

This wasn't going to work. I had seen it before, leaders who let power go to their heads. Little warlords who wanted to set up their own little kingdoms. I despised them. Still, I had to try.

"General, let me explain something to you. Right now the U.S. Army is fighting a massive brawl down by New York City. Last year we retook Denver. Next year we'll be taking back Northern California. We seized the oil fields in Mexico. It may take a year, or two, or even three years but the Feds will be here. You are sitting on top of a vital transit route and shipping line, once we get the canals back in order. Oh and in case you hadn't noticed, we settled the whole secession thing more than a century ago."

He stared at me, glaring, then walked past me, looking out at the lake. The colonel, who I assumed was his Chief of Staff, walked over to him and talked to him quietly. After a minute, I broke into their conversation.

"General, regardless, you and all of your troops were recalled to Active Duty two years ago. I know you have radios and you heard the broadcast. Right now, you and all your men are in a state of rebellion against the United States. I can't hold your men responsible, because, for all I know, they think they are acting under legitimate orders, but you, as their commander, are liable. I'm giving you one chance. Stand down, turn over control of the island to the civilian population, and things can go back to normal. I won't say anything about what happened before we made contact. This is a fight that you cannot win."

He turned to me. The colonel put his hand on his shoulder but he shrugged it off. "My men know full well what they are doing. You have a lot of balls, sergeant, I'll give you that. It's going to need an extra strong rope to hang you. We fought, all by ourselves and survived. Where the hell were you and your precious federal government? No, we don't need you. As far as those civilians you're whining about, they're a bunch of useless sheep who got us into this mess in the first place."

He took a deep breath and shook his head. "No, the time for those things have passed. The U.S. was rotting a long time before the Zombie Apocalypse and I'll be damned if I'm going to let myself be ruled by a bunch of Liberal, west coast retards. You're just another one of those New Army touchy-feely punks, coming here with a bunch of women to back you up. In fact, it will feel GOOD to hang you. Your friends, too."

"Then, sir, I have no option but to place you under arrest for rebellion, treason and murder. You'll be coming with us, back to Albany." I placed my hand on the stock of my rifle but I kept my eyes on Danny, wondering which way he was going to jump.

Danny stepped forward. "Sir, it's time to let it go. Turn it over. What you did, hanging those civilians, was wrong. Nick is giving you an option. Please take it, before things get worse."

"Sergeant Westbrook, your opinion is noted. Corporal, please arrest him and Sergeant Agostine, also."

One of the brute squad reached out to grab Danny and all hell broke loose. Time seemed to slow down and speed up at the same time. Danny leveled his M-4 and pointed it at the corporal. "Stand down!" he yelled.

The colonel pulled out his pistol and fired at Danny, catching him in the neck in a spray of blood. Danny spun around and fired a full auto burst toward him, emptying his magazine before he fell and rounds tore through the General's legs, hurling him down to the ground.

The first guard brought his pistol up to fire at me and his head exploded in a pink mist from a sniper round fired by Ahmed. Ziv hit the other guard on the side of his face with his handcuffs and then started wrestling with him, trying to choke him, slamming his head against the ground and cursing at him in harsh Serbian.

The .50 caliber at the guard started hammering but Hart was faster on the trigger and a string of 40mm grenade rounds slammed into the sandbagged position, chewing through the bags and striking the gun, silencing it.

Brit slammed the boat into high gear towards the dock.

As he fired at Danny again the colonel grabbed a Motorola two-way on his harness and hit the transmit button, causing a muffled BOOM rolled over the water. I shot him through the head and he fell to the ground.

Doc rolled over and kicked the guard struggling with Ziv in the head, stunning him.

Ahmed took out the remaining three guards in as many seconds with sniper fire.

I ran over to Danny, pulling a field bandage off my kit and pressing it to his neck. Blood was everywhere. He had been hit in an artery and was bleeding out quickly. I pressed my hand over the wound but it kept squirting out. Not again. Just like that kid on the barge.

"DOC, HELP ME!' Doc crawled over and pulled my hands off Danny's neck.

"He's dead, Nick. Let him go. We have to get out of here." He was right; the flow of blood had stopped, my friends' eyes had glazed over. I reached up and pushed his eyelids closed. Then, with a ripping sound, I pulled the Velcro American flag off my uniform sleeve and put it on Danny's chest.

"All enemies, foreign and domestic. You did good." Then I stood up and helped Ziv carry Doc to where Brit had pulled up to the dock.

As we passed the General, he tried to lift his pistol and aim it at me. I kicked it away, then tied tourniquets around his legs. Each had a bullet hole through them, one in his thigh and the other through his kneecap.

"Help me!" he moaned.

"Fuck you, you traitor, I hope the zombies take a long time eating you. You swore an oath to your country and your state and you broke both." Then I kicked him in the wounded kneecap and he screamed.

"That was for Danny. And this is for Doc," and I kicked him again. He screamed even louder.

I started back towards the island and Brit shouted at me, "Nick, where the hell are you going?"

I yelled back, "I have to warn the civilians!" As I spoke, a UH-60 rose from the back side of the island and thundered off in the direction of Isle Le Motte. An air raid siren started sounding and I looked over to the right and saw that the zombies were swarming down the causeway. I stopped, turned around and ran back towards the boat. I guess they knew now.

As I ran down the dock, a crowd of civilians appeared, running for the gate to the fortress. Before they got there, it slammed shut and a stream of tracers reached out into the crowd, chewing through their bodies. The crowd broke and ran but the zombies were among them, biting and clawing.

Hart had cast off the line holding the boat to the dock and Brit yelled at me "Let's go, you fat old slug!" I fell more than I jumped, landing on Ziv, who cursed me in Serbian. We pulled away and raced back over the water to where we had left Red and Ahmed. The spot where they had been was swarming with a nonstop stream of animated corpses, heading onto the island, but we picked up the two of them floating on their inner tubes, kicking hard away from the causeway.

"Hart, can you blow that bridge?"

"Sorry, Nick, my mouth just isn't that big," Hart deadpanned, then got serious. "How much C-4 do you have?" Brit handed her a brick, about a pound or so. "Oh, hell yeah, that will work."

She slipped over the side onto an inner tube and paddled over to the bridge. We backed off another hundred meters while she worked, packing the C-4 under one of the bridge pilings. As she did so, zombies were reaching down to grab at her. One got hold of her hair and she coolly fired her pistol straight up into the zombie until it let go, then finished what she was doing. I guess she had gotten over the shock of seeing her teammates killed and was back to being a smooth operator.

When she got back to the boat, I nodded to Ahmed. He leaned forward with his rifle resting on the bow and fired. A puff of dirt shot up just above the C-4. When Red snickered, he muttered, "damn waves," and fired again.

The C-4 exploded with a dull crump and the bridge shattered into a million pieces, throwing wood and concrete into the air. The rush of zombies stopped short, some falling into the water, the volume of their howl kicking up a notch and carrying across the waves.

"Whoohoo, Hart! Put Red on your shoulders and I'm going to call you Master-Blaster instead of Lady Brienne!" She ignored her and we watched as the pieces fell down into the water.

"You know several thousand got onto the island. Those civilians are dead," said Ahmed.

"Yeah but there is one thing I can do for them."

I reached for the radio. "Orion, this is Lost Boys. Execute Arc Light, Target AA 2375, over."

"This is Orion. Roger, execute Arc Light, Target AA 2375, out."

Three miles up, a mix of a half dozen B-52H and B-1B bombers had come back on-station after carpet bombing a zombie horde outside Newburgh. They had been patrolling over the Adirondacks for the last two hours, ready to support combat operations anywhere in the Northeast. Scout teams had priority of fire if there were massed targets and I had worked with these guys before. When we had first started, before we met Brit, the team had extracted the navigator and copilot when one of the overworked, sixty years old B-52s had come apart midair and their chutes had carried them down onto some flatland just outside Syracuse. Before we had left Albany, I had given a target list to the Air Liaison at the Task Force Headquarters.

Now, fifteen minutes after my call, from the open bomb bay doors spilled dozens of two thousand pound dumb bombs, falling in a steady stream towards the island. Each plane made several passes, laying a string of explosives from one end to the other, south to north. The heavy ordnance blasted huge craters into the bedrock and an eruption of dirt and stone leapt high into the sky.

I took the controls from Brit and headed west, full speed. We skipped over the waves and, behind us, the island shook and turned into a cloud of dust.

Brit sat next to me, helmet off and red hair whipping in the wind. "WE GOTTA GET DOC TO SOME MEDICAL CARE, ASAP!" she yelled over the concussion of the two thousand pound bombs pounding the island. "WHERE TO?"

"ISLE LE MOTT, AROUND THE NORTHWEST SIDE!" The S-2 had forwarded me some satellite recon photos and there had seemed to be some settlements and fortifications on the island, although much smaller than on Grand Isle. I just hoped we got a better welcome than we had here.

I looked down at Doc. Red was bandaging his fingers where the nails had been torn off. Ziv sat in front of me, looking backwards, smoking a cigarette, watching the bombs fall. Hart was helping Red, handing him bandages while holding up an IV that ran into Doc's arm. Ahmed looked out over the bow, scouting ahead.

For better or worse, the Lost Boys were together again. We sailed on into the falling darkness.

Chapter 135

Long minutes passed as our zodiac cut around the northeastern edge of Grand Isle, out of range of any snipers that might be hiding among the trees. The wind that blows perpetually across the northern end of Lake Champlain whistled eerily in the dark. Isle la Motte gradually came into view, or what I thought must be Isle la Motte; what looked like a concrete wall obscured the interior. If S2's recon photos were correct, there should be settlements there and if so, that wall was a pretty good way of keeping anyone out. Still jumping on adrenaline, I worried maybe the General had controlled this place too.

I glanced back at Doc, lying across the inflatable seats just in front of Hart, who had one hand on the motor and the other holding up an IV bag. Doc looked like hell and Brit, temporarily on nursing duty, looked up at me with eyes full of worry. I couldn't hear his breathing over the motor but I could see even in the failing light that one side of his chest was rising out of sync with the other. If he didn't have a collapsed lung, he had at least three broken ribs on that side.

The remains of the Vermont Bridge loomed to our front, creating mini-rapids in the current flowing north towards the Richelieu River; the Vermont National Guard having blown the bridge when the Undead made it to northern New York before northern Vermont, in the vain hope of defending Burlington from that direction.

The lake was deceptively peaceful. Ziv was sitting just in front of me, facing the way we had come, watching in silence as secondary explosions continued to eat away at the island - South Hero, if I remembered right. North Hero was connected to it by a causeway. And if the General was as big an SOB as I thought, hopefully he would have placed explosives on that causeway as well. Maybe north Hero Island could avoid the pounding its sister just caught to the south. If not... I pushed away that line of thought and hunkered down next to Doc.

"How bad?" I shouted to him above the engine noise.

He just shook his head. He didn't have the breath to try and shout an answer to me. I placed a hand on his shoulder, not daring to squeeze reassurance for fear of hurting him worse. I turned instead towards Ziv, who pitched his cigarette into the lake and leaned his head back against the rubber sides.

Asking him if he was injured would be useless but I looked him over. His face wasn't smashed in like Doc's and I remembered from the fight that his arms and legs worked, at least; but I wouldn't put it past him to fight with broken bones. The way his left arm was socketed tight against his chest suggested a fracture of some kind. Whatever, we'd deal with his injuries when we got to Isle la Motte - if we were able to get any kind of help there, that is.

It was maybe half an hour or forty-five minutes from the southern end of Grand Isle to the remains of the causeway between Isle la Motte and the Alburgh Peninsula but it felt a lot longer. When we got close enough to the peninsula, I had Hart cut the motor and we used the paddles. There was no sign of life anywhere but the gap between the two wasn't more than two or three hundred meters and I didn't want to alert anyone to our presence until we had to.

Up close, I could see that the wall was maybe twenty feet high and made of cinder blocks and cement. The exterior was incredibly smooth, even the cement between the cinder block joints had been carefully set; the effect was of one flat, even surface. After a few seconds' staring at the thing in stupefaction, my brain kicked in and I realized that no zombie would be able to climb the wall. Pretty slick, no pun intended.

"Ahoy, the island!" I shouted when we were about fifty meters away. Behind me, Brit snickered. Two heads popped up from behind the wall and one of them shouted to me.

"Qui est-il?" The voice switched to English. "Who are you?"

We'd heard rumors for several years that the Quebecois

north had managed to remain organized and it didn't surprise me to hear French; it stood to reason they would want the Vermont farmland as much as we did, especially after the fall of Montreal. The Canadian Parliament had the city nuked, ostensibly to contain the plague up there. However, from the paranoid mutterings of the few survivors to make it south, after Toronto succumbed to the plague moving north from Buffalo and Niagara Falls, Quebec had tried to secede and seal up their own borders. It may have worked. Despite the destruction of their capital city, regular radio traffic could be heard from French news channels. Reportedly, Newfoundland and Nova Scotia remained zombie-free. Ottawa was now its own glowing lake of glass thanks to the Chinese but the Frogs had evidently survived.

"United States Army! We have wounded here!" Hart had pulled out the flag we'd used down south at the ambush site and was waving it madly.

The two heads disappeared for a second, then a series of ropes were tossed over the wall and one of the men rappelled down easily, stopping just short of the water. Several more heads appeared over the edge of the wall. We paddled the boat over to him and he shone a flashlight into each of our faces. The light paused on Doc.

"Is he bitten?" This man, for sure, was Quebecois and it took a minute for me to understand him through the thick accent.

Brit astonished me by rattling off a string of French to the man. After a few minutes of back-and-forth, he nodded and shouted back up to the others. A second man rappelled down with a collapsible stretcher and after a minute or so we were able to wrestle it atop the Zodiac and carefully set Doc onto it. The stretcher was tied off and lifted to the parapet with a crude pulley system. The rest of us, even Ziv, were harnessed in and carefully lifted one at a time to the top of the wall. The two Frenchies remained below, attaching the boat to a series of lines before lifting it clear of the water, winching it into a makeshift gantry.

After I untied myself from the swiss seat, I looked around. Each of the local men was armed with a rifle, their pistol grips and butt stocks shiny from use. Radios beeped, the volume barely loud enough to register. The first man, the one to hail us, untied himself and stepped towards us. "What are you doing here?" His voice was not friendly but neither was it openly hostile. I saw immediately that they had saved our lives but didn't yet see a reason to keep us breathing.

"Do you work for the General?" I asked warily. He hawked in the back of his throat and spit over the wall. "I guess not," I murmured. "You see those explosions to the south?"

"Oui. We are not blind."

"The General and his men are dead. The causeway block failed and the island has been attacked by zombies."

He swore in French and yanked his radio off his shoulder, barking into it. The voice that came through the radio was American and speaking English. "Do they have wounded?"

"Oui."

"Get the wounded to the doctor. Hold the others there. Five minutes."

Brit and I glanced at each other. The man clipped the radio back in place and extended one hand to me. "I am Pierre." He said. "We will get your wounded to our docteur. You wait here for Cassandra."

"Who is Cassandra?" This could either get better or it could get worse, really fast. "I'm not letting you take my wounded away."

Something in his expression softened. "We will care for them. Cassandra, she is one of you. Do not be afraid." He touched the flag on Red's uniform. "We have been waiting for you Americans."

We all shared wary glances. He wasn't exactly clarifying the situation. A few minutes later a cart drew up, led by two horses of the same huge breed as those monsters we'd seen outside Schuylerville a year back. Belgian war horses, I think they were called. Doc's litter was carefully lowered, set perpendicular so that he was not lying directly in the cart, cushioning him from the worst of the jolting. "Ziv, go with him," I ordered quietly. He might not admit to being wounded but I wasn't going to let him stand up here with a broken arm, either. "No one is alone until I sort this out." For once he didn't argue with me, just jumped down into the wagon and took a seat next to Doc. The driver clucked to the team and slapped them with the reins.

A trim woman of perhaps sixty was climbing the ladder to the parapet. In looking her way I saw that the entire wall, what I could see, anyway, had a deck, maybe four feet wide, running along the inside. When I'd climbed over, I'd seen that the wall was actually a type of permanent cofferdam: two separate walls of concrete blocks with tons of gravel fill between them. The wall was nearly three feet wide, a more permanent version of the HESCO barriers that had been everywhere in Iraq and Afghanistan.

"Name," she ordered when she reached us. She wore old-style Multicam pants, the ones with the knee pads sewn directly into the fabric and the brown cotton undershirt.

"Sergeant First Class Nick Agostine, United States Army."

Chapter 136

The woman searched my face intently. Pierre shone his flashlight in my face, not aggressively but so she could take my measure.

"What just happened on Grand Isle?" she asked.

I gave her the short version but before I could finish she turned to Pierre. "Get our boats to the junction between North and South Hero. Blow that bridge. Get on the radio and inform the north of what's happened and tell them to get to stations. Expect contact with the Undead before morning. Broadcast South that any survivors should head for the west shore and to get in the water if zombies come at them. We'll pick them up in our boats. And tell that fucking pilot to get his ass back in the air and give us a proper recon!" She had to shout that last, because with a "Oui, oui, madame!" he'd already slid down the ladder and hauled ass to what looked like a guard shack a couple hundred meters away.

She turned back and surveyed my team. "Your wounded have been taken to my farm for treatment," she informed me. "The rest of you will join them once another wagon has arrived. It will be maybe a half hour wait."

I cut her off. "No offense but who are you?"

She eyed me. "Before all this shit, I was Sergeant Major Cassandra McIntyre. Retired. Now I'm what you'd call the Mayor of Isle La Motte."

My eyes narrowed. That name was familiar. "I think we've met."

"If so, it was long ago. I don't recognize your face or name. The plague broke out just as I was leaving Fort Detrick, my last duty station. Unless you were stationed with me at some point, I doubt we knew each other. And I remember every soldier who was ever under my command."

I shook my head. "We probably didn't but I might have heard of you, if you were in Iraq or Afghanistan." I hesitated a second. "Some people say the plague started in Detrick."

She nodded once, crisply. "They would be correct."

I leaned back, shocked at her casual answer. In the three years since the zombie outbreak, there had been a million theories to how it had happened. "So how did it start?"

"Madame, madame!" The shout came up from below. "General Dupúis!"

"Dammit," she hissed, leaning over the side. "Tell him Allen is dead and our position is precarious. Tell him to continue mission but we cannot join him for three days. He will have to hold his own until then."

"What the hell is going on?" I demanded.

She turned back to me. "Long story. I'll tell you in the morning."

"You are aware of the call-up of retirees three years ago? You should be back on Active Duty right now, Sergeant Major. You're breaking the law by remaining here."

"I hadn't heard, as a matter of fact." I couldn't tell if she was lying or not. "But my duty is here and if the U.S. government wants to retake New England in the next century, they'll be smart enough to leave me here. You said Allen is dead. How do you know?"

"We shot him in both legs and left him on the south side of the island. He's probably a zombie by now."

Her face was unreadable in the darkness, which by now was total, the guards having switched off their flashlights and gone back to patrolling the deck, excepting one young trooper who stood at the Sergeant Major's left shoulder. Her bodyguard, I assumed.

"Good." She managed a world of satisfaction in that one word.

I relaxed. Whatever the whole story about her presence here, she wasn't connected to Allen and my wounded were getting treatment. She glanced over her shoulder. "Your ride is early."

Sure enough, another wagon pulled by those giant horses had appeared. One by one my team climbed down and pulled themselves into it. Padded with straw, it wasn't too bad even with the jolting. I pulled myself up towards the front, hooking one elbow over the front of the wagon, at her left side. The Sergeant Major drove, clucking gently at the team and occasionally slapping the reins against their backs. The rest of the guards we left behind and I looked back to see them spreading along the wall to their original positions. Next to the Sergeant Major sat the young trooper. We jolted along the remains of a paved road for perhaps an hour, gradually turning away from the edge of the wall. "What is that?" I asked over the clopping hooves.

"A twenty-foot sea wall." She replied over her shoulder. "In the days after New York City fell, people in the biggest towns in Vermont took the hint and started leaving in droves. Even though the locals knew we were here, most fled east and north. Only a couple hundred made their way to us and most of them stayed in Grand Isle. There was a window of about four weeks between the zombie plague spreading north and their arrival in Burlington. We took advantage of that and looted every construction site we could find. Most looters were taking things they could cart away in sedans and SUVs. Since we are mostly farmers, we went in there with trucks and trailers. It took over two years, long after we had to start defending ourselves from the Undead, to steal enough cement blocks to circle the island but now the wall is complete. We also excavated thirty-foot deep trenches into the lakebed. No one can reach us from the lake, unless they've got a naval fleet." This struck her companion as funny, somehow and he laughed. I had to give her credit: it was no small feat to circle an island, however small, with that kind of defense. If nothing else, she could organize a work force.

"You know the Zs don't like water. Was it worth the effort?"

She nodded. "There are worse things than Zombies in the world, as I'm sure you know, sergeant."

Eventually she pulled into a long driveway that snaked this way and that through a line of trees, dead-ending in a stable yard. There was a huge, three-story barn on one side, some sort of walled-off enclosure directly in front of the drive and a third, smaller structure to the left. When I jumped off the back of the cart, I landed on cement. A glance at the constellations told me it was well on towards dawn and in the growing light I could see the dark circles and haggard expressions of my team. None of us had slept in better than thirty-six hours and it was starting to catch up with us.

Several young guys had come out from the barn and unhitched the team, leading them away. The Sergeant Major and her companion slung our packs over their shoulders. "This way," she said. We followed her up.

It might have started life as a barn and the horses might bed down below us but the top half of the structure had, at some point, been turned into living space. In a world where people lived badly and a bath was usually a dream, I could only be amazed that she had managed to maintain this place. It was clean – not just the half-assed clean you get by removing muddy boots at the door and maybe sweeping around with a broom made of twigs – but clean. I hadn't seen anything like it outside Seattle. There was even a TV on the wall and a pool table near a tall bank of real windows on the opposite side of the room. I looked around. The space beneath stairs leading to the third floor was filled with books, facing a small kitchen that had, from the sound of it, a working refrigerator. She looked at my astonished face with amusement and I hastily shut my trap. The others were just standing there, heads hanging, so dog-tired they couldn't even drum up the enthusiasm to look around for themselves.

"You can sleep here tonight," she said. "There are enough beds upstairs for you all. Do me a favor and strip out of your clothes and we'll have them clean in the morning."

I just blinked at her, stupidly. The combination of a week's poor sleep, high-alert while teasing out Westbrook's squad, then a two-hour adrenaline rush escaping a pack of zombies had all cost me. Seeing this place was my limit. It was all I could do to stand upright with my eyes open. Processing information was out the fucking window. For a half second, I thought maybe I was really dead and this was just one messed-up stop in purgatory. By the time I understood what she was saying, she was already headed down and the others were stumbling their way upstairs. It was Brit's hand in mine, pulling me towards the stairs, that got me moving at all.

Twenty minutes later, I tossed our combined uniforms into the hallway, truly glad the reeking mess wasn't in the same room as me and passed out next to Brit where she lay, dead to the world, on the double bed upstairs. If they were going to kill us in the morning, I didn't give a shit about it tonight.

Chapter 137

Around 04:00, Red shook me awake for my watch. I got up groggily and he slipped down the hallway into Hart's room. Good for him, I thought. Good for them both. The hour of my watch passed slowly and I was close to nodding off again when Brit stumbled out to relieve me. Even though we seemed safe, we could never let our guard down. I had spent that hour pacing the hallway, worrying about Doc and Ziv. Hopefully they were being treated well but I wasn't going to go stumbling around an armed camp at zero dark thirty to find them. I fell back asleep almost instantly, once I was sure Brit was awake and ready for watch.

I actually woke up to the sound of Brit's "Holy shit, would you look at that!" as she stood naked at the window, nose mashed against the glass, looking down.

I scrubbed sleep from my eyes and caught sight of her. "You're probably giving those farm hands a cheap thrill standing there like that."

She either didn't hear me or, more likely, didn't care. We might love each other and all that sappy-happy crap but she still enjoyed giving total strangers awkward hard-ons. "Get over here and check this out." Less of a hedonist than her, I wrapped the sheet around myself before stepping up beside her. I glanced down and immediately saw what had caught her interest.

At three AM, the place seemed like a farm. At a quarter past eleven in the morning, I could see that it was much more than that. The walled enclosure I had spotted earlier was at least an acre in size and filled with raised beds of vegetables. This late in the season, it was a riot of green. Between the garden and the barn, outside the wall and almost directly beneath us, I could see the curve of greenhouse glass beneath a deck off the second story. A walk to the window against the east wall showed me the smaller barn and beyond it, at least twenty acres of pasture in which a herd of beef cattle were grazing, four or five of those giant horses mixed in with them. The thought of a steak filled my mouth with saliva. A couple of cows, a different breed to the cattle, were grazing in a separate pasture but mooing at the huge bull bellowing at them from the other side of the electrified fence. Brit was bouncing up and down on the balls of her feet like a three-year-old, although the effect was quite different in the nude. "Look at that orchard!" she squealed, pointing out her window. Sure enough, long rows of fruit trees stretched out past the garden.

"Where are we?" I wondered.

She shook her head in wonder. "I don't know but I can die happy now. Fuck the Army, I'm not leaving this place ever again."

I just shook my head. A glance outside the door showed me that the Sergeant Major hadn't been kidding the night before; clean, folded uniforms were waiting outside each door. After a long shower and the delight of toilet paper (seriously, you have no idea how important toilet paper is post-zombie apocalypse. None of those movie directors got that right), my team assembled in the main room on the second floor. None of the people I had seen the night before were to be found but there were scrambled eggs, fresh bread butter and a toaster sitting on the kitchen counter when we arrived and Doc's medical bag was neatly unpacked and laid out inspection-style on the coffee table.

That reminded me that neither he nor Ziv were anywhere in the building but after I caught sight of the Sergeant Major's Wall of Pride that Red was examining; the long lines of military guidons and other goodbye-plaques that most soldiers end up with after a couple decades of Army work, or used to, back when places that made that useless shit still existed, I figured she was legit enough I could trust they weren't buried in shallow graves somewhere. From my vantage on the insanely comfortable leather couch, I spotted at least half a dozen deployment-related shadow boxes and twice that many from various Army posts. It seemed the Sergeant Major and her husband, from the look of the name plates, had been stationed almost everywhere.

The rest of our packs were resting neatly in a line along the wall. I could tell at a glance that they had all been searched but when I went through mine I found everything was there. "Nothing about this place makes sense," I said as I repacked.

"What do you mean?" Brit and Hart had set up the pool table and a sharp crack echoed through the room when Hart broke the triangle. At least three balls, two solid, one striped, landed in the pockets.

"Look around. I haven't seen any place like this since the plague hit. We've got two ex-military with nine deployments between them living on a farm with more food than I've seen in years, at least four farmhands, herds of cattle, horses, you name it, surrounded by a sea wall of all fucking things and zombies on either side of the mainland. What sort of crazy shit is this?"

"The dead are walking the skin of the earth, Sergeant. This place is no stranger than the rest of reality." Her voice, crisp and clear, cut across the noise from the pool corner. Brit paused halfway through her shot, the white ball landing in the center pocket, unnoticed. Hart straightened up, leaning her pool cue against the window and opened her mouth to say something but Ahmed beat her to it.

Whatever you can say about our resident terrorist, he's not a woman-hater. For all that he and Brit call each other names, more than once he's risked his life to save hers, so maybe I shouldn't have been as surprised as I was when he stepped towards the Sergeant Major and bowed from the waist, placing one hand over his heart in the Afghan gesture of respect. She smiled at him, the lines in her face softening. "Ahmed Yasser," she said, returning his bow. "You are the absolute last person I ever expected to see here."

"I am glad to see that you have survived, Sergeant Major. You were a worthy adversary," he replied. She chuckled, then seeing our confusion, explained. "I met Ahmed Yasser near Kandahar in 2004. I was with the 82nd then, a battalion Sergeant Major at the time." She nodded at Ahmed. "He was a frustrating opponent. It wasn't until I finally sat down with the locals in his area that I learned why. We pulled back some of our COPs off his land, because I had a hunch, we could trust him to take out the Taliban without our involvement. He proved me right and shocked us all when he met with me at a meeting of the local headmen to negotiate a treaty that spared our soldiers' lives, while killing all the Taliban that came close."

Ahmed nodded. "The agreement worked while you were there. When you left, your replacement was, how do you say…less accommodating."

She sighed. "I was afraid of that. From the bottom of my soul, Ahmed, I did what I could to convince them to trust you. But old habits die hard and my replacement had just come from the invasion of Iraq. He was too stupid to listen."

Ahmed nodded. "We learned that. It is what drove me into the hills and why Nick there sent me to Guantanamo three years later."

Her glance towards me then was more of a glare. "You don't acquit yourself well by doing that, Sergeant Agostine."

"Water under the bridge, Sergeant Major. They kill us, we kill them.'"

"Typical Combat Arms mentality," she answered.

I scowled, crossing my arms. I couldn't say why but the old woman made me nervous. "Ahmed and I have worked it out."

She didn't rise to that, simply shook her head, then glanced around the room. "We searched your bags to see who you are and to ensure you had nothing dangerous to us. You are clearly military, or most of you are–" she eyed Brit for a second, "–but I saw no unit markings beyond the tags on your uniform. What unit are you assigned to?"

"We're Irregular Scouts. Technically we're not in the Army at all, though for Big Army's purposes we fall under JSOC."

She nodded slowly. "Your two soldiers are at my house,

a few hundred meters from here. They are both doing fine, although Master Sergeant Hamilton needs some time to recuperate. The General was not a gentle host."

"Thank you." I could not hide the relief in my voice at knowing they were still alive.

"We were able to recover sixty-eight people from South Hero," she said after a moment, moving over to the kitchen to clean up our mess from breakfast. We followed her, Brit and Red snagging the chairs on the opposite side of the bar.

"There were a thousand people on that island," Red said hoarsely.

"We hope that more were able to make it to north Hero before the bridge was blown. I have heard reports that some of the residents there went south to see if they could find more survivors. Hopefully we'll find more." She scraped the leftover food into the sink and stacked the plates into the dishwasher as she spoke.

"As for Allen, I met that son of a bitch when we first bought land up here, ten years ago. He was the head of the Vermont National Guard, lived on Grand Isle and heard, probably through our land agent, that we were both military. He tried talking me into transferring over once I dropped my retirement papers. I wasn't interested. I could tell the man had an ego but even I hadn't expected him to turn into a tinpot dictator so quickly. I think I was blinded by my belief that someone with that many years of military service wouldn't forget his obligations to the American people so easily." She shrugged, as if to put it behind her.

"He'd blocked off the highway leading from the mainland onto South Hero, you saw that. But he sent his people out in forays to what's left of Burlington in order to pick up supplies. We do the same thing but we move by boat, so we land south of the city, away from his scouts. He knew about us, of course and we had to give him a third of our harvest every year just to keep him away. Had he only ground troops, I would have told him to go to hell but he had air support and was perfectly capable of killing everyone and simply taking over the land. So, I negotiated with the bastard."

"Only sixty-eight? Sixty-eight?" I persisted, taking notes on my iPhone.

Her mouth compressed into a thin line. "You saw what those JDAMs did, Sergeant. You ordered them, did you not? I am surprised so many survived. We'd blown our bridge when the plague reached Burlington. One of my men stole six pounds of C4 from a construction site but none of us had much experience with demolitions. I was in electronic warfare before I got promoted to Command Sergeant Major, so I had no experience with the stuff. We packed three pounds on either side of the causeway over a hundred-meter distance."

I winced. Six pounds of C4 would have taken care of that causeway and probably everything around it for half a kilometer. She grinned outright at my reaction. "It destroyed the entire causeway and dug a crater sixty feet into the bed of the lake. We'd bricked up the entrance to the island, so most of the debris hit that instead of us behind it but we had to rebuild the wall afterwards. You could have seen that plume from southern New York, I imagine."

"We've informed North Hero that we've blown the causeway to their south, so at least our sister island is safe." Her eyes darkened. I felt myself start to sweat as I imagined the scene and was grateful I had not been there. "But we had so little time. My men reached the bridge an hour before the first zombies came crawling out of what was left from your bombs. The few dozen survivors jumped into the water and they saved as many as they could but some were too afraid to risk it. I finally had to order my troops to fire on the crowd at the edge of the lake, because dying is better than … than that."

She was silent for a minute, then gave a little shake of her head and looked at us. "Grand Isle is finished. We'll start looting tonight. I want their ammunition stores and equipment and we got incredibly lucky. Two of his pilots fled with full crews and UH-60s. We've parked the birds in one of our open spaces, since we don't have anything like a parking lot on the island. The pilots will help distract any surviving zombies while we find what we can find to salvage. I suspect it won't take long."

"Then what?" Red asked, his hands clenched together as he listened.

"We'll burn the island. It's the only way to clear the zombies off of it and I want that land. The soils are better there and it gives us more breathing room. I don't expect, after your little display, that consolidation will be much of a problem. And with three islands, we'll be able to hold out indefinitely."

"That might not work." I said. "The government is going to want the land too and our job was to figure out how useful it is for a base in this area."

"The Army will have nothing to collect but ashes," she said simply. "And I don't think they're coming. They are, after all, the ones who just turned it to glass."

Chapter 138

We were all silenced. With the bombing of South Hero and the death of Allen, that was one problem solved. I didn't like the idea of some wannabe-dictator controlling innocent civilians; it reminded me too much of what LTC Jackass McDonald would have done if he'd had a chance. At the same time, it was sickening to realize that a thousand people were now dead. They'd survived four years of this shit and thanks to one man's blind ego they were gone. Even Brit was subdued. Hart had her head bent over her entwined hands, maybe praying. Red was staring out the windows and Ahmed was studying the Sergeant Major with his usual closed-in look, expression unreadable. The Sergeant Major was looking at me, one old NCO giving another the time to absorb what she'd said.

I finally sighed. "Well, this mission is over."

She nodded slowly, studying me. "To be frank," she said. "I've been wondering how you managed to continue as a scout missing one foot."

Brit stirred. "We're supposed to be retired," she replied, "but those asshats down at Fort Orange wanted to collect on a debt."

I gave Brit a look that told her to play it close. "We're here because Doc was here. I don't leave anyone behind. After this, we're out for good."

"Stay here instead," the Sergeant Major suggested gently. "I've got six hundred and forty-two lives to worry about, more, now, depending on how many are on North Hero. I could use a few more people to patrol the walls and help with the defense. Your training is priceless, even if you don't know this end of the lake. If nothing else, you could teach our younger ones to dodge zombies and help us when we have to make supply runs." I hesitated. What we'd seen from our window upstairs this morning had been encouraging but there was more to this place than one farm. She might be doing fine but what of the other people living here? Perhaps she was no better than the General, another little dictator making a play for our sympathies. Six well-trained soldiers would give her one hell of an advantage. She must have read what I was thinking, for she straightened up. "If you doubt me, come outside. There's more to see here."

She led us over a dirt path from the courtyard through a little grove of trees to the main house. It was a one-story building, almost rambling in its many corners and rounded edges. An elegant deck with a round seating area dug four feet into the ground sat off the back of the house. A firepit in the center was stacked with birch wood. A grill and brick oven had been built into one wall. Climbing the stairs, we followed her into a spacious kitchen, all clean stainless steel and dark wood cabinets. Again, the sheer cleanliness of the place struck me more than anything. It was like being in the world before the plague hit, as if the world in which the rest of us existed had not touched this place. I had to remind myself that if I looked past the trees, I'd see the seawall protecting the island from external attack not a quarter mile away.

We trailed her towards a bedroom in the back, past an impressive wine collection. Brit had the grace not to just grab a bottle but I saw her eyeing them. The Sergeant Major opened a door and ushered us through.

Doc and Ziv were laying on military-issue cots, Doc with two IVs in his arm and a bandage around his ribs. His uniform had been recently cleaned, the jacket hanging on a nail above his head. His color had come back and he clearly had a good night's sleep. Ziv, in no more than his boxers, had one arm behind his head and was staring at the ceiling but he got up and came to greet us when we walked in. Brit did the unthinkable by giving him a hug, although she was careful about it once she saw the bruising on his abdomen and back. His left arm was in a cast. On the other side of the room, a man in his mid-fifties was staring into the eyepiece of a microscope. I looked around. The room might not have been the island's hospital but I got the impression that it was the first place anyone injured found themselves. A row of shelves held glass bottles and random instruments, including scalpels soaking in some kind of solution. A stethoscope hung from a nail under the shelves and those lights doctors used to look in your eyes and throat sprouted from a mason jar. It was a clean and serviceable room, if decidedly rustic. The chairs against one wall were all home-made, clunky but looking like they could hold the fattest person with no trouble, not that there were many fat people around these days.

The doctor stood to greet us, offering his hand. "Hi, Alexander Brundage," he said, politely.

We clustered in the center of the room. "We need to take blood samples from all of you." She told us. "It's just our policy. Doctor Brundage did the same to the refugees we recovered last night, before we sent them to stay with families throughout the island. It won't take long."

The others glanced at me but I shrugged. What would a blood sample hurt and it wasn't as if they'd actually see anything. The doc pulled a sterile lancet from a sealed package for each of us and pricked our fingertips. He squeezed a drop onto a slide, labeled each one carefully, then sat down before the microscope. I walked over to Doc and looked him over. After a moment, Cassandra joined me at his side. "He was beaten pretty badly," she said, including the others who had taken seats after giving the doctor their blood samples. "The fingernails on his right hand were pulled out, probably with pliers. They may or may not grow back, so he will have to be very careful for a while. No broken bones, although he's got a couple of cracked ribs. We aren't sure if his eye orbit is broken but it will be a few days before the swelling goes down and he can see out of that eye again. He's not going to be able to eat solid food for about a week, just to save his jaw from the trouble. One molar might be cracked. There's a dentist on North Hero we'll try to bring over to check the rest of his mouth. I'm hoping he won't need that tooth pulled." Doc woke up as she described his injuries and gave me a thumbs-up.

She nodded at Ziv. "This one was luckier. His elbow is fractured but we put a smaller cast on it so he can use the arm. That shouldn't keep you guys here more than a couple of weeks. He won't say but I think they beat him with a metal pipe. No lacerated organs or internal bleeding but his spleen is enlarged and there may be some damage to his liver. No vodka for you, Soldat."

Ziv scowled at her. "Vojnik. I am Serbian, not Russian."

The Sergeant Major's expression did not change but I sensed some disdain in her tone when she replied. "Perhaps I should have guessed. I knew that accent reeked from someplace familiar."

"What is that supposed to mean, Woman?" Ziv started up from his bed, reaching for the big knife strapped to his pack.

Before it broke out into violence, Brundage leaned back and smiled at us. "None of you are infected," he said. "Although I'm sure you knew that. I can say that you all could use a few good meals and some rest." I nodded. MREs did not a fat man make and we were all on the edge of malnutrition. I was secretly hoping some of the vegetables in her garden would be ripe enough to eat, because I was sick of MRE #11, the Sammich. Man cannot live on Spam alone.

The Sergeant Major tapped my arm. "Hamilton and the other one can rest here for a while. I doubt they're up for dancing. But if you would like, I can show you the rest of Isle La Motte."

Chapter 139

Sure enough, we got a tour of the island, although from horseback. The only one of us who could ride competently was Ahmed and even he was intimidated by the horses when the two young men from last night brought them out. "They're Shire horses," she told us as she easily swung up into the saddle. "About the same size as Clydesdales, those big horses you used to see in the beer commercials. They eat everything they can reach but they don't balk at the sight of zombies and I've trained them to fight. Their height means the rider is more protected from attack, although a horde would bring horse and rider down easily enough."

Uncomfortable though it turned out to be, I did bask in the luxury of riding instead of walking. My prosthesis wouldn't fit in the stirrup but I found I could ride a half-assed sort of sidesaddle when the jolting got too rough and I didn't mind Brit's teasing too much after she fell off twice. "You could sell these to the Army," I pointed out when we stopped for lunch at the home of another farmer on the north side of the island. "It would be the difference between life and death for scouts."

The farmer, a big bear of a man with the proverbial farmer's tan, guffawed loudly as he left the table for his plowing. The farmer's wife, a lady who looked older than she probably was, shook her head and followed her husband out. "These horses are bred for war, that's true," the Sergeant Major explained. "They might do you good when it comes to scout work but they aren't easy to care for. You'd spend half your time just searching for grazing and frankly we don't have enough to lose. If it wasn't for the fact that Burlington was mostly empty when the infection reached it, we wouldn't have enough gas to run our tractors. Eventually we'll run out, even if we can resupply from South Hero, which I doubt. In two years, we'll be out of fuel. These horses don't breed every year and we need them for the plow and for clearing fields. We won't sell them and we'll fight to keep them."

I shrugged. "Oh well. It was worth asking."

She grinned. "It was sheer luck that we have them. If my husband hadn't retired before me, we wouldn't have had time to build up the farm and bring in the horses before the plague hit. He spent the last five years of my career up here."

"Is he that man, Pierre?"

She shook her head, her smile fading. "He died of cancer three years ago. He was halfway through chemo when the plague hit."

"I'm sorry." Brit spoke up, the first words she'd said all morning. Her sympathy was real enough but it was so rare for her to express genuine emotion that even I glanced at her askance.

The Sergeant Major shrugged. "The last months were easier without the drugs and radiation. He said there wasn't too much pain but he was tired all the time. I do miss him but I'm glad he didn't live long enough to realize how bad things would get."

"What were the first couple of years like here?" Hart asked as we remounted and carefully turned the horses back south.

"We didn't starve, I can tell you." She was at ease on the back of the big gelding, a red roan whose size dwarfed her as a rider on his back. She swayed with the horse's gait, comfortable on what was essentially a half-ton of solid muscle. "Most of the island had been farmland in the past and once the community realized what was happening and what would happen if we got overrun by refugees, it was easy to organize everyone. Bryan – my husband – we didn't have much trouble with that. It was lean, the first winter but between foraging expeditions in what was left of Burlington and Champlain in New York, we made it through. Eating badly for six months convinced everyone else to clear their own land, get together to clear marginal land and acreage that belonged to people off-island. The next fall, we had a surplus and no one starved. Even with that third handed over to General Asshole, we've done fine."

She wasn't kidding. What had struck me from the first person I saw that morning was that everyone here was healthy. It wasn't the stick-thin-barely-surviving that my team and I looked like on a diet of MREs and it wasn't the almost-obesity you saw among cannibals surviving on an exclusively meat diet. Everyone here had real muscle, the strength that came from eating well and working hard. As we trotted past well-tended fields and over the one bridge, spanning a wide creek whose sides were carefully brick-lined, I was impressed again at the strength of will it took to organize an entire community in the face of overwhelming odds and succeed, especially in a world where the normal rules had gone out the window when the Undead started hunting the living. I suspected, looking at her upright back, it cost her more than she would admit to keep six hundred people working together, particularly with zombies not more than two or three miles offshore, the last military presence gone. Whatever her feelings about the General, I knew in my gut that he had still supplied them with security, even if it cost more food than they had wanted to give.

But she wasn't a dictator either. Anyone could see that. The men and women working in the fields waved and called out when they saw her astride the horse and she waved back. More than once she enlisted us to help a farmer pull a stuck machine out of the mud. Kids chased after us as we trotted down the road and when she checked on the guards along the wall in the late afternoon, they spoke to her with real respect. Everywhere you looked, her hand was on the community and it was a hand they evidently welcomed. Brit pushed her horse up next to mine as we waited while the Sergeant Major spoke with those guards, perched on the wood scaffolding that placed them just high enough they could sprawl out in the prone, their bodies protected by the wall and snipe anything they could see with minimal danger. "We should stay here," she said softly, her knee touching mine. "We could live here, Nick. No more fighting, no more starving, no more nothing. This place is paradise compared to what we've been through."

"What about the Army? What about all the Soldiers we've supported for the three years? Major Flynn down in Fort Orange is still waiting for our report."

She gritted her teeth. "We did our part, Nick. And she's right, she needs more people. Six hundred isn't enough, this place has to be at least thirty square miles to farm, fortify and patrol. Six more who can train dozens is a godsend to her, you can see that."

"Let me think about it." I cut her off as she opened her mouth to argue. "I'm not saying you're wrong, I'm just saying we may not be able to ride off into the sunset just yet." She grimaced but shifted her horse away as the older woman trotted back to us.

Later that evening, I saw what the woman had meant by surplus. She led us back to the main house to check again on Doc and Ziv but also to gather up supper and Brit damn near swooned when she went into the pantry and saw floor-to-ceiling shelves of canned food. Our resident vegetarian started crying as she looked over the long lines of every vegetable and fruit you can imagine, all pickled or canned or piled in baskets. We all stood there in stunned silence for a while, I don't mind telling you, because it was more food than any of us had seen since before the plague. "You weren't kidding," I said softly. Brit had already snagged a bag of dried apple slices and was alternating them with a huge potato that she simply bit right into, making grunting noises of appreciation.

The Sergeant Major shook her head, her expression a mixture of amusement and exasperation at Brit's antics. Red was busy destroying a can of what looked like sliced peppers and the only one who seemed determined to keep his hands to himself was Ahmed, his arms folded as he stared in mute fascination at a jar of diced tomatoes. His favorite, I knew; his wife, long ago, would make him a dish of stewed tomatoes on his birthday, or he had once told us on a long-range patrol. I hadn't eaten a fresh tomato in three years.

Our host just shook her head. "Grab whatever you want, within reason and I'll start on dinner." We needed no encouragement and presented her with twelve different vegetables and six bags of various dried fruit. We followed her like ducklings back to the barn and to our absolute delight found Pierre grilling steaks on the second-story deck. She had Red spear the vegetables onto sticks for grilling and after a whispered word from me, cooked a dish of stewed tomatoes with curry sauce for Ahmed. He did not say a word when she set the bowl in front of him but the hidden expression in his eyes told me his undying loyalty had switched to her. Traitor.

Doc was carried upstairs on a litter and was able to join us at the table, although an IV bag was hooked over a nail on the wall and Brundage gave him some sort of broth to sip, so he could at least feel like he was part of the celebration. Ziv's arm was in a sling but he took to the steak with uncivilized gusto. There was nothing said for at least an hour but we all ate as we never had before, not even in Seattle. Everything was fresh, except the meat, which had been frozen immediately after slaughter and tasted like the cow was still mooing downstairs. Nothing I ever ate before that night, not even before, tasted like that food. The Sergeant Major ate sparingly, although her companion went through his steak with the same enthusiasm we did. Brit had commandeered the largest bowl in the kitchen and was rapidly destroying the biggest salad I've ever seen. When we finally sat back, full, the table was almost empty, the sink was full of empty jars and I had had to remove my belt. Red let out a long, loud, appreciative belch, apologizing sheepishly when the Sergeant Major gave him a dirty look.

An awkward silence fell. Pierre stood and Brundage excused himself after adjusting Doc's IV. Pierre said something in French that we didn't understand but it seemed to be friendly. We all gave him a short wave before he went inside to clean up. I saw Brit and then Ahmed glance my way and I gave in to their stares. "You said last night that you know how the plague hit."

Three empty wine bottles cluttered the center of the table; her collection in the main house was impressive and even though I had preferred Jack Daniels back in the old world, it wasn't bad. She lifted her glass and swirled the red liquid around before draining it. "I did say that," she admitted as she carefully set the glass back on the table. "Perhaps a better question would be: Do you want to know what I know? You won't forget it and I may not be doing you any favors by telling you."

Chapter 140

It was Brit who broke the silence and in her haunted expression I saw the girl Doc and I had rescued from the remains of Syracuse years before. "I was going to the stars, Lady. I was the top of my class in Physics, I was a week out from an internship at NASA when the zombies showed up. I want to know what stole my future."

The two women shared a long, considering glance. I thought that perhaps the Sergeant Major, a woman who had somehow retained the vestiges of real elegance despite the dirt under her fingernails and the world-weary expression that creased her forehead, was the kind of woman Brit would have admired, if the world were sane and God was paying attention. Finally, the older woman nodded.

"If you insist. My last assignment, as I told you last night, Sergeant Agostine, was at Fort Detrick. By then I was twenty-six years into the Army and I'd gone as far as I could, even among Sergeant Majors. I had no intention of continuing and the only logical assignment left for me would be at Division level. But I had dropped my retirement packet after Bryan was diagnosed with brain cancer, our dreams of building a farm here to putter around gone along with his health. For the last nine months, ticking down to the day I'd leave, they asked me to run the Inspector General's Office. Hardly a glamorous assignment and not the one I should have gotten but by then the only thing a bad NCOER could do was give me a paper cut." Doc and I chuckled, Doc's ending with a wince as he curled one arm around his ribs.

"Detrick was the home of the Army's bioweapons program, despite all denials of it and at my level I knew the basics of what was going on. There was an entire complex beneath the fort, something like six or seven stories below the surface. Supposedly it was capable of containing any virus that might have been accidentally released. It had containment levels and eradication protocols so complex I don't think any one person could have understood them all. I think that's why what happened is so horrifying to contemplate: the release of the 'reanimation' plague was intentional."

We sat in stunned silence for a long moment. "No. Fucking. Way." Red finally whispered hoarsely. "How could someone do that – on purpose? Who would even think of that?"

"This woman should never have been employed by the U.S. military. She should have been killed at birth." The Sergeant Major said softly, with venom.

I knew the name, I spoke it at the same time she did. "Doctor Morano."

I felt her glance pierce me. "You know her?"

"She did this." Brit lifted the damned pirate eye patch I had never been able to break her of using and the Sergeant Major leaned forward to examine the white eyeball, the iris so clouded it was almost invisible.

"That looks like it hurt," she said, settling back into her chair. "You know, a question a lot of people asked after World War II was how Mengele could get away with his work. Everyone wanted to know if the times made the man, or if the man took advantage of the times. You could ask the same question about her. Her reputation on post was such that everyone referred to her as 'Doctor Moreau.' I suspect she took it as a complement."

"She's a fucking psycho," I said, hoarsely. My dead wife's face flashed in my mind. Our daughter's arm in her hands, the splash of blood across her torso, the red eyes. I had married her with so much love and hope for the future, our daughter's birth had been the best day of our lives and thanks to one mass murderer all that was gone. I loved Brit but there was nothing I wouldn't trade, not even her, to have my family back. My old life and the old world back.

"She's a sociopath for certain. I never understood why no one suspected her after the parasite was released but I suppose in the general chaos no one got around to asking questions and if she's popped back up on the government's radar, as she seems to have done, they may not care so long as she appears to be making progress towards a cure."

"She's based out of Seattle now but she hops around the country. She's got two Delta goons for bodyguards," I told her.

Our host nodded slowly. "That's enough to keep her in funding and to give her whatever guinea pigs she wants."

Ahmed leaned forward and said, "Tell us about the beginning, please."

The wind had died and just as she opened her mouth, the faint zombie howl echoed across the water. We all jerked upright, reacting on instinct to the sound but our host only turned her head slightly, as if to hear better. She raised one hand to keep us in our seats. "What you're hearing is Chazy, New York. The wind drops in the early evening and you can sometimes hear it across the water. We're safe here." Pierre stepped back out on the porch to listen himself, his shotgun strapped across his back.

"The wall is fully guarded in the evening and there is no way across the water. You're safe." The sun was almost fully down, the sky a pale lavender in the west, fading to deep indigo. The moon was still new and the stars blazed. Above our heads the Milky Way splashed rich and bright and Brit sighed softly as she looked at it. The Sergeant Major continued her story and slowly we all felt the chill of her words take hold.

"Even as Inspector General, I had no influence or authority over the complex beneath us. It was administered by DARPA, I think in conjunction with JSOC and it was made clear to me that the limits of my authority ended at the surface. Frankly, I didn't give a damn. All I really cared about was counting down the days until I could get back here and be with Bryan for the last half of his chemotherapy. My stepson was up here with him but he had his own life as a photographer in Florida and we knew he would be flying back south as soon as I left the military. There had been persistent reports that soldiers were disappearing from

Detrick and I had noticed on the local news that the number of homeless in surrounding cities was also dropping. There was no explanation for it but many were of the opinion that it had something to do with Detrick. The base was gradually developing a rather sinister reputation. I'm a practical woman but even I began to suspect. I asked around among the other Sergeants Major on post – there's nothing to match the E-9 mafia, I can tell you – and finally one of them admitted that the disappearances had started about the time Morano arrived."

"Finally, she snatched the wrong soldier: my NCOIC at IG. Before, she'd been careful to take soldiers already known as trouble-makers, choosing the drug abusers, recently

Chaptered troops, or those who were most likely to be reported as AWOL. People that were sick and unhealthy. But I knew Staff Sergeant Roberts and he was utterly dedicated to the Army. Not married, no children, he had nothing but the Army and he worshiped it. Now I was pissed. It was one thing to hear rumors but another thing to take one of my soldiers, steal him out of his own apartment and experiment on him."

Even now, years later, I saw the NCO come out in her face, the old rage that someone had hurt one of her people. No NCO worth their stripes took the misuse of a subordinate by someone else, anyone else, lightly. "I confronted the Sergeant Major who supervised the bioweapons complex. We knew each other from Iraq, Harold Schumaker. He had balls, let me tell you. When Hasan Akbar fragged those two tents, Harry apprehended him in flip-flops and PTs. Get Harry drunk and he'd tell you he clotheslined the little bastard as he ran between two tents after tossing his last grenade. Harry wasn't scared of anything. Mortars, IEDs, suicide bombers, you name it: everyone and everything that tried to kill him failed. But when I confronted him about Roberts, he begged me to let it go. Begged me." She shook her head, incredulous.

"Why the fuck should I let it go, Harry? She took my troop for her experiments. He's not a lab rat, for Christ's sake.'

"But I looked in his face and I saw real fear, the kind of fear that keeps a man up at night. I saw a terrified child staring back at me. 'You have to let this go, Cassie,' he said. 'I'm sorry about your soldier but you have to believe me, he's beyond your help now.'

"Not much frightens me but the sight of this huge, hulking man scared out of his wits, scared me. 'What did she do to him, Harry? Why won't you tell me?'"

"He could only shake his head. 'You don't want to know, Cassie. I swear to God you don't want to know.'

"'We have to stop her, Harry. Whatever she's doing,

you have to stop it. If there's protocol, ways to seal her and her little Nazi scientists in there, you have to hit that button. How many victims is it this year alone? The cops are saying three dozen homeless people are missing. If I go through the MPs' records, how many more victims will I find?'"

"He wouldn't answer me. He just shook his head and told me to leave. I guess the best thing about that conversation, the only good to come out of it, for me at least, is that I confronted him the day after my retirement party. It was Friday and I had cleared out my quarters that morning. I had ridden to post on my Harley, my truck parked at a hotel near Catoctin Mountain Park. I climb, you know and I wanted to climb that one before I left for home. Since I lived off-post, the bitch didn't know that I was already moved out and miles away. I drove back to the hotel, tired and pissed-off, after dark. I figured I'd climb the mountain the next morning, then be on the road by 1500 or so. Instead, I got a call around zero one hundred. It was Harry."

Chapter 141

We sat in silence, unable to turn away. I realized dimly that the island was pitch-black around us, all lights doused and that eerie howling a gruesome accompaniment to what I already knew, in my heart of hearts, what she would say. Her face was pinched with old pain. "He was terrified, crying with fear. I could hear a pounding on a door somewhere in the background, with that same scream we hear right now. I could barely hear him. 'Get out of your house!' he cried to me. "For God's sake, you have to run!"

"Run, Harry?' I shouted down the phone. 'What's going on? What is that noise?'

"It's too late for me.' He sucked in a huge, sobbing breath and spoke as calmly as he could. 'I'm so sorry, I should have done what you asked and long before this. It's all my fault.' I could hear him loading a pistol in the background and he came back on the line. 'Forgive me, Old Girl. I hope you're right and God forgives all sins, because what's about to happen is on my head.'

"'Harry!' I yelled at him. 'Don't!'"

"'I have to. You don't know what will happen to me otherwise.'

"The gunshot was loud on the phone, louder than I expected. I heard the phone drop and then the sound of the door smashing in and a howling noise. It sounded like his office was being torn apart. Then the phone went dead." The expression of bitter grief on her face gave me the shudders. She wasn't just telling us this; she was reliving it.

"I didn't know what he'd been screaming about and I had no idea what that noise had been. But I've learned, over the years, to trust my gut. Better, I knew to trust him. I packed my bag, turned in the hotel key and got the hell out of there. I didn't know how much time I had, so I ditched the trailer with my motorcycle in the parking lot and left in the truck. I was on the road twenty minutes after his phone call. I called Bryan and my stepson answered. I told him I was on my way back north and he needed to keep one eye on the news. I turned on NPR and less than an hour later the first reports came in. I set my speedometer for ninety miles an hour and drove without stopping for eight hours, taking back roads. I got here in less than twelve hours. By then the infection had spread to Baltimore and D.C. The island had a meeting in the schoolhouse and I told them what I knew. We started planning the wall that night. Two of our people are general contractors, so we took all of our trucks to their sites and loaded up as much construction material as we could fit, load after load for eighteen hours straight. After that, it was only about a month and a half before the plague reached Burlington. We've been walled up here ever since."

"Fuck me, that's hideous," Doc said hoarsely.

She leaned forward and speared each of us with her intense gaze. Pierre had lit candles after the sun fell and it was in their flickering light that she stared us down. "Doctor Morano condemned our entire world to satisfy her ego. I don't think she released the zombies because I started asking questions. Harry had told me a few days before I confronted him that the funding was going to get cut in the bioweapons program. The staff were subject to the same furlough as every other DA civilian. Morano released her test subjects because she didn't want to lose her job." She leaned back, bitter. "Six and a half billion people are either dead or in some grotesque half-dead limbo because one woman wanted to play God at her own whim and get paid to do it."

"It can't be that simple." Red protested. "There's no way she could do something that horrible just to keep her job."

"Hitler became Hitler because he couldn't get into art school." Brit said grimly. "Sometimes it is that simple, Injun."

"And the Army is still paying her." I breathed. "She's been crisscrossing the country, testing 'cure' after 'cure.' It must all be an act."

"Remember the VX nerve agent that killed Mya?" Brit reminded me. "She probably did it as much in the hopes of killing us as to see if it worked on the Zs."

"She's a sadist." Doc said. "She gets off on inflicting pain. It must be a wet dream, to wake up every day and know she made this world."

"I'm going to kill her." I said simply, my wife's face hovering again in my mind. "I'm going to wrap my hands around her throat and choke her to death slowly."

"Get in line," Brit said, grimly.

Hart stood up and leaned over in the Sergeant Major's face. "Goddamn YOU to hell. You could have called it in, could have stopped it at the start. You ran. You fucking coward!" She slapped the Sergeant Major hard across the face, knocking her out of her chair, then ran from the room, tears streaming down her face. Red got up and followed her out.

"I suppose I deserved that," said Cassandra. "Not that it would have made any difference. You know how fast it spreads." She rubbed her face where the imprint of Hart's big hand was turning red. "Still, she's right."

Ahmed broke the uncomfortable silence that followed. "So, now what?"

Chapter 142

Outside the room there was a large crash, followed by a gunshot. Then the door burst in and we were staring down an old Thompson submachine gun. The .45 caliber barrel looked like a train tunnel and it was pointed directly at me. Behind it stood Pierre, glaring at us. Behind him, on the floor, I could see Hart buried under a pile of bodies and Red was slumped on the wall, blood running from his forehead, smoking .22 still clutched in his hand. One of the islanders sat next to him on the floor, holding his arm where, I learned later, Red's shot had cut a groove out of the muscle.

The Sergeant Majors' voice rang out like a pistol shot. "STOP!" Ahmed immediately lifted his gun into the air; it had appeared in the instant Pierre had kicked the door in. Pierre looked over at McIntyre. "Madame, are you alright? We saw the woman strike you, on the camera and got here as fast as we could. I had to hit the Indian with my gun stock."

"I'm fine, Pierre. A misunderstanding among old soldiers, that is all." He stepped back, lowering his gun but still eyeing us warily. Brit rushed into the hall, where Pierre's men were getting up from the prone figure of Hart. She kneeled in front of Red and lifted his eyelid, checking his pupils, then gave me a thumbs-up sign. Despite the blood running from her own split lip, Hart knelt next to her and started pressing a bandage to his forehead.

I let out the breath I didn't realize I had been holding. Pierre's finger had been on the trigger and my stomach was a knot. Damn, that was close. He would have swept the whole room with .45 caliber slugs. Ahmed may have gotten him but not before he had me and maybe someone else. I was getting too old for this crap. I waved my hand in a stand down sign to the team.

"You have very loyal people, Sergeant Major McIntyre."

She looked at Ahmed, putting his pistol back in its holster, then at Ziv, who was placing a steak knife back down on the table. He had had it held back over his shoulder, about to throw it at Pierre. "So do you, Sergeant First Class Agostine."

"Well, I'm glad that didn't end badly. Though I think Red is going to have a bit of a headache in the morning. "

"I will have Doctor Brundage keep an eye on him. After all, we all know how important Specialist Redshirt is, don't we?" She said, raising her eyebrows at me.

I looked at Doc. He looked back, understanding my thoughts exactly. She knew about Redshirt's immunity to the infection and Doc understood the look I had given him. If the next minute didn't go well, I would give the word for the team to kill everyone in the room and anyone in the way as we got the hell out of Dodge. I tensed up and my voice turned cold.

"I don't know what you're talking about, Sergeant Major."

"Don't be an idiot, Nick. We ran blood tests on everyone. Brundage told me before dinner. I congratulate you on keeping him safe from the authorities for so long."

I knew what this meant to her. If they took Red and turned him over to Doctor Morano, the island's safety was assured. Weapons, ammo, food. Whatever they wanted. I studied her lined face for a moment, noticing the creases around her eyes and I took a chance. "Thanks. I trust you will keep our secret."

She looked back at me and her face broke into the smile that I had seen worn into her eyes. No one who smiled and laughed often enough that it wore into the lines in their face could be evil. Hard, yes but not evil.

"Of course. I would see Morano in hell before I turned over anyone to her experiments. I would suggest that after she is dead, you allow us to send our sample of his blood into the government. We can say it was from one of our islanders who died from an accident. Drowned, unfortunately, his body never recovered."

"Sounds like a plan. Now, let's see what we can do

about getting your people some supplies. Do you have a length of road that a C-130 can land on?"

She motioned to Pierre, who jumped at the chance to leave the room. I turned to the former Serbian Special Forces soldier sitting next to me. "Ziv, can you go with him? You know what we need. And please don't kill him. Make nice with the Frenchman."

"He has more balls than any Frenchman I have ever seen," growled Ziv.

"I am NOT French! I am Quebecois!"

Brit walked back into the room, followed by Hart, who was holding a bandage to her own face. The Sergeant Major looked at her and was about to say something but I broke in first.

"Hart, the next time you act without orders, you are off this team and on your own in the wilderness. Had we been in a combat situation and you had done something so foolish, I would have shot you myself. You put the whole team in jeopardy by antagonizing our host and I'd like you to apologize to her. Now."

Hart looked at me for a second, then she turned to McIntyre. "I'm sorry, Sergeant Major. It's just that, well, I lost everything."

"Apology accepted. We all did and we're all a little crazy these days."

Doc whispered to me "She should see Brit in action if she wants to see crazy," followed by a sharp "OW!" as Brit smacked his damaged hand with a plate.

Chapter 143

FROM: betrayer47@gmail.com
TO: Danielle.morano@amriid.army.mil
SUBJ: IMMUNITY

Doctor Morano,

I have information which you will pay gladly for. I know where there is a person who is immune to infection. I want 30 pounds of gold and passage to England. In return I offer you this information, his location and help in capturing him.

> *FROM: Danielle.morano@amriid.army.mil*
> *TO: betrayer47@gmail.com*
> *SUBJ: RE: IMMUNITY*
> *How do I know you are for real? Contact me through Facebook. Look me up with this email address.*

Sasha Zivcovic: I want 30 lbs of gold up front.

Danielle Morano: I know who you are.

Sasha Zivcovic: Gold and a passage to England. I want to go home to Serbia.

Danielle Morano: Who is it?

Sasha Zivcovic: I want your word that you will pay me.

Danielle Morano: Tell me who it is first.

Sasha Zivcovic: Why? So you can just come wipe us out? You think I am stupid, woman.

Danielle Morano: So what do you propose?

Sasha Zivcovic: When you come to get him, I will help you from the inside. It is someone on the team. If I do not help you, then most of your team will die and he will die also.

Danielle Morano: Tell me. Then I will send a team.

Sasha Zivcovic: The Indian. Redshirt. I have seen this with my own eyes. He has been bitten many times.

Danielle Morano: Why do you want to betray your

friends? How can I trust you?

Sasha Zivcovic: The woman, Brit O'Neill and that Muslim pig, Ahmed. She is a whore and he is an infidel. I slaughtered many of his kind in the war and I want her for myself. If I cannot have her, I am tired of this place and want to go home.

Danielle Morano: I have plans for Nick Agostine. Leave him, I will deal with him. The rest, I don't care.

Sasha Zivcovic: Leave the gold at Grid NZ 15875-45627.

Danielle Morano: It will be there in three days. We will be there two days later.

Sasha Zivcovic: How will I know?

Danielle Morano: You will know.

1800 hours, two days after the gold.

*****

Dinner to me had always been the best time. The whole team was together in the kitchen of our farmhouse and Ziv and Doc were recovered from their injuries. Joe stood guard on the rooftop and Brit was fixing a plate to bring to him. The rest of the team sat around the table, joking and telling lies about the things we had done in the past.

"Make sure you put some meat on there."

Brit tore a leg off the turkey that sat on the counter and set it on the plate, muttering "barbarians," under her breath. I looked at her from across the table as the setting sun cast its rays through the window, setting her red hair on fire. She turned to face me and gave me one of those awesome smiles.

As I smiled back at her, I heard the window shatter behind me and her head vanished in a pink mist as a heavy .50 caliber bullet punched through her forehead. Her body catapulted backward with the force of the round, to wind up against the kitchen cabinets.

At the table, Hart pitched sideways as another round tore into her shoulder and out the other side of her body. Ziv punched Red hard across the skull with the hilt of the big combat knife he always carried and followed through the stroke by burying the blade in Ahmed's chest. With his free hand he lifted his pistol from under the table and shot Doc twice in the chest and the big man fell forward even as he started to rise. A puddle of blood spread out over the tablecloth.

I stared at Brit's body, unable to move. The gunshots still echoed in the kitchen as Ziv stood, holding the pistol directly at my face. Behind him, the kitchen door crashed open and half a dozen black-clad soldiers stormed in, laser sights cutting beams through the gun smoke.

Ziv was putting handcuffs around Reds' wrists. He shook his head at me, a look of regret showing on his scarred face. "Sorry, Nick. It is nothing personal. It is just about money."

"YOU BASTARD!" I screamed and leapt out my chair. From the doorway, a slim figure in green fatigues fired a compressed air gun at me. The dart hit me in the chest and everything went slack as I fell to the floor, my face landing in the pool of cooling blood. Unable to move, the only thing I could see in my field of vision was Brit's small boot, the laces lying open. How many times had I told her to tie them up properly? I couldn't move but I could smell. The metallic tang of blood, a whiff of cordite, a faint odor of corruption where someone's bowels had let loose the moment they died.

As I lay there, someone kicked me in the head, sending stars shooting across my vision and I heard Doctor Moranos' quiet voice.

"I have plans for you, Nick. Such amazing plans." And she laughed, a deep, evil sound that made my skin crawl.

Chapter 144

I woke up with a scream and Brit immediately sat up in bed, scanning the room with the .38 revolver she kept in a holster on the night table. Seeing nothing, she turned to the light on and put her arm around me.

"Nightmares again?" I nodded my head. Despite her being right there next to me, I could still see her body lying on the floor of our kitchen.

"Nick, I know you don't like it but you have GOT to take the Prazosin that Doc gave you. When the shit DOES hit the fan, you're going to be less than useless if you don't get any sleep."

I knew she was right but I hated taking that crap. It left me completely groggy when I woke up in the morning and I felt less than useless, unable to think.

"Brit, it was fucking horrible. You were dead and Ahmed and Hart and Doc and Ziv betrayed us."

"You're just worried about tomorrow. Ziv isn't going to betray us, this whole plan was your idea in the first place. We have to get that woman into the open, you know there is no way we can get to her in Seattle. Sure, we might take her out but then we would be done. This way we're fighting her on OUR ground."

I was still shaking and I felt weak inside. Outside, an early summer thunderstorm sent flashes of lighting across the night sky.

The plan, so far, was on schedule. Ziv had picked up the gold two days ago and had been in further communication with Doctor Morano. We knew when she was coming and how, courtesy of Major McHale at Flight Ops in Albany. She would be bringing in some heavy hitters, a squad of mercenaries (sorry, "military contractors,") and her two Delta guys to act as snipers. Their LZ was a half mile upriver, on the Stillwater side.

We were going to hit them before they even got into position to hit us. Ahmed, with Red as a spotter, had built a hide site 300 meters away on the second floor of an old building, covering the entire LZ. His orders were to take out the two Delta operators as fast as possible. Ziv, good with a rifle himself, was paired with Brit, in a basement window that had a good line of sight covering most of the open space. Myself, Hart with a SAW and Red were one assault team. Jim and Donny the Butcher from the Mechanicville salvage crew, along with my farmhand Joe, made up the other, forming a classic L shaped ambush. Doc was on standby as our medic. Our ace in the hole was Major McHale, who knew to vacate the area as soon as the drop off occurred, denying them any kind of top cover.

I ran over the plan in my mind, unable to fall back asleep. The nightmare of Ziv betraying us kept running through my head but I had to trust him, he owed me his life. I couldn't think of any other contingencies. It was going to fall to surprise and intelligence about their movements, like Sun Tzu said in the book. Just in case Morano had outthought me and had recon on the building, we had captured several Zombies and were going to let them loose on the first floor, locked up. That way their heat signatures would look like there was someone still in the house, moving around. We could take care of that when we got back and we would swim the river the night before to get into position.

One aspect of the plan was Morano herself. I wanted her alive, if I could but I wasn't going to take any chances of any of the team getting hurt just to capture her. If she died in the first round of gunfire, so be it but I counted on her being last off the chopper, after he goons hard secured the area. If that were the case, McHale and his crew chief were going to lift as fast as possible before she got off, hopefully trapping her onboard.

Brit had, of course, fallen back asleep. I looked at my

watch and saw that it was 03:27. I was due to relieve Doc, who was on watch with Ahmed, at 03:52. Might as well get it over with now, let Doc get some extra sleep. I sat on the edge of the bed and strapped on my leg, then pulled on my multicam then checked my weapons, loaded and on safe.

On the roof, Doc was grateful for a chance to get some extra shut eye. He still wasn't completely healed from the torture he had gotten on Grand Isle and he gingerly let himself down through the trapdoor in the roof.

Ahmed sat watching the woods and fields through his scope mounted on his rifle and I picked up the NVG' Doc had left. "What's going on, Ahmed?"

He didn't take his eyes off the scope. "Having trouble sleeping again?"

How did he know this stuff? Before I could answer, he said, "I heard you scream. Well, I heard Brit scream, too but that was much earlier and probably for a different reason."

I laughed. OK, so maybe we were a bit noisy. "Yeah, well, I had a hell of a nightmare. Dreamed Ziv betrayed us and most everyone was dead."

"Really? How did I die?" he asked, with real amusement in his voice.

"Ziv stabbed you in the chest with that big Rambo knife of his."

"Ha, I like the thought of that. Traditional, almost like dying in a sword fight like my ancestors. I would like to fight Ziv one day, with swords. Christian against Muslim, like in the old days." He chuckled quietly, never taking his eyes off the scope.

"Lunatics. My entire frigging squad. All of you."

His laughter stopped short and I felt him tense up. "Nick, we have company."

"Zombies?"

"Yes. Maybe two dozen. Behind them, there are hotter figures, looks like six, following. They have just appeared out from behind the rise, maybe five hundred meters. Due east."

"Take out the hot spots. Those are Morano's mercenaries. Shit shit shit. I'm on my way downstairs. Stay in radio contact, report anything else. I'll send Joe up here to watch the other side, make sure they aren't trying to sneak up from the river. Remember, claymores at the field wall, one hundred meters."

Ahmed didn't say anything, just started firing. I slapped the alarm button, sending a siren shrieking through the farm. On the way down the stairs, I threw the breaker on the outside floodlights. They were angled to cover the grounds outward, blinding any attackers. Also attracting any Zombies within ten miles but that was a chance we had to take. Return fire started thumping into the house, then died off when the lights powered up.

I met Joe coming up the hallway. "Back up Ahmed, watch for an assault from two dozen zombies approaching from the east, backed up by mercenaries. Go!" He took off down the hall and started up the stairs to the roof.

Brit and the rest of the guys were busy slamming the steel shutters shut over the windows. I had installed them a few months ago, cut from used sheet metal. They would stop everything up to a 7.62 round. Just as I thought that, a loud BANG sounded from one of the windows on the west side and a hole appeared in the steel. The round buried itself in one of the kitchen cabinets as we hit the floor.

"Barrett .50 cal!" yelled Doc. That was not good. Another round smashed through the wall and gouged its way across the kitchen table, shattering it.

I got on the radio to Ahmed. "TAKE OUT THAT .50!" I yelled probably way too loud.

Joe came back on the radio. *"Nick, Ahmed is down. I have movement on the west shore of the river, looks like a Zodiac boat, maybe another six guys. They have the .50 cal."*

Damn. We had to act. "Ziv, take Brit and Red. Go south and then cross the canal. Wait. Wait a minute."

I wasn't thinking straight. Of course. We were on a frigging island. The attack from the east, the harassing fire from the Barret, were all just diversions. There was no way the zombies could get across the canal; the doors were open and we had used cutting torches to take out the foot bridges. The only way onto the island was by boat or by foot or vehicle from the north, or by ...

"Ziv, head south. Take Hart and Red with you. Cover the south field, expect an airborne or helo insertion. Take the 240, GO!" They rushed out the back door, Red grabbing extra ammo cans.

"Jim, you and Donny deal with the boat, I'm sure a couple of 40mm grenades will discourage them." The big former Marine nodded. Donny laughed his retarded laugh and started fitting an HE round into the M203 under his rifle. Frigging weirdo. "Then head north, cover the road. I don't think they can get through the wall we built with anything short of a couple pounds of C-4 but just make sure."

Turning to Brit, I ordered, "Go see how Ahmed is, see if he needs any more help."

"Where are you going?" she asked, checking her weapon.

"I'm going zombie hunting, baby. Give me a kiss and give me some cover from up top."

"Nick, if you don't come back, I'm going to kill you."

I grinned at her and then had a thought and turned toward the radio. "Orange Main, this is Lost Boys, over."

"Orange Main, this is Lost Boys, over!"

Figures. Stupid RTO was probably asleep or playing XBox. Not to worry, I had a backup plan. I flipped frequencies.

"Sheriff, Sheriff, this is Lost Boys, Over."

"Lost Boys, this is Sheriff, what's up, Nick?"

High over the Hudson Valley, running a racetrack pattern, an Air Force EC-130H "Compass Call" aircraft was providing radio retransmission and coverage for the Upper Hudson Valley and the forces operating in a 150 mile radius from Albany. Their call sign was "Sheriff" and ANY unit in trouble could reach them, twenty four hours a day.

"Kevin, I have unknown forces attacking my position," and I quickly told him the grid to the island, which I had memorized long ago. "Do you have anything on call?"

"Roger, Nick, I have a AC-130 gunship returning from Z suppression in NYC, ETA Albany in 5 mikes. I can divert but only for a few passes, he is almost bingo ammo."

"That will be fine, tell them to run on any hot spots east of my grid. One or two passes will suffice."

"Roger that, our TAC has handed them off and they will reach you in about eight, I say again zero eight minutes. Can you hold till then?"

"Check. Thanks, Kevin, I owe you one."

"You owe me three, now, Nick but I'm not counting, over."

"Come by the farm someday. Lost Boys Out." I love it when a backup plan comes together.

I ran upstairs, passing Brit along the way as she and Joe carried a bloody Ahmed down the hallway. "How is he?" Brit shook her head, not taking her hand off the wound in his shoulder area. Damn.

As I reached the roof, I heard several grenades detonate, their flat CRACK muted by going off in the water. A red glow started behind the trees that shielded the house from the river. Something hot had set off one of the gas tanks in the Zodiac. Nothing to worry about from that end.

Almost at the same instant, a long stream of tracers suddenly ripped across the south field. I hurriedly put on the NVG's that Joe had left on the roof, just in time to see another short, three second burst dance its way through the figures that were struggling out of parachute harnesses. One started to fire back, then crumpled to the ground as rifle fire joined in. Two of them ran south for the river, away from the gunfire. I guess that mercenary paycheck just wasn't enough.

Two sides secure. I looked north but I could see nothing on the road, so I turned east. Overhead, I could hear the drone of the AC-130 approaching from downriver. A few more minutes and the zombies and mercs prowling the woods and fields out there would be smears on the dirt, fertilizer for next year's corn crop. What I wanted had to be somewhere past them.

I took off the NVG's and lifted Ahmed's rifle to my eye. He used an infrared scope, rather than an ambient, low light one. I scanned the far fields until my eye caught two figures, far behind the attacking force. One was bulky, wearing combat armor and a helmet. The other was smaller, not even carrying a weapon.

I could settle it right here, right now. I'm not the greatest shot in the world and it was well over seven hundred meters away but I thought I could make it. Laying the crosshairs right on the smaller figure's center torso, I let my breath out and slowly squeezed the trigger.

Chapter 145

Seven hundred meters is a long way for anyone to shoot and, well, I missed. Correction, I sort of missed. The larger figure, which I took to be one of her ex-Delta Force goons turned bodyguard, partially hid Morano's body as I fired and I forgot to take into account the windage. A strong south wind, unusual for this time of year, caught the round and moved it about eight inches to the left. Enough that, instead of seeing Morano's slight form crumple to the ground, the big, beefy soldier folded in the middle, probably gut shot. I had been aiming lower because of her shorter stature. When I had settled the scope again from the recoil, both had disappeared into a dip in the ground.

"Dammit!" OK, well, that's the way shit happens sometimes. I scanned the field for the vehicles that must have brought them there and in the far distance I saw two 5-ton trucks. I may not be a great shot when it comes to people but I can hit a truck. I emptied the magazine into the engine compartment of one, then the other. Hot radiator fluid spilled out onto the ground, making a bright white splash in the infrared spectrum. I wished for a tracer round to set them on fire after I had punctured the gas tanks but they were probably diesel anyway. Bullets never set gasoline on fire, unless you got lucky and a steel jacketed slug struck sparks off some metal. Even then, no huge explosions, just a hot fire. Another Hollywood myth. Either way, Morano might still be alive but she wasn't going anywhere.

I turned the scope southward, to the field where the mercenary team had tried to parachute in. I could see a single figure walking toward the remains of the paratroopers, followed by the short / tall team of Red and Hart, pulling security. As I watched, must have been Ziv, fired a short burst into each of the bodies on the ground. Cold bastard, he was but he was right. We had other things to worry about than someone faking death and sneaking up on us behind.

Lifting the scope higher, I searched for the two that had

run away. I saw one floating in the river, unmoving. His heat signature was fading as I watched. This time of the year, the Hudson was still very cold and he probably had been wounded anyway. The other one was trying to hide behind a tree, so I shot him. Such were the wages of being a mercenary and I had no sympathy for the ones that hired themselves to someone like the Doctor.

As I made to head back down the stairs, the ground to the east rocked with a rhythmic pounding as the 40mm cannon on the Spectre gunship walked its way across the fields, followed at intervals by the big BOOM of the 105mm howitzer. I ran down the stairs, passed Doc and Brit frantically doing CPR on Ahmed and flipped the radio to the TACAIR frequency.

"Spectre, Spectre, this is Lost Boys, over."

The copilot of the gunship immediately came back over the radio. I could hear the rumbling of the engines and the hammering of the guns over his headset. *"Go ahead, Lost Boys."*

"Spectre, what's the situation, over?"

"Lost Boys, we are engaging approximately two – four, I say again, two – four undead and receiving small arms fire from a group located about 100 meters from the undead, break,"

After a second he came back on *"Be advised, small arms fire no longer a problem. Will continue to engage the target area until heat signatures are gone, over."*

"Roger, Spectre, much appreciate the support. Be advised there may be heat signatures seven hundred meters east of my position. DO NOT, I say again, DO NOT engage. High Value Target. Will attempt capture."

"Roger, will not engage."

"Also, consider heat signatures on the west bank hostile, over."

"Roger that, Lost boys. We will be on station for approximately ten more mikes. Spectre out."

I dropped the hand mike and raced upstairs. Brit sat

crying in the hallway with Ahmed's head cradled in her lap, covered in blood, his eyes closed. Doc was stripping off his gloves. He also had blood up his arms and it was pooled on the floor.

"He's gone, Nick. The round hit him in the shoulder, penetrated his chest cavity, down to his heart, I suspect. There was nothing I could do. He was dead before we brought him down here."

I sat down next to Brit and put my arm around her. She was sobbing hysterically. "Brit." I squeezed her shoulder. "Brit." She shook her head. I grabbed her jaw in my hand and turned her face towards me. "Brit, he's gone. We have work to do. Let's go."

She looked down at Ahmed's peaceful features, all the color drained away from the massive internal bleeding. She made a pillow out of her hoodie and set his head down on it, then leaned down to kiss his forehead, a strand of her red hair brushing across his still face, tears mixing with the blood.

"Morano is out there, probably still with some of her goons and maybe some Zs. I wrecked her transportation, so they aren't going anywhere." I listened but the explosions outside had stopped. "Air support is done. We need to get the team together and go after her."

Doc stood and then lifted Ahmed's body. "I'll take care of him. I'm still no good in a fight anyway, with my hands like this. I know what to do with his body." Even more so than I had, Doc had spent a ton of time in Afghanistan as a Special Forces medic and had fought and lived with the same kind of people Ahmed's tribe had been. He knew their ways and I could trust him to show the proper respect. Even more than that, Ahmed had been, with Doc and Jonesy, our original teammate and it was an obligation he willingly took on.

I took Brits' hand and led her down the stairs. Halfway down, I had to stop and retighten my leg. As I sat down on the stair and worked the straps, Brit sat down with me. Her tears had stopped and she put her arm around me.

"Nick, I can't go out with you. I'll stay here with Doc."

"Why not?" I asked.

"I'm not risking it."

"What do you mean?" A dawning suspicion grew on me.

"I was going to tell you after the guys had left but I want you to know now. I'm pregnant."

I sat there on the stairs, looking at her. Outside, zombies were howling. Blood was leaking down the stairs, one of my best friends' lifeblood. He lay dead upstairs. Outside, corpses were strewn around our farm. I could hear Ziv and the others coming back into the kitchen. There were hundreds of bullet holes in the house. An evil psychopath was somewhere out in the woods, possibly with heavily armed troops, and corpses animated by a genetically engineered parasite were crawling around. Brit was pregnant. This was the only thing tonight that had thrown me for a loop.

"How?" Well, that was a stupid question. We had talked about it and I wanted a family but she had been scared of being pregnant so far away from real medical care. I had told her that it would be up to her.

"Probably when you bent me over the couch a few weeks ago." She laughed and then started crying again.

"Oh." OK, I felt like an idiot. "Brittany Karen O'Neill" I whispered to her, "thank you." She squeezed my hand and I got up off the stairs. She sat there, looking at me, the blue in her eye rimmed with red from crying.

"I, I just wanted you to know. In case you didn't come back."

"I'll try my best, beautiful girl," I swore to my wife.

"Go get her, Nick."

Chapter 146

The sky was growing light in the east as we started across the drawbridge. We had built it earlier in the year to reach the catwalk across the canal doors, which we had cut away halfway across. Ziv took point and after we had crossed, Brit and Doc cranked the wooden plankway up. As we passed over the canal, Red shot at several zombies that had fallen into the water, more out of frustration than anything else.

I missed Ahmed. I had been on countless missions with him and it was hard to believe he was gone. I put it aside, deep down. I would think about it tomorrow, or later today when we buried him. For now, mission first.

We crossed the Hoosic River by wading through a low spot I knew of. Ahead of us the field of corn that I laboriously planted was torn to pieces by 40-millimeter cannon fire. Small green shoots were scattered around and craters were all over the field, mixed in with body parts from the zombies. Further on, in the next field, a clump of bodies lay around a crater from a 105mm howitzer shell. Those would be the merc squad that had been firing on the house.

"Spread out and shoot any of them that look alive. Watch out for unexploded ordnance." Ziv turned and walked backward for a second and the light had gotten strong enough that I could see the grin on his face.

"We will be making a soldier out of you yet, Nick." He turned just in time to step over the rock wall bordering the field and continued patrolling forward toward the tree line. Red laughed as he passed me, since I had stopped to give Ziv's back the finger.

Hart walked next to me for a bit. "So, what's the deal, Nick? Does this crazy psychopath have some kind of personal beef with you guys?"

I nodded. "Yeah, we've run into her several times. Know that eye patch Brit wears?"

"Yeah. Did she give that to her?"

"Yep, back in Seattle. She also killed one of our teammates, Specialist Mya, with some bullshit neurotoxin 'cure'. That and Ziv mixed it up with one of her bodyguards too."

"Bodyguards?" she asked, with a raised eyebrow.

"Yeah, she goes everywhere with two guys who were Army Special Forces, Delta, back before the plague. I'm pretty sure they've gone rogue. Every now and then an occasional asshole slips through selection." More often than every now and then, when the war had been going on.

Ziv had reached the cluster of bodies in the field and he flipped one over, then started kicking it as hard as he could in the balls. A groan escaped from the prone man. Red rushed up and took a knee, his back to Ziv, rifle at the ready, scanning for targets.

"I think Ziv found one of them." As I watched, he knelt down and made a quick cut across the guys' throat. His boots drummed for a second in the dirt, then fell still. Ziv spit on him.

"He doesn't screw around, does he?" said Hart.

From behind us came, "Nope. He's my hero!" Donnie the Butcher laughed that weird laugh of his and Jim smacked him in the back of the head.

"Shut the fuck up, you weirdo, and watch your sector. And DON'T touch those zombie corpses."

"But Jim, they might have jewelry and like, gold teeth."

"I will butt stroke you. In the teeth." Jim carried an M-14 with a wooden stock and he knew how to use it. Donnie grumbled but kept walking in a straight line. We moved toward the tree line and a fog seemed to follow us across the field, rising from the river.

"Keep it tight," I ordered. "I'm pretty sure I hit the other bodyguard but I could be wrong. Might have nailed him square on the ceramic. Noise discipline from here on out. Jim, you, Donny and Red circle around and try to cut them off. Assume that neither is wounded but I doubt she can move through the woods like we can. He's gotta be hurt, any which way I hit him. Even if hit his strike plate, he's gonna have some busted ribs. Make SURE you ID your targets, no friendly fire. Say it back."

Ziv repeated it back to me and the three of them set out at a fast, airborne shuffle around to the Northeast, through the woods. They would parallel the road until they got to the next field, then keep a line of sight down the opposite side of the woods. The anvil to our hammer.

Red, Hart and I moved through the woods, making noise as we went. We would hopefully drive them out towards Ziv and the rest of the guys. I wanted them alive.

We had only gone a few dozen meters into the woods when a shot punctured the morning stillness. All three of us rushed forward, in single man overwatch, rushing from tree to tree, till we broke out of the thin belt of trees.

Ziv and the others were approaching from the north and in front of us two figures knelt on the ground, half hidden by the scrub growth that had grown up over the last two years. We met the others and together approached them. The soldier had thrown his weapon down and stood slowly, hands raised.

"Hart, cuff the Doctor. Be careful, she might stick you with something. Ziv, what do you want to do with the bodyguard?"

"I will do it the old way, the way Ahmed would have wanted."

*****

Morano looked daggers at Hart and the big woman punched her across the face, knocking her down. Red covered her with his rifle and Hart knelt on Morano's back, wrenching her arms behind her, not gently, and cuffing her with a zippy tie.

Ziv walked over to the bodyguard. "You and I have unfinished business, my old friend. Does your head still hurt from the punch I gave you? Yes, pig?" He drew his knife and motioned for the other man to come at him.

"Ziv, are you kidding me?" I slipped my finger onto the trigger of my rifle and drew a good sight picture, but Ziv waved me off.

"No, Nick, do not interfere. Look at the rifle. This one killed Ahmed. I must do this."

The man laughed. "Ha, good, I thought I got a hit on that Muslim piece of shit. Sniper, my ass. I can't believe you had a hard on for a raghead. I thought you Serbs were tough."

I stepped back and lowered my rifle, worried, because in a knife fight, everyone gets cut. Yeah, one person may come out the loser and wind up dying but the winner, often as not, comes off pretty badly himself.

I nodded to the man. "You know if you win, I'm going to kill you."

"Yeah but I'll go out in style. Killed the famous sniper Ahmed and now I'm going to slice up Sasha Zivcovic, notorious Serbian Special Forces murderer." With that, he slipped a bayonet from where it was strapped onto his boot and went into a crouch, left arm extended; right arm held in close, bayonet pointed down. Ziv walked towards him, the big knife held at the low ready. Damn, this was going to suck.

The shot from the house, fully a thousand meters away, took off the top of the bodyguards' head and he threw his arms up in the air and toppled over to one side, his brains splattering out the huge exit wound. My radio crackled to life and Brit's voice carried over the air.

"Whoops! Must have squeezed the trigger in all the excitement. Excuse me, gotta go pee. Brit Out!"

Ziv stuck his knife back in the sheath, then spit on the corpse. "Nick, I am going to have a talk with your she-devil. Gah, impudent American women."

We walked over to where Doctor Morano sat in the dirt, hands cuffed behind her back. She smiled at me as I approached. "Hello, Nick. Long time no see." She started laughing. "Tell Ms. O'Neill I said that. No see! Hahaha!" She peeled off into hysterical laughter and I had to wait for her to stop.

"You should have stayed in the lab, Doc. Picked the wrong ground to fight on, my ground."

"So now what? You shoot me?" she asked, still smiling.

"No. Not yet, anyway. Back to the house, for starters."

Hart grabbed her hands and lifted her, pulling hard, making Morano wince in pain. We frog marched her back to the house and Doc lowered the bridge, allowing us back across the canal. Brit met us at the far end of the span.

Doctor Morano started to speak, "Ah, Miss O'Nei-" but before she could get the words out, Brit took an icepick and poked her in the eye, puncturing it. Morano fell to the ground, screaming. Jim grabbed Brit's hand but she stepped back.

"It's OK, I'm done!" she said calmly.

"Doc," I said, "treat that. Get her patched up. I want her alive."

Doc got out a field dressing and started to wrap it around her head, holding it to her bleeding eye. As he held her face with his free hand, she twisted her head and bit down hard on his fingers.

"OW! FUCK!" Doc pulled his hand away and Morano laughed. Hart kicked her in the shoulders and she fell to the ground, still laughing.

"Crazy bitch!" He was holding his hand and I could see the blood welling up from the teeth marks.

"Go get that cleaned up, Rob. Leave her eye the way it is." Doc walked over to the well pump, muttering to himself and I turned back to Morano.

"You're an evil snake. Gotta get one last ounce of pain in, don't you?"

"You have no idea, Nick. No idea." She licked at the blood running down her face and kept laughing.

Brit screamed my name and Doc hit me from behind, knocking me down into the dirt. I felt his hands wrap around my neck as I rolled over. Training kicked in and I jammed my arm up into his mouth, the kevlar inserts in my sleeves keeping his teeth from sinking into my flesh.

"I CAN'T GET A SHOT!" yelled Ziv. "MOVE!"

I dragged my pistol out with my free hand and forced it slowly up under his chin. His red eyes burned at me from inches away and his hands were choking me, jaws reaching for my neck. Everything was going black, hazy around the eyes. Out of the corner of my eye I could see Red with his hammer looking for a way to swing. Behind him Morano started to run but Brit tackled her and started banging her head into the dirt. I kept forcing Doc's head back, trying to get the pistol up, working the hammer with my thumb, cocking it back. I finally got it jammed under the skin of his neck, pulled my arm out of his jaws so I didn't shoot myself and pulled the trigger, sending the .22 slug through his lower jaw and into his brain. I pulled it again and again until the magazine was empty and the thing that had been my best friend rolled off me and fell to the ground.

The sky seemed really far away as I lay there, tears running down my face.

Chapter 147

I flicked on the light and Morano squinted up at me from where she sat in the basement, cuffed to a chair. Not bothering to strap on my leg, I hopped down the stairs. Brit followed behind me and we each took a seat in a chair facing her. She stared at us, her eye socket bloody and a half mad grin on her face. On a table in front of her sat a leather wallet, open, showing half a dozen syringes.

"So, let me get this straight," I said, "you're infected?"

She gave me a look like I was an idiot. "Of course, I am. How else could I do my research?"

"You did this to yourself?"

"Why, yes. It would be inhumane to not experience what my test subjects were going through, right?" she answered with a straight face.

Brit leaned over and whispered in my ear, "She is freaking nuts."

I nodded. "So, what's in the syringes? A cure?"

"Not that you would understand it but no, not a cure. A preventive. It keeps the parasite at bay. I need to have it every forty-eight hours. You'll be happy to know that I perfected it from your friend Mya's blood."

Brit stood up, pulled on a glove and jammed her finger into Moranos' bloody eye socket, making her scream in pain. I grabbed Brit's arm and pulled her back, but not a fast as I could have.

"Sit down, Brit. I know what we're going to do," I said, reaching for the medicine.

Morano leaned forward in her chair, new blood pouring from her ruined eye. "You have to let me go, you know. I'm very close to a cure. The government needs me. I could have even saved your friend Doc. You'll of course have to give me Specialist Redshirt. He will be vital to our program. I'll forgive Ms. O'Neill. Eye for an eye, you know."

One hundred percent, batshit crazy. I dropped the syringes on the floor and ground the glass vials into dust under my boot, then spread the liquid around on the brick. Morano's mouth opened and then closed.

"Forty-eight hours you said? Must be at least twenty-four since you had your last shot."

"You can't do this. The world depends on me!" she yelled. For once, something seemed to have gotten through to her.

"Not this world, Maybe the next one." I called up for someone to come down and give us a hand.

Ziv came downstairs and grabbed her by her feet, dumping her out of her chair. Despite her kicking and screaming, he dragged her up the stairs, making sure she hit her head on each step. When we got outside, he locked her cuffs to a tree with a bicycle chain. Then we went to bury Ahmed and Doc in the field just outside the house.

In the end it took less than a day. Maybe the adrenaline from the firefights purged the preventive from her system more quickly, I don't know. I sat and watched, with Brit, as a red light started to appear in Doctor Morano's good eye. At first, she begged, then cursed us to hell, then laughed hysterically.

When the dark had fallen and the red light was shining out of her eye in a full blaze of hunger for flesh and the intelligence was gone, I took out the ten foot pole we used to corral zombies and slipped the leather loop on the end around her neck. Pushing and pulling, we managed to get the thing to the flatbed trailer hitched to my Jeep. We roped her down, wrapping duct around the snapping jaws and drove into the night, crossing over the river and into the hills on the west side. After a few miles, we stopped and all climbed out. Ziv, Red, Hart, Brit and myself. What was left of our team. We unhitched the trailer and Red poured a slight acid solution on the ropes. In a few hours, the acid would eat through them, weakening them enough that the reanimated corpse of Doctor Morano could break free. From there, as far as I was concerned, it could wander the earth for all eternity, her evil soul trapped in the hell of her own making. Hopefully, somewhere inside, the thing that was Doctor Morano lived on and knew what had happened to her.

We drove back to the farm in silence, until Red switched on the radio for the 23:00 BBC news broadcast.

"... Scientists in America released the news that a vaccination against the so-called zombie parasite had been successful in clinical trials using United State Army volunteers. Production of the serum will proceed at full capacity and World Health Organization officials say that enough can be produced to vaccinate the remaining world population by this time next year. Spontaneous celebrations have broken out in Seattle, Liverpool, Auckland, Singapore and other remaining cities around the globe.

In other news from the Americas, riots continued for a third day in Portland, started by protests against the continued emergency suspension of the United States Constitution. The office of interim President Taylor downplayed the riots, saying the suspension would be necessary as long as the zombie threat existed.

European Union troops have secured the island of Sicily, in preparation for a major clearing effort on the Italian peninsula. A United States Marine Amphibious Unit is assisting with operations, the first time a major U.S. combat unit has been available to work with... "

Red turned the radio off and Ziv turned it back on. Red turned it off again and Ziv reached over and punched him in the shoulder as hard as he could. The two started cursing each other, one in Navajo and the other in Serbian. Brit laughed at both of them.

Outside the Jeep, the ghosts of Ahmed, Doc, Esposito, Mya, Hernandez, Killeen and Jonesy laughed silently. Even Zombie Killers can die; but like all our brothers and sisters we learned to love in the fires of combat, they will also live forever.

Epilogue

"Lost Boys, Lost Boys, this is Empire Main, Over."

I sat up in bed. The radio sparked to life again. *"Task Force Empire Main calling Lost Boys, Over."*

I glanced at my watch, 02:36 in the morning. I reached out and turned the radio off. Then I rolled over and put my arm around Brit, where she lay cuddled up with our month-old son, little Nate.

"What was it, Nick?" she asked, drowsily.

"Nothing, Brit. Somebody else's problem now. Go back to sleep. We have fields to plow tomorrow and corn to plant." She muttered a sleepy "OK" and pulled the baby closer to her. He squirmed a bit but stayed asleep.

Somewhere, far off in the distance, on the other side of the river, a zombie howled, faint in the wind.

The Grunts

It was hot in the cockpit, despite the air streaming past at almost a hundred miles per hour. Flying up and behind the other UH-60 in the flight, the pilot could see the hot engine exhaust of the lead Blackhawk being blown downward by the rotor wash. The turbulence shook the bird and he ignored the warning lights on the dashboard.

"Goddamned missing spare parts," he said into the headset when the copilot tapped the lights. "Can't get a replacement until we get back to Fort Orange and there isn't any at FOB Castle. We should be OK on this flight." He went back to concentrating on following the path of the Hudson River as it passed beneath them.

In the back, Staff Sergeant Mowers ripped off another piece of green hundred mile per hour tape and wrapped it around a hydraulic line that was leaking purplish orange fluid. He grinned at the trooper who sat on the canvas seat next to him, who looked like he was ready to puke. "Kid can't be more than seventeen years old," he thought to himself.

The trooper, Private Henry Boudreaux, gripped the stock of his M-4, pointed down on the floor and prayed a silent prayer with his eyes open. The crew chief held up his hand with one finger. One minute out, oh Jesus Christ save us. The helo tilted to the right and the crewman on the other side opened up with his 240B machine gun as they circled the landing zone. With a flare they came down on the cracked pavement of the parking lot and his squad leader, Sergeant Ramirez, punched him hard on the shoulder and yelled, "GO GO GO!" in his ear. He unsnapped the crossed seat belts and grabbed the rucksack full of extra magazines for their rifles, then jumped to the ground, turned left, ran five paces and down, scanning for targets.

Sergeant Ramirez fell to the ground next to him as the Blackhawk increased power and lifted off, nose pointing back up river. Ramirez was yelling into his headset, giving a situation report to the company commander back in the TOC at FOB Castle. He glanced around, counting off the squad. One, two, three, six total plus him. They had hit the ground short of a full squad, as usual. He stood and pumped his fist towards the target building, then fell into the middle of the column as they rushed the front doors of the four-story apartment building.

"Team one, GO!" he yelled and the first team crashed through the yawning front door, clearing the lobby. One shot rang out as the second man in fired into a zombie that came down the stairway. The remains of the obese woman crashed to the floor.

"Up the stairs, to the roof!" They knew what to do but his command reinforced the urgency. Boots pounded up the stairwell. As he passed the bloated corpse, Private Boudreaux vomited onto the boots of the man in front of him. Team One stayed behind, watching out of the doorway.

"Thanks, you, asshole noob!" yelled Specialist Schride, glaring back at him over his shoulder as they hit the second flight of stairs. By the third landing, they were all out of breath. Seventy-five pounds of ammo, water and food on their backs, plus a survival kit around their waist, weapon and the extra ammo many of them carried in bags. That, along with the short rations everyone in America had been living on for two years combined to make them more tired than they should be. When they got to the top, one of them collapsed on the tarred blacktop, chest heaving, face red with exertion. PFC Johnson, the only woman on their squad.

"GET THE HELL UP!" yelled Ramirez, kicking the prone soldier until she rose to her feet. The others were already scanning their sectors, looking out over the tops of their ACOG sites.

"I GOT MOVEMENT. IT'S THEM!" PFC Johnson, on her second mission with the squad, was as keyed up as Boudreaux and her voice cracked as she yelled it.

Ramirez barked at them "Make sure you ID your target!

Remember what we came for!" He leaned over the parapet of the roof and yelled into a bullhorn.

"CIVILIANS, MAKE FOR THE FRONT DOOR. RUN!"

A group of a half dozen civilians, dressed in ragged clothes and armed with a variety of makeshift weapons, ran toward the front of the building as fast as they could. Behind them, rotting figures started lurching quickly towards them.

Johnson opened fire without orders from Ramirez and her first shot hit one of the lagging civilians in the hip, sending him sprawling to the ground. He fell with a screech and before he could rise, the zombies ripped him apart.

"God you stupid puta!" yelled Ramirez and he smacked Johnson hard across the helmet, yelled, "RUN," over the edge of the parapet, then started firing at the zombies. Downstairs, as the refugees cleared the door, Team One, the more experienced, disciplined fire squad, opened up, a rolling crackle of shots that started dropping zombies. More appeared at the edge of the woods and the team rolled back from the doorway to follow the civilians up the stairway. They left a tiki bomb on a trip wire in the looby, set to spread a hundred steel pellets at head height. It detonated with a muffled BOOM as they rounded the second landing.

The civilians huddled on the roof as the second team fired at a measured pace into the horde crossing the parking lot. POP POP POP. First team took up a position over the stairwell, shooting downward into the zombies that were climbing the stairs. In a minute, the pile had grown so great that it blocked the stairway.

Ramirez popped orange smoke into the center of the roof and the first Blackhawk thundered down, sucking the smoke into the updraft. It hovered over the roof and the crew chief hopped out and started hustling the civilians onto the bird. The last one in, a tough looking bastard with a crooked leg and scars on his face, looked around to make sure his group was all in, then hopped on himself, riding the edge like he had done it before.

The second helo dropped down onto the roof as the first circled around, firing into the horde. First squad piled into the open doors, then turned and kept firing at the zombies that burst through the doorway of the stairs. Second squad fell back from the roof top to board the other side of the helo.

Boudreaux reached over and grabbed Specialist Schride by the carry strap on his body armor as he tried to clamber onto the UH-60. Rotting arms grabbed at him and he howled in pain as jagged, rotten teeth tore through his leg. "Let me go you stupid fuck!" he yelled at Boudreaux and threw his weight back against the strap, breaking it free from Boudreaux's grasp. The helo rose above Schride as he fell to the roof and started swinging his rifle at the Z's clutching at him.

Ramirez grabbed the gunner and yelled in his ear, pointing at the roof as they spiraled away. The gunner nodded and opened up with a long burst of fire that chopped Schride down as he fought, already infected.

When they touched down at FOB Castle twenty minutes later, a medical team had already moved the refugees off the landing pad. Ramirez jumped out of the helo and walked across the pad, then slammed his helmet on the ground, screaming curses in Spanish. Johnson grounded her gear and slumped off towards the tents.

Corporal Snow, First Fire Team Leader, lit a cigarette and put it in Boudreaux's shaking hands. "Welcome to the Wild Wild East, noob. You did OK. Not great but OK. You'll get better but it's gonna get worse."

A Very Zombie Killer Christmas (a separate short story)

It was cold. Upstate New York cold. We sat in the ruins of a house, holed up on the second floor, shivering in our inadequate shelter. The horde of zombies outside shuffled around the house, their ghastly moans competing with the wind that howled through the mountains.

There was nothing solid to build a fire on. If we had tried, the whole house would have gone up in flames. We had to be quiet, after our running shoot house with the horde that had chased us in here. For the tenth time, I pulled the magazine out of my rifle and counted the rounds. One, two, three, four. Not even enough for each member of the team to take the easy way out.

I took off my pack to root around in it, to see if I had any more loose rounds hiding down the bottom. Beside me, Brit shivered, her red hair catching snowflakes from the holes in the roof. Ziv looked out over the horde, impassive as ever, trying to match the undead stare for stare.

Specialist Redshirt, not used to these cold New York winters, was the farthest gone. His bronze Navajo face was pale with the cold and he had fallen through the ice on our retreat across a creek, soaking him. He started chanting under his breath, something I suspected was a tribal death song.

Doc knelt next to him, took his pulse and shook his head. "He's not going to last much longer, Nick. We gotta do something." Ahmed crawled over to Red, ignoring his broken arm and huddled against him, trying to raise some body heat. Doc sat down on the other side, lending his burly weight.

We had been so tired from a weeklong trip through the mountains that the horde had surprised us walking through a ruined town. They had risen up like ghosts from under the snow, the infection keeping their body heat just at freezing. Hundreds of them and we had run, run as hard as our tired bodies would allow. Ducking into the last shattered house on the street after gaining some distance, we had smashed the stairs and barricaded the doors. Now, well, now we were screwed. Out of ammo. Too far from a firebase to raise anyone on the net. Freezing to death. The undead started banging at the door, smashing against it. Eventually it would shatter and they would pile themselves up on the missing stairway as we killed them with two by fours and rifle butts. Then they would feast and we would either die or be turned.

I took the four rounds out of the rifle magazine and placed them in my pistol mag, then racked the slide. One for each of them, since I knew that Ziv would prefer to go out fighting a horde, risk be damned. I looked at them each in turn and each one nodded back.

"Anyone this net, this is Lost Boys, Indian Sierra Tango One. Need extract, over." I repeated it again and again, knowing that no one was flying in this storm. Brit's hand closed over mine. Since the Denver campaign last summer, we had become close, far closer than teammates should be. We had tried to fight it but now, I regretted the wasted opportunity.

"Nick, don't bother. You're just killing the batteries."

I sighed. She was right. I looked at them all again and continued to rummage around my rucksack. I had about given up, when my hand closed on Gerber multi-tool stuck way down in a corner. I pulled it out and in the glow of the chemsticks, opened it. Inscribed on the blade were the words "YOU WORRY TOO MUCH!"

I laughed to myself. Jonesy, who had died so valiantly at West Point, creating time for us to escape another horde, had given it to me when we first formed the team, what seemed a lifetime ago. He had given it to me for Christmas.

"Hey! I just remembered! What time is it?"

Ziv looked at his watch. "Zero Three Thirty," he said and looked at me like I had a hole in my head.

"It's Christmas!" That brought a ghost of a grin to all of us, even Red. "Well, it's the shittiest Christmas I've ever had but screw it. I've been wanting to do this for a long time."

I got down on one knee in front of Brit and said,

"Brittany O'Neill, will you marry me?"

Her mouth opened and closed like a fish. I had never, ever seen her at a loss for words, but I guess there is a first for everything. She said nothing, just bent down and kissed me and buried her face in my shoulder. I looked at the rest of the guys, who all had shit eating grins on their faces.

"About effing time!" said Doc.

At that moment, the radio crackled to life. *"Lost boys, this is Odin Six, over."*

I stared at it in amazement. "ANSWER THE GODDAMNED THING, YOU IDIOT!" said Brit. I could see that the magic of my proposal had lasted all of twenty seconds. Grabbing the hand mike, I called back, "Odin Six, this is Lost Boys, are we glad to hear your voice, over!"

The heavy thud of rotor blades sounded in his transmission as he called back. *"Heard you need some fire support. Pop a flare to your position, over."*

We wasted no time in complying. The eerie red light reflected off the slowly breaking clouds of snow as stars started to shine coldly overhead. In answer, a green shaft of light danced a circle all around the house, six thousand rounds a minute from a minigun chewing through undead like a lightsaber through a Sith. The aircraft made several passes, hunting down individual undead with short bursts from the door mounted gun and several other machine guns. While they were doing that, we lit the house on fire, not caring if it burned. We had to get Red warm again and he quickly revived under the scorching heat.

The pilot deftly set the big CH-47 Chinook down in the snow in front of the house. A team of riflemen spread out, making sure there were no live undead. Then the pilot walked out of the lowered ramp in the back.

He was a short, fat dude wearing Colonels' rank and sporting a red and white aircraft crewmember helmet. "Geez, they sure let the standards slip. Look at how fat that dude is!" said Brit. I shrugged, not willing to complain about the help. He had saved our asses.

With a grin and a twinkle in his eye, he took off a fur lined glove and shook my hand. "So, the famous Nick Agostine and the redheaded wrecking machine Brit O'Neill. I hope you're going to make an honest woman out of her, Nick!"

"Do I know you, Colonel?"

He waved his hand dismissively. "You know how the military is. When you've been around forever, like I have, eventually you know everyone. I can't give you kids a ride back, I've got places to be but I can give you some supplies." He whistled and some of the bird's crew started tossing crates of ammo and boxes out the back. My team carried them into another house, this one much more solid than the one we had hid out in. He stood and watched with his hands on his stomach until everything was out and then called his crew chief.

"Sergeant Dancer, load 'em up, we have other places to be. Well, Nick, Merry Christmas! You've been a good boy this year but put a ring on it as soon as you can!"

"Can do, Sir. What's your name? I'd like to buy you a beer if we ever run into each other again."

"You can call me … Chris." He laughed and ran up the ramp. I saw him again at the cockpit window and he saluted me. I saluted back and the engines powered up, sending me back into the house to avoid the blowing snow. Inside, the team was going through the packages, reloading magazines and breaking open MREs.

"Hey, Nick, check it out! This is weird." Brit held a long package in her hands. She tilted it to me so I could see in the light of the fire we had going in the fireplace. On it in big letters someone had scrawled, "O'NEILL".

"Look, here's one with your name on it!" Sure enough, a box was marked, "AGOSTINE."

She grew as excited as a kid in a candy store, ripping into the stack and throwing boxes at people. "REDSHIRT! HAMILTON! YASSER! ZIVCOVIC!" she called as she found each one.

"Well, don't just stand there, open it!" I ordered her. She did and pulled out an Italian made Benelli Vinci 12 Gauge Tactical Shotgun.

"OHMYGOD!" she squealed and started jamming rounds into it. "NICK, LOOK! It says SOUL STEALER on the stock!" She ran over and kissed me hard. "I don't know how you did this but THANK YOU!" I didn't spoil it by saying I had no idea what the hell was going on.

"Careful, you'll shoot your eye out!' said Doc.

"Ha!" she laughed, "Screw shooting my eye out, I'd blow my head off!"

One by one we opened the boxes. Ziv had a custom made 14" combat knife, forged by Mike Williamson. He laughed and threw it as hard as he could and it THUNKED into a wooden beam an inch from my head. I ignored this, having had it done to me dozens of times before.

Doc got an expensive new leather jacket with "ZOMBIE KILLERS MC," hand stitched into the back. His old club had pulled a spectacular ride through a horde when things fell apart and he had been the only one to make it through, his leather jacket shredded. He had been looking for a replacement for two years now.

Ahmed pulled a hand-woven prayer rug that still smelled faintly of the desert, to replace the one he had lost only last week. He immediately took out a compass, laid the mat in the direction of the glowing crater that was Mecca and started praying.

I waited until last. My box was small, not much larger than my hand. I opened it slowly, gently. Inside was an envelope. I opened this carefully too and a piece of paper fell out. On it was printed one word.

Brit put her arms around me and asked, "What did you get, oh fearless leader?"

I turned the paper up so that she could read the one word printed on it.

"The best gift ever," I said and kissed her. The paper fell to the floor between us, landing right side up. The flickering firelight played on Brit's red hair and illuminated the word.

HOPE.

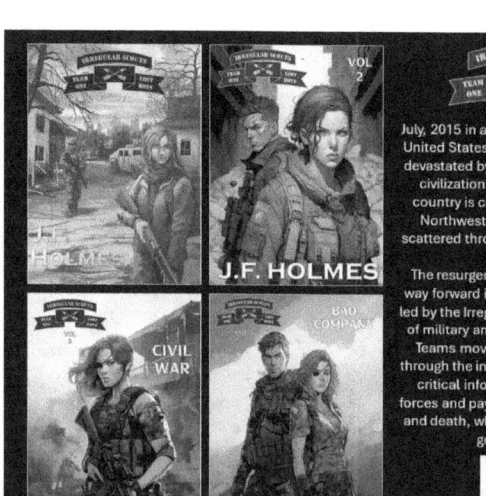

www.ingramcontent.com/pod-product-compliance
Lightning Source LLC
Chambersburg PA
CBHW070749280626
47162CB00018B/2788